Deception In The
Shadows

Gerica's Tale

S.Robichaud

To the best
Mom in the
whole wide
world !
I ♥ you.
S.Robichaud

First Published in 2019 by Blossom Spring Publishing

Deception In The Shadows, Gerica's Tale Copyright

© 2019 S.Robichaud

ISBN 978-1-9160320-0-2

E: admin@blossomspringpublishing.com

W: www.blossomspringpublishing.com

Caleb and Kk- I'm so glad that I was able to show you two that no matter what, you can do what you set your minds too. Never give up, I love the two of you so much.

Daniella Mason & Melissa Ryan- Thinking about my time in school, it's you two that have stayed in my heart this whole time. Ms. Mason, when you see this I hope you smile. And Ms. Ryan, if you see this, I hope it makes you proud.

Chapter One

*To understand the tragedy that took place within the
castle walls of Leward kingdom, you must understand how
the King single handily ruined the very thing he tried to keep
dear.*

Inside an enormous castle that could easily
house several hundred people, lived King
Beckford. A tyrant, who ran the Leward kingdom
with a suffocating fist. This King was not loved by
many, but he was certainly feared.

Nuzzled amidst cherry colored trees and
plum tinted shrubs, his castle stood alone and
unbothered, in the city of Bales. Black marble
floors, large white stone walls, and windows that
stretched from the floors to the white marble
ceiling, made up the domain. Lights of all colors
danced on the walls as the sun shined through the
pained glass windows; their different sizes and
pictures all told their own story. All the wings of
the castle held unique tales and the dungeon held
secrets.

His riches were what most could only dream
of and he only wore robes made of the finest silks
and crowns made of the purest gold. His throne
was his most precious of processions, made up of
gold and diamond covered edges.

The Leward kingdom provoked envy in the hearts of on lookers in surrounding kingdoms; they failed to compete with Leward. Its mega city Bales was the largest city of any kingdom near. It consisted of shops and business that brought financial gains to the King from his citizens and citizens from far away. The town of Carmin, two towns away from Bales, had the largest lake known to the any of the surrounding kingdoms; filled with fish, and fresh water; a financial pot of gold. The more wooded areas on the outskirts of the town were home to the farms that kept most of the citizens fed.

All the houses and store fronts had to pay rent to the King; along with any taxes on purchased items. Beckford also had laws in place that would prohibit any citizen from being able to run a business without his knowledge and his many guards worked to ensure his laws were obeyed and his demands for money were met.

Not a single kingdom around had the means to take over Leward. King Beckford was never worried; in fact, he invited trouble. Sometimes he would get bored with his perfect kingdom and he secretly wished a war for his land would start or there would be an upraise in rebellious citizens. He loved exercising his power and it had been a long time since someone had felt his wrath. No one dared however, aside from all the random rebels refusing to pay taxes, which did not happen often, King Beckford lived a life of silence. For someone that lived to use his power, that life of silence was painfully boring.

On a sunny rather cheerful day, while King Beckford was pondering new ways to squeeze more tax dollars out of his citizens; he heard yelling coming from the corridor. And his brainstorming was interrupted by two castle guards rushing a man into the throne room. The man was tall, with a thin build, wearing a bright yellow robe that reached down to his ankles; on his feet were a pair of furry black house slippers. He had very light skin, as if he had not seen the light of day in ages. A shaggy mane of blonde hair sat upon his head, under his yellow hat that resembled one a chef would wear. Light Blonde facial hair had taken up space on his chin and his eyes were the color of pearls; white but not nearly as beautiful. He was frantic, and utterly confused. His presence and persona puzzled the King.

King Beckford was not to be interrupted by anyone no matter the issue but since this man had persuaded the guards to allow him to enter, the only right thing the King could do was entertain the man's reasoning for being there.

"Are you lost, boy?" King Beckford asked in a harsh, raspy tone.

"Your Majesty, we found this intruder lurking around the gate on the far western end of the castle. We were going to take him to the dungeon but he was rambling on and on about your kingdom being dethroned. We thought this might be of interest to you." Interrupted, Samuel, the newest, and brightest of the castle guards.

"I believe Samuel; I was speaking to someone other than yourself. Do you find it in your rights to speak when not spoken to?" King Beckford snapped at Samuel.

Samuel was never a timid man, until it came to the King. He was tall with a very athletic build; like a farmer who was able to lift large rocks with ease and throw them long distances. His head was covered in straight, jet black hair; that reached his shoulders and was pulled into a bun at the back of his head. His face had the same black hair and was well trimmed. His skin was the color of bark on the trees in the forest; his eyes were black as coal. Even with Samuel's intense look, when the King spoke he lost his frightening appeal.

A look of fear shot across Samuel's face; he bowed his head to the floor and exited the throne room. Without a word the second guard, Stetson, followed Samuel. Stetson was older than most of the guards in the castle; he had been serving the King from almost the start of his reign. He was not a weak man, but not as fit as Samuel. His brown, wavy hair was spackled with gray strands that reached to his ears. He kept his face well shaved and never had facial hair. His eyes were like snake eyes, an incredible emerald green that glittered any time he laughed. His face was wrinkled; his age was nothing that he was able to hide.

After the guards turned to leave something happened to the King; his attitude changed and the look of interest took over his face. He was curious what this man could possibly have to say. He was up for a good laugh, or fight for that matter.

"Speak!" demanded King Beckford.

"My lord, my name is Anders from the Southern corner of Carmin. I, sir, am a psychic and today, my lord I had a vision which I assure you will be most grateful to hear." Anders spoke these words clear as day, even though his hands were uncontrollably shaky.

The King let out of small chuckle. "Excuse the doubt, dear boy. I do not have any interest in anything you may have to say… Unless of course, you are going to give me advice on how to raise more taxes in Leward." The King's words dripped with arrogance and his eyes rolled back into his head while he tried not to laugh harder in Anders' pale face.

"This morning, Your Majesty. I was awoken by a dream that frightened me. I saw you in all your glory, sitting on a throne; wearing a purple silk robe and having guards surround you. There was a war going on and the outside of the castle was being attacked by all the villagers. The strangest thing about the dream was the leader was a teen girl; maybe early twenties, but still very young. She was in a dark robe with a hood pulled over her head. Her face was a blur and there was not any noise. I saw the villagers come from the woods in every direction. There were too many for your guards to fight. They kicked in the front door, and many even climbed into the castle by the windows. They came with bows, and arrows; used their brutal weapons, slaying every guard, servant, and finally, Your Majesty. When I awoke, I rushed to my books and charms to try to make sense of this dream. There seemed to be key information I was missing because there were no helpful answers in my books. I was able to conjure a remembering potion to revisit this dream. I put myself back to sleep and watched the same dream. Everything had happened the second time in the exact order as the first dream, and by the end of both dreams my lord, you were dead. This time, however, it had sound and that was the scarcest part. You see my lord, the young girl, was able to take your kingdom from right under your nose. She was made the ruler with the help of Leward's citizens; they made her queen." Anders completed his speech with a look of uncertainly in his eyes; he did not seem to believe the words coming out of his mouth anymore than the King would believe them. He knew it sounded insane. He knew what he was saying was beyond unlikely; yet he stood there, giving the King his whole story.

"Ha! Dear boy, please remove yourself from my castle." King Beckford dismissed his revelation and assumed this man was not well.

"Your Majesty; I have lived here my entire life, and I need you to save our home." Anders tired to catch his breath between each word he spoke. His excitement and fear had made it hard to complete a sentence without stopping for a breath. "I understand this may sound insane, insanity was my first thought upon waking this morning for the second time. I do assure you, King Beckford; this is as real as you and I standing in this very room. Her name is Gerica; she was born almost two years ago to a peasant family on a farm in northern Bales. She has unique gifts; the strength found in this girl, both physically and mentally are unknown to man. I do apologize for how this may sound, but Your Majesty, there is no way to stop her from becoming the Queen of Leward. She will not fear you when she comes of age; nor will she abide by your laws. This single girl can ruin the entire kingdom you are so proud of." As Anders went on, his mouth spoke words that haunted the King to his core.

King Beckford was beginning to worry; *is it possible that a child, a girl, would be able to take me from the very throne that only my family had ruled?* His mind began racing as he called for his guards.

"Samuel, Stetson! In here at once!" He yelled at the top of his lungs and then looked Anders right in the eye, focusing on his pearly irises. King Beckford rose from his throne and inched his way closer to Anders, his entire body filled of anger and rage. *This pathetic worm invited himself into my castle, and insulted the very thing I value the most, this man is no psychic; he was a lunatic!*

"I will tell you this, even speaking of someone thinking of removing me from my throne will get you killed in this kingdom. You idiot, have you any idea the things I have done to worms like you? Did you fall; perhaps you knocked your head on a rock. No, sir, you are surely mistaken if you think this kingdom will be in anyone's reign but mine." Just as the King spoke these words, there came a slamming from the front doors to the throne room.

Stetson was trying to get in the unlocked door, but the door appeared stuck. "What is going on with you, have you forgotten how to open a simple door?" The King huffed as he made his away to the door. He braced the cold knob in both hands and tried to pull. While he pulled, Stetson pushed, but the door would not move. At that moment, the King realized the door had no lock, but was being kept shut by something more powerful. He felt a thousand eyes on his back when he realized that Anders was still the only person in the room with him.

King Beckford was overcame with fear, "you lunatic! What have you done to my doors?" He screamed as his fear turned to rage; he stormed closer to Anders with fire in his eyes.

Anders was now nose to nose with the King and shaking harder than ever before; but held his ground, "I need you to listen to me, my lord. I need you to trust me." Anders began to beg with a soft voice. "You need to know the fate of the kingdom if you do not choose to act on the matter of Gerica. It is my duty as a citizen of Leward to put the kingdom's interest ahead of my own." Anders did not move as he spoke; he was scared but he needed the King to hear him.

The King was beyond irritated at this point in the conversation; and very concerned how Anders, who was nowhere near the door, was able to keep it closed. *This man was obliviously not a typical insane person; there was knowledge within this man.*

Only when he realized that he was not able to open the door did he take Anders seriously. He remembered stories from his own father and Kings from different places about psychics, and their abilities. He recalled being told that psychics were powerful people that could help in the ruling of a Kingdom, a way to keep ahead of wars and such. King Beckford never took that advice, but something in his stomach told him it was time to listen to this man.

King Beckford took a long, deep breath, collected himself and looked into the eyes of

Anders. "This is not something that has ever happened to me in my time ruling this kingdom. Anders, is it? I will need to know more about your dream; I will need to know the choices I have. I will not give my kingdom up, no matter the cost. Now, this girl Gerica… is she capable of running a kingdom?" The King would plan his attack on Gerica based on the answers he received from Anders.

"Your Majesty, from the dream that I had there is hope for your kingdom. It also, however, comes in the form of Gerica. She is the determining factor in the future of this kingdom. You will have no choice, someday you will pass on and as of this date, you have neither wife nor children. There are no siblings, there is no one that can or will take over this kingdom in the midst of your passing. She will have rule of this kingdom, in one way or another. The good news is my lord; you can choose how that is achieved. When the time comes, if you do not intervene, she will gain the trust of all the citizens in Leward, and with their help, she will attack this castle and they will take your throne; making her the new queen of Leward. However, she was born into a poor family; perhaps, you could barter with her parents. Offering financial help in exchange for giving you their daughter. You would be able to raise her as your own daughter. You could teach her the way you want this kingdom run. She will be a mold of you, my lord. The tight hold that you have on this kingdom will remain. You would be able to keep your throne until the very day you pass on. Essentially, there will be nothing you have to lose, should you choose that option. I understand that this is not something a King would normally do, but weighing your options, it may be in your best interest. The choice is yours, my lord." Anders felt like he was being heard, but he was not sure how the King would handle his suggestion.

The King sat on the floor, in the middle of the throne room to collect his thoughts. The silence in the room was thick; the air became warmer as the room started to spin. The King could not make sense of any of this news he was receiving at this moment. He balanced his head in his hands as he tried to catch his breath.

This was his kingdom; since he was twenty years of age. His father, King Blair had died in his sleep. The morning after King Beckford's bedroom filled with ministers and councilman. They told him the kingdom was now his, and he was free to do what he wanted to within the kingdom walls. Now he sits in his throne room, at a mere forty-one years old, learning that someone else will be in control of determining the kingdom's fate? Then he got an idea; the most sinister idea that his twisted mind could come up with.

"I shall have her murdered." He declared. He had never killed a baby; men, in abundance. Never any babies, however this may be the day that would change.

"Your Majesty, I fear that is not the salutation to this problem. You could kill her, yes but I assure you that would upset the order of how events will take place. I fear that would cause an uproar among the villagers. She is already such a loved member of the Bales town people; nothing but devastation will come from such a reckless act." Anders assured in his most convincing voice.

"So, I should buy this brat from her peasant parents, raise her as my own to ensure that all I have worked for will not be in vain?" The King found himself asking this question aloud only to try to make sense of it for himself.

"Indeed, Your Majesty. That would be the surest way to keep your hold on this kingdom," Anders replied. He had an endearing look on his face as he stared at the King.

An odd sensation took over the King; he felt comfortable with Anders. He learned to trust him quickly but then a thought crept into the back of the King's mind. *Why does this man care, what does Anders have to gain if this prophecy if fulfilled in either way?*

"You, Anders are a man of wonders. You show up uninvited and unannounced to my kingdom. You bring me news that my kingdom will be under attack, and yet you look at me, with all the faith in the world that everything will work out should I choose the path you are encouraging me to follow. I must ask you what your motive is. How will changing the fate of this kingdom impact you?" The King questioned.

"King Beckford, I can tell you that the kingdom will be a happier place for the citizens. If Gerica takes over the kingdom on her own free will. There will be fewer taxes and more freedom for citizens. However, these perks are of little concern to me; my business has little to do with money, or taxes. I fear that should she take over, without your guidance, she will not allow people such as myself to practice our gifts. To some, people with my abilities are seen as evil. That is not the case I assure you but I fear from my vision she is of a pure heart. Untouched of anger, or hatred

14

and she will not understand someone of my background. I do have a selfish reason for making my appearance here today, but your hand will give me promise." Anders confides in the King his worries, and suddenly, the two men have a mutual motive.

King Beckford grinned and understood Anders' dilemma. "Ah, yes, that makes perfect sense. Now, the question will be how to make this happen. How can we get Gerica into my care?"

"As I mentioned before sir, her family is in dire need of financial help. There has to be something you can offer her family in return for their daughter. These are simple people and they might not understand everything that I have told you. Offering them something that they will not be able to refuse is surely the way to have Gerica in your castle, my lord." Anders reassured the King that this is the plan to put into action.

There was a silence in the room as the King sat and thought about his options. "Then my mind has been made up for me. I shall make this family an offer they will not be able to turn down. You now have to prove yourself useful to me. I assume you will stay here at the castle with my guards and myself?" The King insisted in a commanding voice. The eerie part of the encounter is that the

King was not scared of Anders; in the beginning when the doors locked, he was slightly scared of Anders. *The doors... Stetson!* The King hustled over to the door, and opened it with ease. Stetson was still trying to open the door by ramming his shoulder into it. He almost fell into the King when the doors finally opened. Once the door opened, he stared at the King with the most puzzled look upon his face that the King had ever seen. Samuel was making his way toward the throne room from down the corridor.

"Your Majesty..." Stetson started to inquire if the King was safe but he soon saw that the two men are standing side by side. "I thought...we tried to get into the room but the door...was stuck."

"I need you and Samuel to go on a trip; to bring me a family that resides in the Northern part of Bales." The King looked at Anders; "I need you to go with them, I shall assume you know exactly where to find them?" asked the King rather cheerfully.

"Yes, Your Majesty. On foot, it may be a day's travel." Anders stated in a matter of fact tone. The city of Bales was the biggest city in the kingdom of Leward; Northern Bales was mostly a wooded area; with swamps and mountains spread out throughout the land.

"You shall take my three best horses. That will give you better use of your time." The King insisted.

"As you wish; my lord." Anders bowed his head with respect and relief; he had been sure this meeting would end in his death.

"As for the two of you, you shall accompany Anders here into the city of Bales. You are to protect him as if you would protect me. He will bring you to a house where a family lives. I will need you to bring back both parents and the child. Each of you will be able to fit one member of the family on your horse with you. I will expect you back no later than one day and a half from this very moment. Go to Lucille, have her pack enough food to get you through your journey." It accrued to the King that he was putting a lot of trust in Anders having just met him. The information that he presented to the King was intimidating, and he was not in a place to ignore any type of warning. *Perhaps I was in the wrong for not having plans for my kingdom after my passing. The work that had gone into this kingdom would have fallen apart once I was dead.* He reflected on his reasons for never having a hire and none of them made sense anymore; he feared having people around that he cared for left he vulnerable to threats or ransom. If he had had a son would that son kill him for the throne? These were the fears that kept him from having his own family.

His mind wandered to Gerica; *she would need to be able to stomach all the things that come with being in power.* He hoped her parents would take any offer he made. The King was prepared to offer whatever amount of gold or land, or both for that matter, that would satisfy the family's wishes. He did not even know the name of the family he would be entraining; nonetheless, he will have his kingdom and their daughter.

Anders' had more than exhausted him with the news; and he was seeing the back of his eyelids flash before his eyes as his head started to nod.

As he made his way down the corridor, his eyes focused on the azure specs that sparkled against the black marble tiles. King Beckford's bedroom was located up long, curled stair cases that lead to the Northern wing of the castle. The Northern wing had fewer windows than the rest of castle and the walls were a light blue, the King's favorite color. The floors were golden tiles that shined in the light, he was always greeted with the delightful smell of vanilla and spring lilies picked fresh from his garden thanks to Lucille. His bedroom was the most remote room in the house; she was the only one ever allowed to enter and even she was limited on her time there.

She is the only person that the King considered himself close to. King Beckford was an incredibly cold individual but for Lucille, he was slightly warmer. To say he was in love with her is an overstatement but he was very fond of her. They had secretly dated for many years and she had spent many nights in the King's bedroom; though, she would never be his wife. He was far too worried that she would not be able to handle the tasks; Lucille was too caring and warm. Like a mother figure but incredibly trustworthy. Trustworthy people were not an easy thing to find; especially for a King. The last thought the King had was of Lucille before he was able to drift into a deep slumber.

The next day started as any other day. Lucille was at the King's door right as the sun was making an appearance into the windows. She had the King's breakfast; a roll and hot cereal; he ate in his bed. He was not someone who enjoyed the morning, and dealing with the servants upon opening his eyes would just annoy him.

"Good day, I hope your sleep was peaceful; I have your breakfast right here, Your Majesty!" Lucille declared in a high pitched, pleasant voice. Her smile spread from one ear to the next. Her scarlet red hair was tied back behind her head in a sliver hairclip, with just a few random strands falling into her face. Light green eyes laid against her fare complexion with intensity. King Beckford always admired her skin, with no scars or freckles, her skin was creamy milk. Everything about her plump, short body was perfect in the King's eye, even if he would never tell her that. He loved the way her modest pale pink dress flowed freely exposing her bare feet.

"Good day, Lucille. How was your night?" The King asked between yawns and stretches.

"Wonderful, there was not any rain and nothing of a cold breeze, so the southern end made for a very comfortable night." Lucille smiled as she spoke these words. She had her own room for the nights that the King wanted to be left alone. This was fine for Lucille on nights when she needed to relax. Her room was the only place she could escape all the duties of the castle. One of the biggest rooms inside the castle; it was her own personal heaven from the lime curtains to the light purple carpets.

"I am glad to hear that, Lucille. Did you have the pleasure of meeting Anders yesterday before he left with Samuel and Stetson?" He asked in a calm matter. One more reason the King wanted Lucille around was she could read people, their eyes and their body language; she was an excellent judge of character. She took note of how they carried their self and how they communicated. When people had an agenda, they would normally have something that would give them away; like a habit of biting their nails or scratching their heads. She paid attention to things he would never think of; she was everything the King was not.

"Yes, I packed them all a great deal of food. Why do you ask?" Lucille replied.

"What did you think of him?" The King was only going to tell her the news that Anders informed him of after she tells him whether she liked him or not.

"He was delightful, and very warm. Respectful; he seemed distracted though. What was he here for? Is he a new business partner?" Lucille asked with a nonchalant tone as she started to open curtains in the King's bedroom. The King enjoyed sun light warming his room as he ate his breakfast.

"I am not sure what I would call him. He came into the castle after the guards found him trespassing. They interpreted me while I was alone in my throne room. He is a psychic and came to tell me of a dream he had." King Beckford stopped talking for a moment to see Lucille's reaction. She was staring at the King; he had all of her attention. After he saw that she is fully involved with the conversation he continued. "He dreamt that a young girl was capable of taking the throne from me. He told me that no matter the way I handled this, the outcome would be the same. The insane part is that I do not feel he was lying. The sincerity in his eyes was comforting. He wanted to help me, in a way that no one else had ever wanted to. Well, no one besides you, Lucille." The King smiled at her as he spoke; his eyes were soft but he was still on edge with all the new information. The King continued to tell Lucille about the events from the day before. "The most convincing part of this man's story was when it was only he and I in the throne room, the doors shut and locked; or at least they were not able to be opened by Stetson or myself. It was clear at that moment that I needed to take this man seriously. It was a little terrifying, if I may be totally honest with you. His white eyes showed passion; like his world was coming to an end if I did not do anything to save both of our lives. There was a sense of desperation in his voice, and it was the same sense of desperation that fell over me at the thought of not being able to save or keep my kingdom."

"I see," was all Lucille had to say.

"Lucille? What is it?" King Beckford asked in a concerned tone.

"I did not get the impression that he was someone to fear, the exact opposite to be truthful. I must ask, why did he want you to know? What was his motive, surely he was not solely concerned with your wellbeing?" Lucille asked the appropriate question at the most appropriate time.

"That was my thought; he must want something from me to be telling me this. Although his reason seemed valid; the girl in the vision was 'of a pure heart' and his style of living is less than pure. He fears that should she take over the kingdom, practicing psychics, such as him will be outlawed. A thought that never crossed my mind. So by coming to me he wanted to ensure his future. I see him as a partner in this journey. We both want to continue living the way we have been all these years. He does not seem to have a life besides practicing his talents." Confessed the King; that moment, he felt he and Anders shared a bond.

"Yes, that makes sense. Now, the question will be how do you plan on handling it? She is a child, you cannot kill her…" Lucille stated as the haunting picture of a murdered child crept into her mind.

"The way that Anders explained it, I would have two choices. Since the outcome will be the same no matter what I choose; Gerica will be queen one day. I could leave everything as is and face her whenever she and the villagers choose to come to the castle and rage a war against me. Or I can face it now. Gerica is coming from a poor family, so I am going to offer anything they may seem fitting in order for me to gain Gerica and raise her how I wish." As the King spoke these words, he watched Lucille's face for her feeling on the matter; her honest nature displayed the majority of her thoughts, but she was unreadable.

"If you know that there will be a war, why can you not prepare yourself?" Lucille asked a question that the King had not thought of.

He was silent for a moment, aware that Lucille was on to something. "I did not think of that possibility however I assume this day will be… when I am fragile." Not wanting to confess his undeniable aging, he knew his legacy could not bear that sort of embarrassment. To be killed by a girl and her village idiots. He needed to remain a strong figure in all the years to come. "I think being the girl's mentor and raising her as a daughter will work out in my favor long after my days are done."

"Raise her? Oh my, Your Majesty, have you fallen on your head? Do you realize you cannot even wake yourself up in the morning! That is why I am here at this very moment; to help you start your day! How will you care for a child?" Lucille was amused by the idea, until she realized that she may have a bigger part in the "raising" of the child than the King would. She looked dead in the King's eyes, as he lifts the corners of his thin lips into a sly grin. "Oh! That was your plan; I should have known there was a catch!"

"Lucille… you know me more than anyone that has ever lived on this earth has known me. Surely you did not expect me to be the one raising this child? I will of course, get her anything she needs but to take care of her is beyond my skill." As the King said this, he inched his way toward her; reaching his arm around her curvy waist and gently pulling her closer to him. When she pressed against him, he placed a single kiss upon her neck. "Lucille," he took a moment to pause, breathing in her sent. "This kingdom and you are all I have in this world; I cannot lose either of you. And I know you deserve a King, so I need you to help me on this journey. I will teach Gerica everything I know and together we will mold her into the perfect queen. This is possible but to ensure that I will need your help." King Beckford whispered in Lucille's ear. Her heart always melted in the rare moments that the King was vulnerable; making it impossible to tell him no.

She turned to look at her love in his eyes. "You should be warned I may not do her justice; I have never raised a daughter," she whispered.

"Anything you touch turns to perfection, Lucille." He smiled as if there were unspoken words in his eyes. Moments like these between the pair were nothing short of magical.

"Then it is settled; I shall help you. I do have to ask, what makes you so positive that her parents will even allow you to take her and raise her as your own? I understand that they are poor, but in all actually, that may mean very little to them." The concerned tone in Lucille's voice was convincing. She knew of his power, and of the fear that all of the citizens of Leward had for him, but she could not help but wonder; after all, money did not equal love.

"Do not be silly, my dear Lucille. Anything I offer these peasants will not be an offer they can refuse," stated the King as he gave a light chuckle, his confidence was clear.

"Yes well, we shall see. When will the gentlemen be returning?"

"They should be here by night fall. The journey was only supposed to last a day or so, but I would assume they stopped to rest." He informed her while glancing out the window nearest him. The sun had moved from his windows and began to dance over the sapphire tree tops.

"Shall we go for a walk in the garden after breakfast? Or would you like to start your day in the throne room? I assume there is not much business to attend to." She asked in a hopeful tone.

"A walk after breakfast may be a nice change of pace." King Beckford agreed.

The afternoon had been dull while the King and Lucille awaited the return of the guards and the parents of Gerica. The longer the King waited, the more anxious he started to become. He had played every scenario in his head. *How will they react when I offer them gold or land in return for Gerica. They could let greed takeover and want both.*

He knew that he could not treat them like he would treat any other person; he needed to treat them gently. As he walked down the corridor toward the throne room, he looked out the window, and realized it had started to drizzle rain. The castle was covered by a dark cloud; a possible thunder storm was on the horizon. King Beckford never made it the throne room because just as he was two steps away, he heard Lucille's voice.

"They have arrived! They have arrived! They are making their entrance now!" Lucille exclaimed with excitement present in her voice. The King could hear Lucille's footsteps running down the corridor toward the front of the castle. He stopped walking to the throne room; turned on his right heal to head in the opposite direction. It was only right to meet the guest at the door.

"Welcome!" the King and Lucille both announce together as Stetson led a man and a woman to the castle's doors; Samuel and Anders followed close by. All five of them were damp and cold from the rain. "Lucille," the King turned away from his guests to face Lucille. "Please, do start the fireplace in the dining hall and start a kettle of tea. Also, if we have any soup or bread, bring that in as well; and perhaps some blankets. We do not want our guests cold." King Beckford added, as he turned to face the couple he did not know how to address; Anders never told him their names. Lucille gave the couple a warm smile and then turned to walk down the hall.

Chapter Two

"Welcome, welcome. I am King Beckford of Leward. What can I have the pleasure of calling you?" The King asked as he shook the man's hand; he had a firm hand shake, showing the King that he was not intimidated.

"I am Earl, Your Majesty; Earl Wood. And this is my wife, Lena." Earl replied as he looked at the King in the eyes and bowed to honor him. When Earl's wife, Lena saw him bowing she did the same. Beside them was the child, Gerica. She was small with short brown locks that hang right above her shoulders. She looked at the King with her big gray eyes; from the look she gave; the King knew she was something special. She held onto her mother's hand; with her other hand in her mouth. She had skin like a china doll, expect on her pink cheeks; they reminded the King of light pink roses that were in his garden. Although, she was there with her parents she looked scared and lost. Her parents did not look intimidated but meek and fragile; their eyes looked up at the King with despair. It was clear that the guards and Anders had not told them why they were called to the King's castle.

Earl was a regular sized man; not tall like Anders, and not chubby like the King. He was muscular. He had black hair, with quite a bit of shinier gray strands, and tan skin. He was a bit intimidating himself; with eyes that reminded the King of Samuel's black eyes. Lena was a beauty; long wavy blonde hair and sun kissed skin. It was clear she worked on the farm along with her husband. She was shorter than her husband and plump; not skinny like most peasants. The most noticeable thing about her was her big brown eyes; they sucked you into a world where you cannot help but want to be closer to her. The King actually had to stop himself from staring. Both were dressed in torn robes, with sandals on their feet.

The King always noticed a person's feet because it showed the type of person they were. Feet support the whole body, they allow a person to move in any direction they want to go. They need to be cared for; pampered. He sat on his throne as much as possible to allow his feet the rest that they deserved. He was pleasantly surprised when he saw that both had clean feet. The observation would seem odd to persons not in high power, but for the King, it gave him peace of mind.

"Please come, take off your top robes. I shall have them hung up to dry and we will sit you down in front of the fire place to warm you up; just follow me." King Beckford said, in a pleasant manner as he went to turn and walk away.

"Excuse me, Your Majesty. Forgive my manners, but I must ask - why have you called for us?" asked Lena in a small voice.

"I will be happy to answer any and all questions you have. But first, let's get you warmed up," with that statement the King starting walking toward the dining hall.

Annoyed that her question was ignored, Lena chose to keep her thoughts to herself. She was a headstrong woman, but she knew better than show that side to the King.

When they reached the dining hall; Lucille handed them soups with bread, and hot tea with maple cookies. She covered Mrs. Woods' shoulders with a wool blanket and wrapped Gerica up with a wool blanket as she tried to sleep on her father's lap.

The King looked at the child sleeping peacefully before he turned to Lucille, "Thank you for everything, Lucille. I will need you to leave the room but stay near incase there is anything we need from you." King Beckford was extra careful to speak nicely to anyone working in the castle at that moment.

"As you wish my lord." Lucille agreed; then turned to walk out the door. She had planned to listen to the conversation from the other side of the door. She did not want to miss a word of the exchange.

"I would first like to start out by thanking you for making the journey to visit me. I understand that you have a farm that you run as a family. How are the crops and livestock?" The King asked, in an attempt to make conversation.

"Well, all things considered, we are managing. It is a lot of work. As long as the rain and sun shine balance each other out, we should not have any issues this season. This past winter was hard to maintain the livestock; we loss several chickens, ducks and even a cow. However, we have faith that everything will balance out later this spring." Earl gave this information without much thought. He was used to talking to many people about the status of his farm. As he spoke to the King, Gerica began to move on his lap, she was waking up. Earl gently patted her head and rub from her forehead to her hair.

"Yes, the wheat fields and apple trees are looking very positive." Lena added as she sipped her tea and adjusted her body nervously in the seat; it was rather clear she was not comfortable.

"What do you think would help make your farm as successful as you would like it to be?" The King asked in a way that confused that Woods.

"Just hard work Your Majesty and good luck… there is not one thing I can put my finger on." Earl stated as if he was nervous.

"I can be sure there is something that would help you achieve the farm of your dreams. Would money or extra land help?" The King was not going to believe that there was nothing that would help the couple. "Perhaps, more hands to help with labor?"

"Forgive me, but I am confused, Your Majesty. What is the point of this meeting?" Earl asked as he and Lena began to grow more uncomfortable.

"I will be honest with you. Recently, I was visited by a psychic, Anders, who told me your daughter will be of great help to me. She is the missing puzzle piece in my kingdom. I was told that she will help turn this kingdom into the happiest place on earth. It was clear that she was special by the way he was explaining her to me. The reason that I sent for you was to make a deal. I will be more than happy to give you money or land in exchange for the adoption of Gerica." The King was bold in his speaking; but he was determined to get what he needed. He did not even blink an eye while lying, one of his many talents.

"You are asking to buy Gerica?" Lena gasped at the idea. Gerica was her precious two-year-old, and Lena was appalled. She reached over to her husband's lap and placed a firm hand on Gerica's back, in a protective manner.

The King was growing annoyed but remained calm. "So to speak Lena, you see, I want to raise her as my own, only for the benefit of this kingdom. There is something very special within your daughter. I understand that I may not have experience with children, but I have Lucille. She will be helping me every step of the way. So, again I ask, what can I help you with?" The King was hopeful that this would go over the way he wanted, and that having Lucille there to help him, they may feel more comfortable with the arrangement.

Silence took over the room that felt much too long for the King. Earl was staring at the King as if King Beckford was a hideous two headed lizards with red eyes and Lena started to shake.

Finally, Lena looked up and rose to her feet. "There is nothing in this world that would justify us giving you our baby. She is our child; if we have to struggle to thrive then we shall do just that." Lena yelled with fear in her voice; Gerica woke from the noise and started to whine.

"Lena!" Earl nervously cried.

"Calm down, Lena; we can figure something out together. The kingdom needs Gerica; surely you can see the dilemma I had even asking you to come. I know that with my guidance, she will be the best queen that Leward has ever seen." The King started to plead. *They could have more children if they wanted, but I cannot replace Gerica. I need her for the sake of saving all of my hard work.* The King thought to himself, *why are they willing to struggle to live instead of having everything given to them?* "I will ask you again... Mr. and Mrs. Woods, what can I help you with. I would be more than willing to give you a tax break on top of anything else you choose to take. As you see, this agreement means a great deal to me." He began to grow arrogant. *I am able to have you both thrown in jail and take the girl,* he declared in his mind, but he remained calm.

Earl rose to his feet. "Nothing; anything we accept from you in return of our daughter would be in vain. Gerica is the very reason we work so hard, and without her, there would be no reason to have the farm. Surely, you can see our dilemma." Earl spoke boldly as his voice dripped with annoyance.

"I am sure that you love Gerica, with all of your heart, but this is my kingdom, our kingdom. She will want for nothing; she will be loved and taken care of. I need you to trust me." The King's voice began to crack and squeak as he pleaded. He was starting to become nervous as the outcome he hoped for drifted away.

Lena walked closer to the King. "Trust you, trust you! You do not know what it is like for your 'citizens' within your kingdom! All you do is raise taxes and give little thought of us when you choose to bleed us dry of the little money we make! Children, mothers and fathers all die because of the living conditions you allow us to live in! You keep your guards in the city streets to patrol and harm innocent citizens for merely walking in a way that the guards do not find to their liking. How dare you ask us to trust you, a King who is so high on his throne that he does not even know that he is hated by his whole kingdom? Why would we give our daughter to your cause? To hell with your kingdom, no one should live this life." Lena had become unhinged and as she yelled these words to the King, she spit in his face. Only when the last speck of saliva reached the King's bottom lip, did Lena realize what she had done; she froze from the fear of what was to come.

"You wretched wench!" King Beckford roared as he wiped his face clean before pushing over the chair at his side. There was a spike of hatred that began to run through every vain in his body as he reached out his hand to wrap around Lena's neck.

"Lena, go!" Earl grabbed Lena's wrist and the two of them run out of the dining hall and through the castle, with Gerica thrown over Earl's shoulders. By this time, she was awake, kicking and screaming. They managed to reach the front doors and escape the castle unharmed.

Lucille stopped listening through the door, and came rushing in. "Beckford! What has happened?" Lucille was confused by what she heard, and more confused that the King is sitting in his chair. "Why are you letting them escape?" Lucille yelled over the sound of the King throwing the bread and bowls of soup at the wall. He stopped and looked up at Lucille.

Veins in his forehead begun to show through his skin as he roared at Lucille; "Silly woman, they cannot run away from me; there is no need to run after them. They have mistaken my moment of kindness for weakness." All of a sudden, the King's face fell back to normal as a smile spread on his face; Lucille could see a plan forming in his mind. "I will have that child, it is not a question of how, it is question of when at this moment."

Lucile felt anxiety running around in her heart as it dropped to her stomach. "What are you planning?" Lucille whispered; she was not sure if she was ready for the answer that would follow.

King Beckford was silent for a moment, as he formulated his plan and dipped his finger into the only tea cup that survived his massacre and stirred it in circles. "They have a journey on foot ahead of them. I will allow them to make the journey home, safely. I will allow them to go back to their everyday life, unbothered. Once they have forgotten about this little encounter, I shall make my move. The one thing the witch said to me that was disheartening, was that my kingdom hated me. I knew that the citizens were not lining up to greet me, but I did not think that there was passion of hatred toward me. I will have to fix that until I get

Gerica; I shall lay low for now. Tell the guards to leave the streets of Leward, and report back to the castle. They shall remain here for the time being. Go now, Lucille and relay my message. Also, please find Anders, I need him to speak to me right away."

"Yes, Your Majesty, right away," Lucille replied as she stood on her tippy toes backing out of the room, never taking her eyes off the King. She started to run down the main corridor while her whole body shook from fright.

As the King sat in the dining hall, he replayed the situation over in his head. He was in awe of how the Woods did not think that he was being beyond generous. *Do they not understand that I could have just killed them both and stolen Gerica? Who would have missed them? They must think that they were in the clear and they will not encounter me again.* He felt the corners of his lips curl into a smile. There was not a doubt in his mind that he would one day have Gerica.

Some time had passed before Anders walked into the dining hall; nervously. "Your Majesty... Lucille sent me to speak with you," he announced in fear.

"I need you to explain to me what the Woods' house and farm look like, and where exactly it is located. This is not over." King Beckford demanded.

Anders sat down in a chair to recall every detail of the Wood's cabin and farm. He begun to tell the King everything he could remember as he closed his eyes and tilled his head back. "It is a small wooden cabin, on the edge on the forest. It sits at the end of a long dirt walk way. There are windows in the front that have blue curtains that hang the entire length. A porch that wraps around the front of the cabin; in some spots the wood is decaying, and you can see boards sticking up in random places. The front door is painted white, while the rest of the house remains brown. There is a well where they get fresh water from that sits to the left of the cabin. Right next to that is the garden, with things like tomatoes and pumpkins that you can see from the walk way. From the walk way you can also see the land that sits behind the cabin. A fence that runs the length of the large field separating the animals and three little stables; I believe this is where they keep the farming tools. There are trees on each side of the yard that provided shade of the cabin. As for the inside, I did not see it. I stood outside of the cabin and Samuel and Stetson stayed with the horses at the end of the walk way. None of us saw the inside of their cabin." Anders had given as much detail as he could remember.

"You said there was a well near the house where they get water from, correct?" Asked King Beckford, his head was a whirlwind of ideas as he came to his attack plan.

Anders nodded his head at the King. "Yes, Your Majesty, we had arrived at the Wood's address shortly after the sun rose this morning. When we got there, Mr. Wood's was retrieving water from it."

"Very well Anders, will you follow me. There are some things I would like to show you." And with that sentence, the King left the dining hall and started down the corridor. The King was filled with rage and hatred; he felt his blood boiling as it ran from his head to his feet. *I had been as nice as humanly possible; the wench and her husband did not see the treasure that I was just going to hand them. They could have another child; they could have ten more children. All I needed was the one; the one girl that could take my kingdom away.* He grabbed a candle stick from a holder that was hanging on the wall, along with matches from a table that laid against the same wall. The more the King walked and thought about this situation the more he became enraged. *Why did*

I even try to make a deal with them, he thought to himself. *I should have just stolen the child. There would have been nothing they could do to stop me. Of course, having a King that was a kidnapper was not going to go over well with anyone. Nevertheless, I will hide in the shadows while the dirty deed is fulfilled.*

Anders, who was aware the meeting did not go well, was unsure why they were walking away from the dining hall. The two men walked down a set of spinal stairs that were behind a brass door he had never seen before. The further down they walked the colder the air got. It was dark; the only light that was available was the single candle that the King was holding. When they reached the bottom of the stair case, the King walked up to the wall, reached up and took the candle he was holding to light more hanging candles. The hanging candles were on gold chains that came down from the ceiling and lined the stone wall. The King lit the candles as he walked, making the room became more visible. The King took the last candle and gave it to Anders.

Now that Anders was able to see, he wished he could give the candle back to the King. Anders could see rats, everywhere on the floor and wall; crawling over each other with their tails wiggling. Anders may not be used to living in a castle, but he was not used to seeing rats run so freely where men walked. He looked at the walls, there were cracks in almost every wall, some big enough for the rats to push their bodies through. The ceiling was dripping water, or at least what he hoped was water, Anders was already feeling nauseous and afraid to look up.

Finally, the two men reached the end of the hall. They came to a gigantic black stone door with gold lock in the shape on an eye. The King reached into his robe and pulled out a key. He took the key and unlocked the black door. King Beckford put both of his hands on the door and pushed it open with all of his strength. It was clear that this was not a room that was used very often. Cob webs cluttered the door way when the door was fully open. Anders' stomach started to turn; it was the most inhuman place that Anders had ever had to experience.

Chapter Three

The King's dungeon looked like a torture chamber. As the two men were fully in the dungeon, the door closed behind them with a bang that rattled the room. Anders jumped when he heard the door slam; causing an instant jolt in his heart as it began to beat faster. The air was colder in this room than it was in the hallway, which created bumps that covered every inch of his skin. Shelves that hung on walls wrapped around the room in its entirety and were filled with jars and books. Anders walked closer to the walls; noticing the contents of some of the jars. His stomach was on the verge of releasing its contents when he saw the fingers and ears. Decaying flesh still stuck to the bones of hands and feet. Anders was confused; he knew the King was a tyrant; but he thought it started and ended with the money the King demanded from the citizens. He never had pictured the King as a · sadistic and disturbed individual. He wondered what had these people have done to be met with such a fate.

Then he realized he was alone in this torture chamber with the very man that kept such items; he was infuriated. In all actuality, the reason that King Beckford was mad was his fault. Had Anders not told the King about his dream, the King would not have had that meeting. He would not have been spit on and thus, they would not be exploring such a hellish place. Sweat dripped from Anders' palms and forehead despite the temperature in the room being cold enough to freeze a thin layer of water.

He felt both pain and nausea in his stomach, "Your Majesty, I apologize for breaking this silence between us. I must ask why you have taken me down here?" Anders' voice trembled with every word. The King walked to the very back and began taking a lid off a barrel that resembled something you would find in town, at a pub.

Holding a candle over it, he demanded Ander's attention, "Come over here, Anders."

Anders had a sensation in the back of his throat that felt as if a rock had been eaten and was clogging his ability to breathe. He took one step and noticed his feet did not want to move. With each step, his balance was interrupted by the shaking of his legs. Nonetheless, he did as the King had asked. "Yes, Your Majesty" Anders mutter in the lowest tone he could manage to come up with. Anders could picture the King attacking him in a fit of rage for bringing this information to him. He was sure the King could hear his heart slamming against his rib cage as it beat.

"Anders, when you first came to me, I thought you were crazy. I thought there was no way a child would take my spot on my throne, in my kingdom. I was ready to have a part of your body hanging on one of these shelves. I trust you know that?" King Beckford was all too certain that Anders was petrified.

"Very much so Your Majesty; may I ask how you feel at this moment? Giving all that has happened? I do pray that you have mercy on me; their reaction was not in my dream. I did not foresee this outcome." Anders proclaimed with the deepest of sincerity in his voice.

King Beckford looked Anders directly in his eyes and gave a devilish smile before he let out a hearty, belly laugh. "My dear boy, I am no fool. I know that you had no idea the outcome. If you had known, you would have brought this to my attention, am I correct?"

"Indeed, my lord. I never thought of it ending this way. I thought I was helping both of us by reporting this information to you."

"I did not have to be a psychic to see that you had no idea. I see something in you that I do not often see in people. It is my belief that the future of this kingdom will be bright if you are here. I want you to be my personal psychic; my advisor. I know that our conversations have not discussed your personal life, so we shall start there. Do you have a wife or children?" The King had just assumed that this man was single in this world. He was an odd lad, and surely not able to convince any woman to marry him.

"I do not, sadly. Before I came here, I had been living with my sister." Anders answered

"I should ask then, your thoughts on moving into the castle. I can give you your own end of the castle, your own servants. Anything that you see fit. You must understand that staying here would make you part responsible for the fate of this kingdom. I see great things in your eyes; I believe that you are capable of helping me fix this current mishap." He did not feel like he was being too forward with Anders; if he had not been frightened away at this point in their relationship, he may never be.

"It would be my honor, Your Majesty. Is that why you took me down here? Was it to intimidate me into saying yes?" Anders felt like it was a realistic possibility.

The King looked at Anders and began to laugh hysterically. "Heavens no, my dear boy; this room holds the answer to winning back the kingdom. You see, there are things in here that I am not proud of. When people steal, they lose a finger or in some rare cases, they lose their life. When people hear conversations that they should not have, they lose an ear. So on and so forth. I would like to point out, that I never get my hands dirty with the blood of my citizens. I do however, order my men to handle that business. And they bring me back a token from their job well done, as you have seen in the jars above. This room has any weapon known to mankind. In these barrels, there is hemlock soaking in water. Are you familiar with hemlock, Anders?"

"It is a plant, sir." Anders answered in a nonchalant voice.

"Hemlock contains poison. Most of the plant's poison is located in the seeds." King Beckford informs Anders, in a sinister tone that brings chills to Anders' spine. "However, the entire plant as a whole is very dangerous. When consumed in small parts, it might not be fatal immediately however, over time it can kill. But these barrels are filled to the top with hemlock. The plants are soaking in water to keep them fresh as possible, but the water now has the poisonous properties of the hemlock plant. When you said that the Woods' had a personal water supply, it was evident that this would be the way they would need to go. There will not be much planning involved with their murder. But no one can know of this plan. Yes I am known as a tyrant, but since Gerica is a special child, I do not want the citizens to know that I stole her in order to keep my kingdom. They might cause some sort of rebellion that my guards cannot handle. This is what you shall do. Two nights from tomorrow night, you are to set out, with a barrel of this hemlock water and on one of my horses. You shall go to the Wood's farm and pour this water into their well. You said that Mr. Woods was retrieving fresh water in the morning time; we shall hope that is part of his daily routine. When you see that he has taken the water out of the well, you are to wait. I assume that he and Mrs. Woods will drink the water with their breakfast. While this happens, you are to find the most opportune time to sneak in and take Gerica. As long as they have drank the water, even if they see you they would not be able to stop you. Within the hour they will start to feel the hemlocks symptoms. You are to tell no one of this plan. When I introduce Gerica as my own, we shall say she was found on a dirt road." This plan was not well thought out but the King had no doubt that it would work. "When it is finished, I want you to sever one finger from each of the parents. Cut the finger off once they both are fully dead, or at least, mostly dead. If one is fighting for their life, just remove the finger. It could help speed the process along if they cannot stop the bleeding."

"I have never killed anyone Your Majesty; this is out of my element." This was not only out of Anders' element, but out of his character. However, he stands by what he told the King. Should Gerica be raised in a family such as the Woods, she will have a pure heart, and thus, ruining Anders' life. Anders also had no choice but to obey the King if he wanted to stay in the King's good graces. "I do not think I can stomach such an inhumane act."

"Normally, I would not send anyone less than my very best guard. There are reasons I am asking you to do this for me. For one, this will prove to me that you are befitting the title of my friend. As I am sure you know I do not have friends. This will be the perfect test. Second, you have powers that my men do not process. I assume that should trouble find or follow you, you will see them before they see you. Am I to assume that these are accurate statements?" The King had valid points, and he knew this was not something that Anders could deny. Of course the King did not mention that should Anders refuse, he would be decaying in a jar within mere moments. The King cannot trust that Anders would not speak of this, another reason having Anders commit this crime is to ensure he keeps his lips closed on this matter.

"Absolutely Your Majesty. I would be able to see any type of threat. I understand why I must go, and I will prove to you that I am befitting of the title. You have my word, I will fulfill this journey for you and it will never leave my lips." Promised Anders. "How will I get the baby to you when I have arrived back to the castle?"

"I shall tell Lucille and the guards that they are to leave you alone, you are able to come and go as you see fit. When you return with the baby, you are to tell everyone that she was found wondering down a dirt road in Bales. No one will know the significance of her presence expect Lucille and I can handle her. When you return, pay no mind and come find me. For now let's leave this dungeon, tomorrow Lucille shall help you pack for your journey."

When Anders reached the dirt road that would lead him to the Woods' house, he started to feel anger the closer he got. He channeled every negative thing that was ever said about his line of work in to hatred. He would use this hatred to help him finish the job. He reached the edge of the woods leading to their farm house; he peered through the trees and walked slowly closer to the house.

Chapter Four

It was about two days before Anders came back with little Gerica. When they arrived back to the castle Gerica was fast asleep against Anders's chest. He did not have any of her belongings, just the baby. Lucille waited for them, anxiously at the front door. She had everything ready, from clothes to toys and blankets. She never had a daughter and she was beyond thrilled to be able to raise one. Considering all things, that was basically what Gerica would be to Lucille; the daughter she never had.

The second that Anders and Gerica made their way into the castle they were met by King Beckford and Lucille. Lucille promptly took the sleeping baby girl and whisked her away to her new bedroom. This was right down the hall from Lucille's bedroom. The King was not interested in losing any sleep, in case the baby should wake up; that was going to be all Lucille's job to handle.

The King looked at Anders, and with a deep voice asked, "How was everything?" It was a loaded question, and the King was not sure how to ask it exactly. This was the ultimate test of Anders. If there had been any doubts in the King's mind, they had vanished when Anders made the safe return of himself and Gerica.

Before Anders even whispered a word, he handed the King a sliver box. When the King opened it, he was pleased to see two pinky fingers. One was a tan, chubby finger with dirt under the nail. The other finger was a pale, thinner finger with a clear, long finger nail attached to it. This gift made the King smile. "It was nothing less than bizarre, how it all happened. Upon arriving to the farm, I creeped into the yard without anyone seeing or hearing, and I poured the water right into the well, per your instructions. I slipped away afterward to watch from the woods. And some time had passed before anything took place. Then I heard the front door slam shut and Mr. Woods had walked outside. He went and checked on his chickens and the like. Then, just as he did the other morning he walked to the well. He dropped a bucket down into the black depths with a splash and retrieved it with the rope that hung from a wooden beam above the hole. Then he took the bucket into the house. At that moment, I panicked because I had not gotten Gerica out of the house. I run around to the chicken hut and allowed them all to run free, knowing that it would take both Mr. and Mrs. Woods to get all of them back into the house. Fortunately for me, Gerica was in a back room sleeping. When they came running outside, I made a mad dash for the house. I took her with me, quickly out of the house. I was careful so she did not wake and start to cry. Afterward, I rocked her to keep her asleep and watched for the next hour from the woods. Once all of the chickens had been placed into the hut both of the Woods reported back into their house. They both sat down at the table to finish their breakfast. Which looked like it was oatmeal that would have been made with well water, and the tea was made with it as well; I could watch through the windows. After they both finished their meal, and their tea, both came outside. Mrs. Woods went off to the garden and Mr. Woods looked like he was about to pick apples from a nearby tree. Roughly twenty minutes had passed before any kind of sign took place. Mrs. Woods started to throw up, she dropped to her knees and begun shaking uncontrollably. This went on for about two minutes, until she fell. She laid flat on the ground and did not move. I stayed where I was. I thought it was too risky leaving the spot I was in, incase nothing was going to happen to Mr. Woods. He was out of sight at the time; after waiting for quite a long time, I started to walk around the house from the woods. I went around to the apple trees but I did not see Mr. Woods. It was not until I heard a gargling coming from the bottom on one of those apples trees that I realized, Mr. Woods was dying also. He must have fallen and landed on his back because he was staring at the sky, with his mouth wide open. It looked like he was choking on foamy saliva that was coming from his mouth. I sat and watched for a moment until he stopped making any noise. Just as that happened, Gerica started to wake up. I had no choice but to bring the baby with me while I checked on her dead parents and removed a finger from each of their bodies. I walked up to Mr. Woods and stood over his lifeless body. I put my boot on his stomach and felt no movement. I bent down and dragged the blade of my knife along the crease of his finger and pressed down until I heard a snap. Then the finger was lying on the ground, detached from his body. Gerica started to cry. The saddest part of this whole ordeal was when she saw her mother. When she saw her mother, face down in the dirt not moving; Gerica begun to scream. A blood curling scream, far stronger than one would expect could come from a baby. I did the same to Mrs. Woods as I had done to her husband. I placed a boot on her back and felt no breathing coming from her chest and removed her finger. I did however; try to shield the baby from seeing the blood that came from her mother's body. The baby was not consolable. Nonetheless, I threw her over my shoulder gently and walked back down the dirt road where I left the horse. Your Majesty, never in a million years would I have ever thought I was capable of such an inhuman act. This is not the person that I have lived my life to be. But once

I did it, I realized that it was little to do with me and my wellbeing; but more for the kingdom. It was easy to find the ability to partake in murder once I started thinking about my life without practicing my gifts. I can say that once the deed was complete, I had an odd sense of accomplishment. However, I do hope this is not a memory that stays with the child, she may never understand those imagines."

It was clear to King Beckford that Anders had an emotional confliction with what he had done. For a brief second, the King had felt guilty that he asked this of such an innocent man such as Anders. The second did not last long, what is done is done. From this day forward, they shall have a happy kingdom. The King extended his right hand to Anders to shake this great man's hand. It was interesting that Anders seemed to get some kind of thrill from this journey. Perhaps murder was much more in his character than he had originally thought. This was a pleasant surprise. The King could see the two of them getting along very nicely.

"Anders, I realize this may not have been in your character, but I want you to know, this is what had to be done. As you know, I was prepared to do anything that it took to avoid a mishap such as this. They gave me no choice. Now from this moment on, you will be looked at as a prince. No one should ever look at you in a way that does not please you. You have earned your spot on my council. I am forever in your favor." The King then bowed to Anders. He had never bowed to a man expect his own father when he was a young boy. The King stood upright, wrapped his arm around the shoulders of Anders, and started to walk Anders to his new end of the castle.

Many years had passed since the deaths of Earl and Lena. They were never spoken of after the day Anders returned to the castle with Gerica. King Beckford made it an unspoken law that there would be no mentioning of their names or the events that took place that day. Gerica was always made to believe that she was found, alone as a baby on an empty dirt road. Gerica grew into a beautiful girl, with a seemly perfect life. But that was only from the outside looking in. Gerica knew of fears that no one else in the castle could begin to try to understand. She had been followed by something that never showed its face. She could never prove that anything was there, but she knew in her soul that she was not alone.

Chapter Five

Fear shot up Gerica's spine the way a snake would attack its prey, fast and unstoppable. The lump of fear in the back of her throat stopped her from breathing. She was frozen; her body stuck, much like the way a tree is stuck into the earth. She was unable to move. She was going to face a shadow; that was not her own, yet she knows it all too well. It has followed her throughout her whole life. Inflicting this paralyzing fear onto her. Gerica would not know life without this fear; it is now a part of her being. She tried to turn her body away from the shadow, but it was moving too fast. It had reached her and forced her to the ground. She closed her eyes and hoped that it would end as the shadow covered her mouth with a black cloth. She was too afraid to look at the shadow so closely. She opened her mouth to scream…

Gerica woke, she realized it was the dream that has haunted her since before she could talk. This being forever engraved into her mind; she could never see its face. The only part of it that she saw was its black cloak. It pained her that her fears and dreams were always dismissed by anyone she told. Her father had no time for her fears, and he never took her seriously. Cloaks are not uncommon in the kingdom, and thus, this dream could not be significant; or at least that was his reasoning for ignoring her.

Gerica laid on her bed; her mind would not stop racing. She thought of the King, and everything he was teaching her. He said she would be alone, without a companion in the world, for the entirety of her existence. This was how Gerica was raised to believe life as a queen was supposed to be.

She already felt so alone in life. She never felt love from the King and was certain that when he did show affection, it was only an act to please the spectators. *I cannot blame him, I am a clumsy girl and always in the way,* she thought. Although she tried to keep to herself, it never seemed to work. She did not talk to the King much because she knew his life was preoccupied with the Kingdom. She knew her place was to continue his reign over Leward when he is no longer here. She was saddened when she remembered that was the sole reason she was saved as a child. She wished she was taken in out of love and compassion; instead it was out of desperation.

The dream had woken Gerica up while the sky was still black. With each dream, she would wake with sweat beads forming on her head and under her nose. She would be hot to the touch but unable to remove the blankets from her body. She always felt safe when she had a cover over her.

She could hear birds chirping and realized that she must have drifted back to sleep. The fear left her body right as the sun peaked into her bedroom. The red curtains lit up by the sun's strong rays, as a hand started to shake her shoulders until she was awake.

"My lady, please feel my hands and wake up. The King has requested your presents in the dining hall and will not wait another moment for your arrival." Lucille was in distress. The King had every servant scared of his temper, and often, his temper is due to Gerica's lack of attention to rules.

"Yes Lucille, I know you are there. How long since the sun rose? Sleep eluded me; I did not realize I that I was still in bed. My dreams, as real as ever, allow me to think I am awake." Gerica said. She tried to make sense of being able to forget the fear long enough to fall back to sleep.

"My dear Gerica, enough with your dream talk. I vowed to watch over you and there is not one thing I would not do to ensure your wellbeing. But take my words; this nonsense will do you no good. The King will not allow any more of this conversation to take place in his castle. Please understand you are nothing short of normal." Lucille sounded discouraged as she made her statement. "Now, please Gerica, get dressed and meet your father in the dining hall before he has both of our heads!"

"Alright, as you wish." She replied with just a hint of fresh mouth toward Lucille, while hiding the rolling of her eyes.

Dressed in her expensive silks, she sat at her vanity to brush her hair. Her gray eyes peered back at her through the mirror, but she felt like they were not the only eyes in the room watching her. Gerica knew that she was not insane like everyone made her out to be, and she could feel herself slipping into a hole of isolation.

When she was done getting ready for the day, she thanked Lucille and left her room. She thought about the walk down the unnecessarily large, long hallway, and how much she dreaded the morning meal with the King; his attitude toward her is one of annoyance. He was not a typical King of the times; most took pride in their daughters and made plans for them to marry right around the time of menstruation. Kings want their daughters to marry someone that will give promise to their kingdom. She was eighteen years of age, and the idea of never marring took Gerica deeper into her hole of isolation.

Gerica's limited freedom had only allowed her off the castle grounds a small handful of times; in the company of Lucille and at least two guards. The King kept her away from any villagers that may put different ideas into her head. She was blissfully ignorant.

Once she reached the dining hall, she saw her father with a look of dismay on his face. He watched her walk in and take her seat at the dark wooden table that spread from one end of the dining hall to a little more than half way toward the entrance. With shaky hands, she begun to eat her meal of porridge and bread, and refrained from making eye contact with her father.

"My dear Gerica, I have awaited you to join me for far too long. Is this disrespectful manner a direct reflection of how you view your father? Do you not take me seriously as King?" The tone in his voice was damaging. Though it was a mistake, he seemed to always make Gerica feel beyond guilty.

"No father, you see, I was unable to sleep last night. However, somewhere during the early morning of tossing and turning, I managed to fall back asleep. I was unaware what time the sun had come up, my deepest apologies." She spoke with a shaky voice because she knew that even in her sincerest moments, he would find fault.

"There will be no excuses, you have known my rules and to not be here when called for means you do not respect my rules." He assumed with a hint of painful delight in his dark eyes and a sting in his tone.

"Father, I assure you, it has nothing to do with not respecting your wishes. I cherish this time I get with you; it only comes in short amounts of times. I pray for your forgiveness." Gerica begun to choke on every word that she said to the King because she knew that he could snapped and that made her nervous.

"Gerica, I pray someday you will learn to be diligent in following orders. As for now, I have business to attend to in the upper part of the country. I will be gone on my travels for the better part of the week. When I come back, I will expect you to have had time to think over your respect for the kingdom and myself." The King announced. It was not often that he had to leave the castle; in fact, Gerica could count on a single hand how many times he had left her alone with just Lucille to watch over her. He hated to leave his throne, and his belongings.

"Yes, father, I will not disappoint you," Gerica replied with promise in her voice; her mouth half full of stale, week old bread.

"You mean any more than you already have. Right, well finish your meal and be off then." His words stung Gerica's heart as she was reminded that she had failed him; he removed himself from the table and left the dining hall.

Chapter Six

It was mid afternoon when Gerica decided to take a stroll through the garden. The mood was lighter when the King was gone; allowing her to explore. Outside she could feel the warm rays of the sun beating down on her face. Rays followed by a light spring breeze that was just enough to keep the day from getting too hot.

She noticed handmaids hanging up cloths to dry in the wind; they were right around her age. She wished so badly to make conversation with them. But servants would pass her with their heads hung low. She thought they assumed she was like the King; and that they did not want to know her anger. The thought broke her heart; she hung her head as she made her way passed them.

Gerica walked along a long line of white and blue bellflowers, marigolds and tulips. She watched her feet and counted the stone steps as she walked. Out of the corner of her eye, she saw something black move; the quick glimpse that made her very uncomfortable. She felt her legs turn to stone, but she needed to run. The wind fell silent; the sun was hot enough to make Gerica feel like she was bread baking in the oven.

Seconds had passed before Gerica heard any noise, then she heard footsteps coming right for her. She was too panicked to see what was coming and she chose to keep her back toward the sound. She jumped out of her skin and her heart stopped beating when she felt a hand placed on her shoulder.

"My mother is looking for you; she told me I may find you here. Is everything alright?" Oliver asked with concern when he saw Gerica jump from his touch. He was the only servant besides Lucille to ever speak to Gerica; though their encounters were brief and sporadic.

Gerica's legs regained their ability to move when she saw it was Oliver, "yes, Oliver. Thank you for asking, where can I find Lucille?" Gerica asked as she tried to remain calm, she felt the color drain from her face in the anticipation.

"Right this way my lady, you shall find her in the den." His reply was short, yet, reassuring. He was such a gentleman and Gerica felt comfortable around him. More importantly she felt safe, she was happy to follow him.

The pair found Lucille cleaning the windows in the den; which were not of small demand. Most of them taller than the King and wider than him as well.

"Lucille, you sent for me?" Gerica managed to keep her composure and regained the color in her face from the episode in the garden. Lucille may be Gerica's personal servant, but she was more like a mother and when the King was gone, she took her role of ruler very seriously.

"Gerica, your father has left for a few weeks, and has instructed me to keep an insanely close eye on you. Have you any clue as to why that is?" She asked the rhetorical question knowing that Gerica knew he was not happy with her when he left. Lucille did not even look up at Gerica but focused on making her reflection sparkle.

"I can only imagine. Though, I would be delighted for you to enlighten me." Gerica uttered, knowing this statement will be taken as being fresh; she could not help it, Lucille was the only person she could be herself around. She would never dare mutter things like that to her father.

"He is worried that you are not happy here, and that is stopping you from listening to his rules. He only put rules in place because he loves you, and when you did not meet him from breakfast today, he was less than excited. Since he cannot be here, it is up to me to make sure you are in your right state of mind. What is going on with you, Gerica?" Lucille spoke and each word shot through Gerica like icicles falling from the frozen trees into the snow during the cold winter months. She played to Gerica's guilt.

"Lucille," Gerica slowly begun to utter, "It is not that I am unhappy, I am so scared. There are feelings that I have to hide from father because he does not understand. He does not care. I am not convinced that expressing these feelings to you will matter much, but I know that I am not alone. Not even when I am physically alone, I am never really alone. There is something that is with me. I call it the shadow, for a lack of a better term. Though, it feels like an entity. Something that has been with me my whole life. He does not hear me. He does not believe me." Her statement turned to a cry for help by the time she had finished.

"My lady, do you understand how preposterous you sound! How is the King going to take you seriously? You have been given a rare and amazing opportunity to be adopted by him. Do you not see that? Do you not understand how differently your life could have ended? There is not anything a young lady in your shoes could want. Instead of loving your generous father; you wish to complain? To make a mockery of what has been given to you?" The annoyance in Lucille's voice as she spoke these words also filled her eyes with tears. "You have nothing more you could want; you would do well to remember that. You will learn a lot from him, and someday you will need to use what he has taught you. Now, run along, I cannot bear to look at you." Lucille had never taken her eyes from the windows.

Gerica ran away to her room with a broken heart; she felt there was no reason to speak her feelings or thoughts to anyone in the castle. It was a silly idea that either her father or Lucille would listen to her. *They have never seen the cloak, nor the shadow. They are not awoken in the dead of night with the paralyzing fear coursing through their bodies, turning their blood ice cold; with beads of sweat rolling into their brows.* Gerica felt like a fool as she reached her room. The lack of sympathy proves her fears of being alone; provides her with a hollow faith.

Chapter Seven

It was a rainy day with dark clouds that hovered over the castle like a bee hovered over a flower; they would move from time to time but they never left. The castle had been kingless and remained dull and uneventful. Gerica spent most of the time he was gone alone in her large bedroom; on the second story of the castle. The four windows in her bedroom were not as big as the rest of the house; they do not reach past her shoulders. It was impossible to see out of entirely unless she stood on a stool. The only way she could see the yard was by her balcony with glass doors. It reached from the top of the wall to the bottom; scarlet curtains covered all the windows and the balcony.

Gerica's room did not have much in it. She had a large bed with several mint silk covered pillows and a large pink silk throw blanket that covered the bottom. A side table sat next to her bed with three draws that contain trinkets that she had collected throughout her life. Her most prized procession was a crystal rock that had a single crimson line that traveled directly through the whole crystal. She had found it in the garden amongst many other stones when she was twelve years of age. The only crystal among a large pile of rocks, and from the moment it was in her hand, a sense of calm took over her body.

As she laid in her oversized bed, she stared at the ceiling; rolling the crystal back and forth between her hands. She was feeling sorry for herself because she was not able to see the world's many wonders; not being allowed to live her life. She would start her preparations for taking over the kingdom on her nineteenth birthday; without knowing anything important. She would be thrown into learning her father's plans for her more in-depth; she was dreading the day.

Dreading that day came hand in hand with dreading becoming Queen. She dreamed of running away since she was a young girl, but never had the nerve. Her survival skills would surely get her killed, or worse, caught by her father.

She started to picture how her teachings would be given to her when she begun to hear scratching noises coming from her doorway. Then boards began to creak under feet that were stomping their way down the hall. She shot up into a sitting position on her bed and placed one foot on the floor. The cracking continued and Gerica begun to feel her heart race as she lowered her other foot to the floor and stood up from her bed.

The cold floor begun to numb her exposed toes as she made her way to the door; the noise grew louder. But just as she reached the door, it stopped. Gerica only heard the rattling of her bones as her whole body shook with fear.

Facing the door, she took a deep breath and begun to calm herself; she thought perhaps she was hearing things until an incredibly loud sound of glass shattering made her jump from her skin.

Placing one hand on the latch to unlock the door with sweaty palms; she forced the door open as quickly as possible. Gerica noticed that the corridor was empty, no windows broken; and she had a clear view to the other end of the hall. The doors to the Western end, the forbidden end of the castle, were ajar. The Western end was by far the most eerie place in the whole castle. There was an ice cold draft throughout it and, even on the hottest days of the hottest summer. There was a presence there, one where you not only feel like you are being watched, but you feel as if your thoughts are not your thoughts; like eyes peering into your soul to find your deepest fears.

Fear shot up her spine like a thousand needles pricking her all at once. She began to convince herself to shut the doors; in hopes to avoid anything getting out. She was terrified, but she started to inch her way closer to the Western end. Hidden behind the blanket of clouds, the sun's rays were dimmed, barely able to penetrate the large windows. She smelt a faint cigar smell in the air as she run her hand alongside the wall of the corridor. She felt every dent and small hole that had ever been put in them. The peach colored walls did good to hide the uneven surface, but not the feeling of it. The dents and bumps were a reason for her to take her time getting the doors; they distracted her, keeping her mind off whatever was in the room.

She made it to the Western end and slowly placed her right hand on the cold, brass door knob. Before she could realize what she was doing, she poked her head into the cracked door; she had only heard about the Western end but had never seen it. Her jaw was shriving as her teeth began to grind; she was awful at hiding her fear.

She first noticed the floor made of mirrors; not wood or stone. She nervously pictured herself falling through as she had stepped on them. She noticed that the first room of this end was very large and had smaller windows than the corridor, and the rest of the castle. She gently pulled the heavy door toward her; closing it. When she turned around to walk back to her room, she saw Lucille walking toward her.

"And what do we have here, Lady Gerica? Are we finally out of the bedroom that has kept you away from the rest of this castle for so long? Have you decided to join us in the dining hall for our mid- day meal? Since your father is away, it will be Oliver and I, unless I can convince you to join us." Lucille extended the invitation with a half-smile and a loving look in her eyes.

Gerica felt Lucille's genuine love at that moment, and it eased her heart. "That actually sounds delightful, Lucille; I have been lying in bed listening to the rain and waiting for it to cease. It would be a nice change of pace." Gerica replied; casually forgetting to mention the Western End and its open doors, Gerica simply did not have the answer to any questions Lucille may ask. Both ladies turned and started walking down the stairs together.

"Lucille, how long have you work in this castle for father? I know that you have been here since I was brought here but I was curious if you were here long before that?" Gerica hoped that starting a conversation with Lucille would keep her mind of the Western End. As they walked farer down the corridor, Gerica would catch herself peering over her shoulder, ensuring the doors remained closed.

"I have worked in the castle for your father since he took over the throne for your grandfather. It was a long time ago; I believe your father was in his twenties; the exact age escapes me. I remember the day the guards bought you into the castle; you looked like you had not had a decent meal all your life, and you were wearing rags that were not fit for a dog to wear. Your father took one look at your gray eyes and realized that there would not be a more perfect child to make his daughter, and the hire in the entire kingdom. You can call it love at first sight. I was there that day, you know; it was a magical time in the castle. Your father knew nothing about raising a child; I had to rush into the town of Bales to purchase any and all clothes, toys and shoes that I could get my hands on. Oh, that day was a highlight in your father's life. He made the announcement of your arrival the very next day. He had me bathe you, dress you and comb your beautiful curls. Then he showed you off like you were his most precious prize. Before you, your father knew nothing of love." Lucille tried to maintain that her father was the most loving, and caring man to ever walk on this earth, but she is wrong. Her blinded love kept her from seeing what he actually was, a tyrant.

"Was he not worried that someone may recognize me when he announced me? He never talks about the day I was found; I have known very little about my life before I was taken here. I do not know who named me, or who found me. I simply know the basics; I was found, alone and abandoned on a road and then father thought I would make a decent queen. Did father name me?" She asked, and as she waited for Lucille to answer, she wondered if she had been told the answer to this very question before, and simply forgotten.

"Your father named you, Gerica; he loved that name. As for who found you, it was Samuel. God bless his soul, he is an honest, hardworking man." Lucille revealed.

Gerica always felt like pieces to her puzzle were missing, she had never felt whole. Perhaps because she knew that deep down, she did not belong in the King's world. She also knew that she did not belong in her birth parents' world; they abandoned her.

Lucille and Gerica reached the end of the hallway and Lucille opened the door to the dining hall. Oliver was alone, already sitting at the table with bowls of soup, little biscuits in a glass bowl, and goblets grape juice. The dining hall was filled with the smell of celery and onion soup; it made

Gerica incredibly hungry as soon as the smell hit her nose. The women sat down at the table, and Gerica took in her favorite sight. Oliver was muscular, with arms that looks like rocks and a tall, lean build. His light brown hair had a very short cut with crystal blue eyes that made everyone want to stare at them. He was Gerica's age and the two had grown up together; she tried to stop staring. He did not notice her eyes peering, he never did. Gerica was sure that he would be the one she would choose in her if she could, although she knew nothing of his desires. There were so many young ladies around the castle that it would be insane to think he would even consider her. Ladies that had his time, and knew him better than she did, it was a heartbreaking motion to have something so close to her reach and yet never being able to reach for it.

She looked away from staring at him dead on to just looking at him out of the corner of her eye. She could see the blue of his eyes sparkling off the glass as her vision went blurry. The idea of running through the castle while Oliver chased took over her mind. She pictured herself hiding behind a wall, trying to stop her giggling as Oliver threw himself on her covering her mouth with kisses from his gentle lips.

"Come on now dear, eat up!" Lucille said, as she stared at Gerica with wide eyes; Gerica had been staring off into space thinking about Oliver; not realizing that they had been sitting there long enough for her soup to begin to chill.

Gerica glanced at Oliver, who as busy dipping his bread into his soup. "I am, Lucille. The soup is delicious, who made it?" Gerica asked to start conversation. If Lucille made it, she will give the step by step instructions of how she made it, and the history behind this specific soup. She took pride in her work and will let any person willing to hear the details, hear them.

"Well I did, of course Gerica! Have you ever known Oliver to make such a pleasant meal?" Lucille looked at Oliver. "Not that I mean any harm what so ever by that statement, Oliver. I simply mean that the way I cut the vegetables and place the stock in the pan to boil is all personal technique. For example, the Spanish onions that I cut up ever so gently, were a little on the too ripe side. So, I soaked them in water to dull some of the flavor. And the stock was a job in its self. I had to dismember the chicken that I used for stew last night in order to make the stock for today's soup." Lucille continued speaking about the stock, onions and such for what seemed like forever.

Gerica glanced in Oliver's direction again; she saw that Lucille's story was boring the poor boy to death; but he played the attentive part very well. Gerica was sure in his head right now he is thinking that if she choked on her soup it would be a peaceful few moments without her voice. Gerica had tuned her out totally at this point; Lucille does not even notice the absence of their attention.

Gerica started to stare at her food, she was too nervous to continue to look at Oliver again, she knew that they would catch on at some point. She begun to day dream of dancing in the rain with girls her own age; friends perhaps; as she listened to the rain hit the windows. The idea of dancing in the rain was a silly one, but one that fairy tales painted to be a beautiful event. Everyone would smile in those fairy tales, but Gerica imagined that they were chilly, with goose bumps covering their skin. Girls dressed in pink and turquoise satin dresses, their hair stuck to their faces as they all laughed hard enough to lose their breath. In that moment, she felt like she was belonged with those girls.

She could hear Lucille's voice in the distance but was not listening to a word that she had said. She had been so deeply involved with the day dream that she did not notice the silhouette standing outside of the dining hall right away. When her eyes focused on it, she quickly forgot about dancing in the rain as her body begun to tighten; it was the shadow, out in the day time. Gerica finally had a clearer view of the being, but it was still hard to make out. There was white around where a person's eyes would be but everything else was dark. Gerica could not catch her breath or move a single part of her body.

"Gerica, GERICA! Snap out of it, child, you are spilling your tea everywhere!" Gerica could hear the muffled sound of Lucille's voice, but she was not connecting to what she was saying. "Hello! Gerica!" Lucille had her hands on Gerica's shoulders and started to shake her; after she took the cup out of Gerica's frozen hand. Oliver was standing on his feet, at the opposite side of the table with a look of fright on his face when Gerica came to. Her whole body was shaking, and she began to sweat.

Finally, Lucille got her attention, but it took a moment for Gerica to focus on only her. When Gerica blinked, and refocused her eyes, the silhouette was already gone.

"I... I... am sorry. I am not sure what happened." Gerica stuttered; she knew that Lucille would not believe her. Gerica hung her head in embarrassment; her goblet had tipped and started dripping onto her dress. She stood up from the table without saying a word and started to walk out of the dining hall while making wet footprints. She was in a daze as she walked out of the glass doors and shut them behind her. She leaned her back against it and closed her eyes. Her heart was pounding though her chest like a drum being beat on. Gerica stayed there for a few seconds trying to catch her breath. Her head hurt; her throat burned and she felt like she was going crazy.

She began to walk slowly back to her bedroom, still breathing heavy and shaking. The rain stopped but the sky was still so dark in the late afternoon. As she made her way down the hall, she felt something graze the underneath of her foot; she looked down and found a folded paper. She bent to pick it up, and once it was unfolded, she read the words:

Dear young Gerica, you are not crazy. We are here, and we have been watching you. Your future is not for you to choose. It has been chosen for you. You will be with us soon.

Chapter Eight

Her body tightened, and her throat went dry; she was not prepared for a note so haunting and raw. The words were so simple, but so horribly frightening. In a split second's time, she had every nightmare that had ever haunted her, flash back in her mind. She saw the cloak; the shadow standing over her bed as she slept. Standing in the middle of the corridor; unable to move and horrified; she became overcome by a sensation thousands of eyes coming from every direction, watching her. The word "We" stood out the most to her, *how many makes up "we"?* She looked up and saw through the glass doors into the dining hall that the only eyes on her were Lucille's and Oliver's. Lucille had the most confused look on her face that Gerica have ever seen, and Oliver was standing at the table with no expression showing.

She took off running with the note clutched in her fist. The faster she ran the less she could feel the floor on her feet. Upon reaching the top of the large stairs case, Gerica saw the Western end in the distance with the door wide opened; she had closed that door. Her body was starting to numb and every hair on her arms stood straight up. Tears rolled down her face faster than ever as she ran from the Western End.

Gerica made her way into her bedroom to catch her breath. She sat down with her back against the closed door. She had a million thoughts spinning around her mind all at once. *Had Lucille seen it, surely, she could not miss something so bold; but she did not have a look on her face that proved she had seen anything. This shadow was taunting me; it likes my fear.* Gerica pulled her knees into her chest and wrapped her arms around them; salty tears started to roll down her cheeks, into her mouth. She was not able to make a sound when she had one more thought. *Perhaps, it is father's doing; some kind of twisted game that was keeping me from ever wanting to leave. It was a reasonable explanation as to why no one besides me ever sees it. And of course, that would be a reason that no one ever listens. Perhaps it was all a game, testing my limits.* Gerica felt like a fool and the only one in the castle to be made a mockery of.

"Gerica, what in the world has gotten into you?" Lucille banged on Gerica's door with an angry fist, yelling at the top of her lungs. Gerica moved away from the door, wiping her freshly cried tears away as fast as she could.She opened her door to find Lucille standing there with her red hair a mess, and her face even redder than her hair.

She stood looking at Gerica with eyes made of ice, as she fixed her hair. She moved a piece behind her ear as she started to walk closer to Gerica. "Do you know the mess you made in the dining hall, young lady? The stains on the floor! Or your dress! You made a mockery of a nice meal that we had planned for you!" Lucille yelled. There was a single vain visible in her head every time she yelled. It is very possible that she could psychically hit Gerica at this point.

"Lucille, you should know that nothing of what just happened was my intention." Gerica mustered the courage to say this in the strongest tone possible as she took a few steps back incase Lucille lunged at her. "I am not sure what came over me, I know that was a bit out of character of me, I am so very sorry. Is there still a mess? I will be more than willing to help you clean it." Gerica tried to sound sincere to hide her fear; but in her head was a far bigger mess than anything from the spilt tea in the dining hall.

Lucille stared at Gerica, and slowly her cold and frightening eyes turn soft and welcoming; she never could stay mad at Gerica for long. "Gerica, if there is something going on, I need to be aware of it. I realize your father is not around, but I can still help you. What is going on with you dear girl?"

"Lucille, there is nothing more going on than what I have already expressed to you." After looking into her eyes, Gerica swallowed her pride and closed her eyes tightly as she begun to speak her next few sentences. "Nevertheless, I will tell you. You remember all of those times I told you and father of the shadow that had always been in my company?" Gerica asked as she paid close attention to Lucille's facial expressions. "Today, while I was in the dining hall, I looked up only to see this "shadow" looking at me through the glass doors. I know what you must be thinking, it is not real; but I can assure you, he or it was there. I am not sure what to call it at this point."Gerica ended her sentence by looking down at her hands. Then she remembered the note, "Not only was I being watched by this thing, but it left this in the corridor. " Gerica pulled the piece of paper from behind her back and handed it to Lucille. Lucille unfolded it and began to read it while not making a sound.

"Gerica, where exactly did you find this." *Her face is unreadable; it is clear that she is disturbed, but what was bothering her? The fact that all of this time, I have not been lying? Or could it be that she now knows that we are not alone in the large castle, and it could be under attack?*

"In the corridor; where I stood, it was just lying on the floor. Where anyone could find it; and the shadow was there, where anyone could see it." Gerica would give anything to make her believe these words.

"I see. Well this obviously changes things. Your father will not be back to Bales for one more week, and this is not something I am prepared to handle in anyway, I will need to consult Anders. For now, you will not be alone. Follow me; you will need to sit in the dining hall while Oliver cleans up the mess you made. He will keep an eye on you; for your safety, of course; come now." Lucille held out her hand to hold Gerica's. They walked down the stairs, and into the dining hall. Oliver was alone, on his hands and knees as he scrubbed the huge mess that she made from the floor; she felt a huge feeling of guilt take over her.

"Oliver, I need to you keep Gerica in your sights; she is not to be left alone for one second. She can also help you clean this mess up; but do not allow her to be unattended for any reason. I need to go speak to Anders about important matters and I cannot take Gerica with me. She is to stay here with you." Lucille ordered as she walked into the hall. Gerica sat down and just looked at

Oliver; who looked annoyed by her presence; but he did not say anything.

"I will, mother." Oliver agreed. Gerica felt horrible watching him clean her mess, but she was not able to say anything. She just sat there with her head down, watching him from the corner of her eye.

Chapter Nine

Lucille walked out of the dining hall and made her way to the Southern end where Anders stayed to himself. He was almost never seen out of his room, especially when the King was not in the castle. Anders was not a people person and could not bring himself to be bothered with small talk. Truth be told, Anders did not want to live in the castle with the King nor did he want to be the King's confidant. He most certainly did not want to murder anyone, and had he known the outcome of him informing the King of his dream that night so long ago, he may not have done it; he felt stuck. Since the very first dream about the Leward kingdom to the present day, Anders' dreams have come and gone without much significance. Since there was nothing more that Anders' felt he was needed for, the only thing he wanted was to be able to live a normal life. He had never dated a woman, or had his own children; was never able to see the world.

Lucille thought regret had cosumed Anders. She could sense the growing frustation for him, and although he never spoke about his own life, she could tell his thoughts. Lucille was able to read people and she had always been good at it. There was something in the way people talked to her, or looked at her with their eyes that made her intuned with their minds. Anders' eyes showed a blank, empty life. There was never a twinkle in his eye, nor a tear; they were as empty as they were white.

Lucille reached Anders room and knocked loudly on the thick wooden door, she saw a pair of creepy white eyes looking through the window in his door. Lucille found it ironic, *since he is supposed to be able to see the future; why does he need a window? He should know I am here.*

"Can I help you with something, Lucille?" Anders asked; not bothering to hide his annoyance or distaste for Lucille. In his opinion, she was only around the King to benefit from what he had to offer. *Why else would she still be sticking around the castle all this time, knowing she will never be more than a maid or a mistress?* She was a tough one to read, however, Anders had no knowledge of her true intentions, so he could not prove anything. His thoughts were mere speculations, and he never did dare mention his thoughts on Lucille to the King because he feared it could back fire on him. After all, Lucille does cook most of the food inside the castle walls; and she had her henchman at her disposal. That little weasel Oliver; he was a smug, arrogant young man and Anders had no use for him. Anders was filled with hatred; being forced to live among people he was not fond of had taken a toll on him.

"Let me in, Anders. This is not a matter to be discussed so publicly." Lucille whispered with a death stare in her eyes and her arms crossed over her chest. For the love of everything good in this world, she did not understand why this man was so guarded. She had tried on several occasions to make Anders feel like part of their world, but he denied her every attempt. When he looked at her, she always felt this uneasy, nagging feeling that something is off. Anders used to be so gentle, and what Lucille had deemed as trustworthy. Those feelings faded with each year he was in the castle.

"As you wish, just do not touch anything." Anders demanded this simple request from Lucille. He had a room full of things like dream books, which described any possible dream known to mankind; spell books; red and purple potions in various bottles on shelves that outlined his entire room. He had a key that with the right spell, could unlock any person's thoughts; he also had a set of dice, with eyes on them. They were supposed to help Anders see where people are, even if they were millions of miles away. But he had not had much luck with any of these things; which made him upset; his whole life was a lie. He was inside his own head, cursing the life he lived when he realized that Lucille was still there, staring at him.

"Anders, are you with me? We need to fix this. I do not want this problem to still be here when Beckford returns." Lucille had been talking that entire time; Anders did not hear a word of it.

"I am sorry, Lucille. You have lost me; why are you here?" Anders was not even going to try to make up a reason for his wondering mind.

"Ah, you were looking right though me. The one thing about your eyes, Anders, no one can tell what you are truly looking at. The reason for my visit is that today, my sweet Gerica was visited. We were in the dining hall and she saw a being, standing there watching her. She did not mention seeing a face, but said it was the size of a person. Not only did it scare the life out of her, as she ran down the hall, she came across this." Lucille pulled the letter from her pocket and handed it to Anders. Anders unfolded it and read it.

"I have two questions. How did something get into the castle, passed the guards and what could it possibly want with Gerica?" Anders asked; knowing the answer to this question before he muttered it; she is in line for the throne. "I lied, I also have a third question, why are you telling me this; it is not like I can physically protect the girl?" Anders was tall and skeleton like, there was no way he could fight off a murderer.

"I am not sure of the how, what or who. The reason for my visit was to try to see if you had some magical crystal ball you could rub and see what will become of this and is there a threat to her life. I will have guards sleeping outside of her room until her father returns, at least." Lucille was not in the mood for witty conversation with Anders, someone was threatening her castle, her Gerica and her King.

"A magical crystal ball; you stand here and mock me so freely to my face? There is no way for me to know the exact reason for things unless it comes to me in a dream, and I have no control of the information that may be presented to me. I do not appreciate the jokes of my practice; and I assure you, if it is something that was let into the castle, then we have nothing to fear; no one would let anything sinter in. If it was something that just appeared, there will be nothing I will be able to do. From the things I have heard, lady Gerica has always talked to being followed and watched. Perhaps, she was right; in which case, this is nothing new, or stoppable for that matter. I can give you this for comfort, I will take a nap, and we can hope for a dream; you will be lucky if that happens." A cold, wide smile spread across Anders thin lips; he knew that there was not much he could do to help ease to Lucille; nor did he want to ease her mind. Her intentions were good, but Anders' problem was solely because of her disrespectful comment. Anders stood waiting for Lucille to turn around and walk away, but she did not move; and she was not laughing.

"The fact that you are not willing to help fix this problem puts the whole kingdom at risk. I hope you understand the jeopardy you are putting all of us in. I will be sure to enlighten King Beckford as soon as he returns. Sorry to bother you and waste so much of your useless time." Lucille's words sting; because Anders knew she was right.

Anders swallowed his pride. "I see, well I may be able to do something. Is she sure that it was a person-like-figure? How do we know she even saw anything?"

"She claims to have seen it, and she had this note." Lucille was convinced of this event because of the note. She knew what Gerica's handwriting looked like and knew this could not be hers.

"Ah, yes the note. I had forgotten that piece of evidence. There may be something I can do; I will have to consult the old spell books to see if there is a light magic that can be used to see where this came from. I will tell you now; I have never had much luck with this type of thing. I do not believe any sort of magic is in my blood. There may be something, however, leave the note with me. I shall try my best." Anders kept the note and ignored his better judgment; he truly did not have any idea what he could do to help.

"As you wish, I will be keeping a very close eye on Gerica, and I assume to hear back from you the second you find anything. Whether it is useful or not, I will need to know about it." Lucille demanded in the kindest tone she could come up with. "Enjoy the rest of your evening, Anders. "Lucille turned and walked away; as she walked down the corridor, her head started to fill with thoughts. *Could there be something with claims on Gerica? Gerica is a special girl; in plain sight, she is a normal child; there is not much to her. No one would have pegged her to be queen one day had Anders never mentioned the idea of it. The truth is, Gerica is not an outgoing; driven person. None of this matters, of course, because when you look into her eyes, you see light. The calming, effect, her eyes have on you is to reassure you that life will be just fine. The power that she possessed is not anything she can control. She does not even know she has it.* Lucille saw Gerica for much more than the meek, shy girl that she showed the world.

The King liked to keep Gerica within the castle walls as much as possible for her safety, and for his. Obliviously, how he came to be her father was not a respectable way. King Beckford did not want to take the chance of someone seeing her and asking too many questions. Lucille's mind and heart were torn.

Chapter Ten

A thought occurred to Lucille as she was walking away from the southern end. When Gerica had been outside of her room, she was walking away from the Western end and back toward her bedroom. Gerica had no business being toward the Western end. It was the end of the house that was once used as a ballroom, and where the King's throne was once kept. Lucille was reminded of what exactly the Western end had been used for as she stood in the corridor. Before Gerica's arrival, the King would throw luxurious parties where many kingdoms' royals would all meet and dance together. The King had also used these parties as sneaky ways to kill off the competition without getting caught. The King kept a dungeon full of poisons and weapons. Every so often there would be a prince, or a regent that would feel he was better than King Beckford. Whenever the King heard of this nonsense, he would invite the royals from every kingdom he could get his hands on to join him for a ball. There would be liquor by the barrels, and food that most people only saw in dreams; roasts and the finest cakes. He would befriend whoever was the target of the night and allow them to quench their thirst for liquor as much as he would like. Not knowing that the King had Lucille mixing a small amount of Hemlock water into their goblet the whole night. By the end of the night, the target would be unable to breathe, speak or even walk. They would start to vomit blood, and foam at the mouth like a wild animal; something that was witnessed by everyone. The King would drop to his knees and scream for someone to help his newly found friend. Being that over the course of the night, this target was being poisoned, he knew there was no help for them. What most people do not know is that hemlock is incredibly dangerous and when consumed can kill a person of poor and even great health. There was always a doctor or two present at these balls, so they would rush to the aide of whoever was dying on the floor. The King was never looked at as a suspect because it was clear that this person had drunken themselves dead. No one was ever pointing fingers at the King, although Lucille doubted that had anyone thought it was him, they would breathe it into words. Lucille sighed with regretted as she replayed her part in all the deaths, the only time she partook in such affairs; she needed to protect her king, she would tell herself.

That went on until the day that the target was a prince from Danielson, Prince Aaron. A kingdom that was three days journey from Leward. The prince was a younger man, whose father was on his death bed. He was too inherent the throne any day. It had gotten back to King Beckford that shortly after Prince Aaron had taken over his father's throne; he would attack Leward and try to stake a claim to everything that belonged to King Beckford. Prince Aaron had already hired a militia and they were being trained to fight. When King Beckford heard that there was to be an attack on his kingdom, he was unfazed; he knew what he had to do.

The King invited Price Aaron to his ball to celebrate his new-found duties. The night was full of life, and every person in attendance was enjoying their self. The King was near his throne entertaining some young ladies, while the Prince Aaron was acting in a less than King like manner. He was drunk, which was to be expected. Prince Aaron went for a walk down the corridor and went into the King's personal bedroom. How he made it that far was still a mystery to Lucille, who was supposed to be keeping the target near. Lucille had looked for Prince Aaron for around twenty minutes before she walked into the King's bedroom, his door was open and she knew King Beckford was not in there. When she poked her head around the corner, she saw Prince Aaron, stumbling drunk and going through the King's jewels. He picked up the King's gold chain that was given to him by his father and Prince Aaron put it into his pocket. Not knowing that Lucille was watching him, he continued to look through King Beckford's things; holding jewels up to a lit candle as he squealed like a young girl.

Lucille quietly went back down the corridor until she found Samuel, Stetson, and Horus. These were some of the King's most useful guards. She told them what was going on in the King's bedroom and to report there at once. As the guards ran off down the hall; Lucille then slipped her way back to the Western end to inform King Beckford of the betrayal. When she reached the King on his throne, she whispered in his ear, quickly so that the onlookers could not make out the words moving from her lips. The King sat up straight and with a stone face waited for the arrival of his guards and the thief.

Before too long, the doors to the Western end were pushed open. There was Horus on one side of Prince Aaron, and Stetson on the other. Samuel followed with a sword to the back of Prince Aaron's neck. Pushed up enough of the skin that it made a dent and discouraged Prince Aaron from making any sudden movements in attempts to escape.

"Your Majesty, this maggot has betrayed your trust in the utter most disrespectful way. He was caught in your sleeping quarters with his hands in your most precious jewels." Horus announced loud enough for the entire ball room to hear. Everyone stood around trying to get a look of the situation without breathing a word.

The King rose to his feet and walked toward Prince Aaron. He looked down with a tint of amusement in his eyes. He was starting to become bored with the normal way of executing his targets and people were starting to question why at every ball there was a royal that turned up dead. Although, no one ever directed the blame to King Beckford, that day was possibly nearing. By Prince Aaron breaking a cardinal rule of the Leward kingdom, the King would have the right to kill him without any backlash or questions formulating. This would take the attention from the King. Most importantly, since the current King of Danielson was no longer able to maintain his kingdom, there would be no one to come after King Beckford. Oh, yes, the King would enjoy this a great deal.

"Prince Aaron, are these accusations true?" King Beckford asked for the purpose of playing the victim and for the audience to side with him.

"Never King Beckford, I was simply lost. Your servant has provided me with much to drink. You see, I had to relieve myself and simply got lost. I am prone to poor vision, and I was unable to see what I was touching. Surely you do not find me capable of such an injustice." Prince Aaron replied with an offended manner.

The King was silent for a single moment while he stared his prey in the eye.

"I suppose I do not. But to prove that my men are liars, you would not mind disrobing. I assume?" The King asked this question just to see the look of fear in the man's eyes.

"I refuse, with all due respect Your Majesty. I am royalty just as you are. And I am a guest among a room of ladies. How rude of a man would I be to simply strip to my flesh with so many innocent eyes?" Prince Aaron was in a panic.

"That was not the answer of an innocent man. Do you see me as a fool, Prince Aaron? Is this not a serious matter to you? Hear me now." King Beckford yelled at the top of his lungs and stepped onto the stairs where his throne was kept. "If I could have every lady that is present in this ball room, please close your eyes and shield yourself from the flesh of this man." The King stepped down and walked toward Prince Aarons. "Now, you shall have no problems or excuses. Samuel, put down your sword and search this man's garments. Leave no pocket unturned." The King ordered as he tightened his arms across his chest.

The King stood and watched as Samuel ripped through the articles of clothing worn by Prince Aaron. In the first pocket, he found nothing; the second pocket was empty as well. The King started to become nervous, *could this be a mistake*, he thought? That would surely make his death look suspicious; by now the poison would be starting to make itself visible, and all eyes were on them.

The very last pocket, inside the robe was the hiding pocket. Samuel pulled out the King's golden chain, and a diamond ring that had belonged to his mother. This was a miracle; King Beckford did all he could to keep his smile on the inside.

"You are hard of seeing? Is that what you said? You lost your way?" The King announced loudly so the whole room could hear him.

"Your Majesty… I do not know what to say. There has to be some sort of misunderstanding." Prince Aaron's voice started to tremble.

"A misunderstanding is it; you mistakenly have my dear late mother's ring tucked into your robes by mere accident? Are you aware that stealing from me means you give up any human rights you have to your life?" King Beckford asked with amusement. "There will be no more discussion to this matter. Samuel, you and the others take this pathetic thief to a holding cell. I will be there once the last guest leaves."

The three guards took Prince Aaron away while he kicked and cursed the King. King Beckford watched in enjoyment and relief at the series of events. Prince Aaron just made his job so much easier. The King returned to his throne, stood in front of it and looked out into the ballroom. All of the guests were looking at King Beckford for some kind of direction. It was clear they were as shocked and confused as the King himself was. He had to speak to them as if he was their King instead of just one of the royals. "It is a shame that one ingrate has brought this ball to a close. It is clear that some people cannot be trusted in my castle, which is unacceptable. The punishment of stealing in the great kingdom of Leward is death by decapitation. It does not matter who the person is that committed the crime. In this case, it was a Prince; someone who knows of riches and jewels; but clearly has no knowledge of respect for his fellow man. Let this be a lesson to everyone that is in attendance at this time. I will not be crossed, and my kingdom will not be threatened in any way, shape or form. This will be the last time a ball will be held to unknown guests in my castle. I now have more important matters to attend to. Please see yourself out." The King directed his guests to leave the castle; he sat in his throne until the last one had left. If he was right, the poison would have kicked in and his problems would soon be solved. The only person that was left in the ballroom with him was Lucille; standing strong to his left side. The King looked at her and was reassured that she had his best interests at heart. She was a faithful and trustworthy servant; she had more than earned her place in the castle.

"Thank you." King Beckford whispered. He was no longer on his throne as he walked toward her. He wrapped his arms around her and embraced her into the tightest hug she had felt in a very long time. The King had to show her his appreciation. "Lucille, what would I do without you?"

"You would have lost your jewels, dear Beckford." Lucille looks up at the King and smiles. She pulled away from him. "You need to check on the Prince. He had a smaller amount of hemlock water than I would have liked. Normally, the target would be lying in a pool of their own bloody vomit by now. I doubt he is in that condition."

"Would you like to accompany me?" The King asked hopefully.

"No, I will start picking up the items left behind by your guests. They are some messy creatures." Lucille answered.

"Very well. Please meet me in my quarters after you are finished.' The King turned on his heals and walked down to the dungeon. He was curious what a partial hemlock poisoning would look like. Maybe he could torture the maggot that thought he was in his rights to steal from the King. Truth be told, the King admired anyone that was brave enough to challenge him or go against him. He just did not pity them when they received their punishment. The King made his way down the long corridor to the dungeon. The lights were already lit and everything was visible; he walked into the door to find all three guards sitting around the Prince as he was tied to a wooden chair.

The King paused in the doorway and smiled. He could see that there was foam starting to escape the corners of the Prince's mouth and beads of sweat had rolled down his forehead. His nose was bloody, and he had cuts on his neck, and his hands. It is clear that the guards had fun with him before they tied him to the chair.

"You three may leave. You have done your work." The King informed them. He did not need an audience when he handled the Prince. They did not say anything; and closed the door when they left.

Knowing that the Prince would not be able to talk back, the King felt that it is an excellent time to enlighten him on everything that had taken place on this night; he wanted to see the fear and hatred build up in Aaron's hazel eyes.

"Let it be known, that you have made my job easier than I had expected when I announced this ball. You see... I have heard many, many things about you, your father and the kingdom of Danielson. Great things, horrid things, and things that I found far less amusing. Not too long ago, I was approached by someone that you had spoken to. Apparently, while you were in intoxicated on gin, you allowed your ego to speak for you. You were going to try to ambush my kingdom; try to kill me and take everything that I have worked so hard for, away from me." The King looked at Prince Aaron with one arm crossed over his stomach and the other holding onto his chin. In his eyes; a stone-cold look of hatred with a sparkle of excitement. "My dear boy, you are a sorry excuse for a Prince; you would make no King. You put the plan of your own murder into effect unknowingly. While you carried yourself in the typical arrogant manner; parading around the beautiful ladies within these walls; I had my dear Lucille making your drinks with something special," King Beckford boasted. He walked over to the barrels that still contained the hemlock water, and he lifted some out into the cup of his hand. "You see, Prince Aaron; your drinks were poisoned with water that had been absorbing the components of the hemlock plant. The death will be slow, and painful. I can see it started to work on you as we speak. The plan was to allow you to lie on the floor of the ballroom, in front of all those guests and die slowly. You changed those plans when you chose to help yourself to things that did not belong to you. You thought that within your first few days on the throne, you could over throw Leward? I will enjoy ending your useless life." King Beckford was delighted to watch the life slowly ebb from the Prince's eyes; however, he did not want to wait anymore. The King walked behind the chair that the Prince was sitting in and reached for his sword. With a clean swipe, the King took the Prince's head off. The King stood there and wondered how he would clean with mess now. He dropped the sword, and walked out of the room, and he was overcome with the sense of success; he felt accomplished and justified. When he reached the end of the corridor Horus and Samuel were waiting.

"You two gentlemen will care take of the mess in there." King Beckford commanded as he walked by. His body was tired and beyond ready for a good night's sleep; after he stayed in the company of Lucille. She was waiting for him when he opened the door to his bedroom; he smiled as he closed the door behind him.

Chapter Eleven

It was because of this night that the Western end was closed down indefinitely. There would never be another ball in King Beckford's castle; it was both a blessing and a curse. Since there would be no more balls, there would be no way to eliminate anyone that thought they were able to match the King. The only positive outcome was that the news of Prince Aaron's death had traveled to all of the kingdoms and discouraged any others from trying to test the King. The saddest part was that now, the western end was closed off. There had been so much work that went into making that room a gorgeous piece of art; the floors were made of a special type of unbreakable mirror, so dancers could watch themselves as they enjoyed the music. It had gold curtains that sparkled in the sunlight and shimmered when the room was lite by candles. The King's throne once sat upon a small set of stairs, overlooking the entire room. Lucille once loved that room and she was still heartbroken over its ending.

She had gotten lost in her thoughts over the Western end, and she had forgotten the task at hand. She did not see why Gerica was near that room. There was no reason for her to be there,

there was nothing in there for her. In fact, there was nothing in there for anyone now; the whole lot was entirely cleaned out. The only thing that was left in there were the mirrored floors. Lucille walked into the Western end and felt an intense burst of cold air on her face as she opened the door. Since it was cut off from the rest of the house, it had not received any heat from the fire places in some time. Lucille glided in the ball room with ease; like many times before, she missed these floors. She looked around to see if there had been anything in there that may have been useful, but the room was uneventful. Lucille gave up rather quickly; *Gerica was just being nosey*, silly girl.

Lucille thought it was best to turn around and walk out of that room. Being in there was pointless; the memories were depressing. But just as she turned to leave, she felt the glares of eyes upon her back. She had never felt this feeling, but she knew she was not alone. Unlike Gerica, she was not afraid; the one thing she picked up from the King after all these years was that she needed to have a backbone. She turned around, but the room was empty, and it was getting dark; there were no longer any candles in this end. She thought it was be best to turn and leave; ignoring any more ideas of glaring eyes. She closed the door behind her; making sure it was latched. Gerica had no business what so ever wondering into that room; and if she had been in there, there would be hell to pay. *It should still be used. There is no reason that it needs to be closed down anymore. Nothing ever came from the death of Prince Aaron, I can understand why the King did not want to have balls anymore, but why keep that end closed off. It may be the memories of a happier time that bothers the King, a time before Anders and Gerica...*

Finally, Lucille made her way down to the dining hall; where she found both Gerica and Oliver in the exact spots that they were in when she left them. She sat down next to Gerica and took both of Gerica's hands into her own hands and looked into her eyes. "Gerica, I cannot tell you what it was that you saw. Nor can I explain this note, but I can protect you. I am planning to speak to the guards and there will be one outside of your bedroom as you sleep all night. When your father returns, he will have the last say in how this is handled. But for now, I shall walk you to your bedroom. You should not wonder the corridors alone."

"Yes ma'am," Gerica replied, she felt warmth in her heart toward Lucille that gave her a tiny piece of mind, but in her soul, she could feel no relief.

The two women headed out of the dining hall and made their way to Gerica's bedroom. All Gerica could think of was what was watching them with every step they took. And all Lucille could think of was when King Beckford would return. They remained silent as they walked.

Upon reaching Gerica's room, they saw Horus already outside of her door. He stood stiff as they approached. "Ah, Horus. I see you received my instructions to watch over Ms. Gerica while she is alone in her bedroom?" Lucille acknowledged Horus with a slight smile and a matter of fact tone.

"Yes, Lucille. I also investigated her room to assure that there was no one or nothing inside; she is clear to go in," responded Horus.

Gerica did not say a word to either of them, and she let herself in her bedroom, their fussing over her made her feel quite uncomfortable. If there really was something that was after her, they would not be able to stop it. It was clear to Gerica that they feel they are doing their job by enforcing security for her; but she knew it was too late.

The moment she entered her room and the door was closed tightly behind her, she ran to her bed. She laid flat on her back and looked at the window ceiling; she had spent so much of her childhood looking through the giant windows. She was comforted by the clouds and stars that she was able to see; it reminded her that there is a world outside of the castle.

Chapter Twelve

The noise started out as if a person was knocking on a door or window. For a few moments, it stayed at that volume, but it was enough to make Gerica jump from her bed; as her heart started to pound. There was no one up at this hour, and no candles shining light on anything. Gerica placed both of her feet flat on the floor; lifting her body off of her bed. The knocking seemed to increase any time Gerica made a movement. Besides the knocking, the sound of intense rain falling down on the castle and the thunder that came after filled her ears. Every so often, there would be a bright blue strike of lightening that would light up Gerica's room; allowing her to almost be able to see. Her hands started to tremble as she made her way to her bedroom door. Every single hair on her body was standing straight up; she had a feeling that tonight would be the night that she would face this shadow. She reached her door and began to push it open. It was not locked, but it would not open; something was stopping it. Gerica started to pound of the door and scream for help. The knocking that woke her did not stop; it grew so loud that she could feel the vibrations in her head; every knock felt like she was being hit.

"Horus! Horus!" She screamed at the top of her lungs as she kicked the door. Finally, there was a noise on the other end, and the door started to slowly open. All of the screaming and kicking Gerica had done stopped and she could hear nothing. When she did, she noticed that Horus was not standing in front of her door, protecting her like he should have been. He was laying down on his stomach to the left side of her door. Gerica walked over to him; *perhaps he has fallen asleep on his watch* duty. She began to shake him and call his name; but that did nothing. He was still without making breathing sounds. Finally, she kneed down and rolled him over on to his back; his head was on her lap.

"Horus!" Gerica shrieked in fear as she noticed his bloody face. There was a cut from his ear all the way to his left eye, which was missing. The right eye was rolled back into his head. His mouth looked like it was sewn together by a piece of white thread. The blood from his wounds drenched her blue night grown. She knew she had to run.

As Gerica ran away from her room and Horus, the rain stopped. The knocking on the doors had all stopped, and the castle was dead silent. Gerica could only hear her own heart beat;

in the most eerie of ways. She stopped dead in her tracks when she saw the door on the Western end wide opened; it had been fully closed the day before. The windows provided the light from the moon, and the strikes of lightening on the door. She had begun to feel like she was being invited into the Western end. She took a quick right and ran down the stairs. She was on her way to find Lucille when the biggest thunder she had ever heard in her life struck the castle. The echo of that noise seemed to have moved the ground. Perchance the movement was in her head, it had not stopped spinning since she found Horus and she was unable to tell the difference.

When she reached the bottom on the stair case, she noticed light. Coming from every end of the castle, in every room; light that she was not able to see from the upstairs. As cold sweat rolled off her forehead, she searched for Lucille. The castle normally had guards on duty at all times; by the front doors, in the throne room, and near every exit. Yet, tonight when Gerica had needed them the most, she was alone.

"Lucille! Where are you? Horus has been murdered! Lucille!" Gerica shrieked and was unaware that her voice could go that high. She started to lose her voice; not from yelling, but by fear. She run into Lucille's room, and found the door was wide open. Her heart stopped banging against her rib cage and froze in her chest as she saw the shadow standing over Lucille's bed, but Lucille was not in it. She was lying on the ground near the doorway which Gerica stood in. "Lucille!" cried Gerica. Gerica turned her head to the right of Lucille and noticed a body hunched over the arm of a rocking chair. It was hard to make out who this person was until lightening had struck just right and Gerica could see it was Oliver's body; only without a face. Gerica could see blood around his hairline where the skin of his face had been removed from his head. Dark red blood dripped from the locks of his hair as his body laid lifeless.

Just as Gerica screamed, the shadow turned around; she could now make out a face. An odd face with snitches where the eyes should be and a nose that looked like Gerica's. Thin lips that curled into the most sinister smile that Gerica had ever seen, with corners that were pointed. She had begun to cry as her legs turned to stone, she was stuck. She watched the shadow as it moved along the edge of the room, against the wall. All the windows in Lucille's bedroom opened at once and a wind with intense force came rushing in, blowing all of Lucille's belongings toward Gerica. Pillows, pictures and candles flew, all aiming right for

Gerica's head. In that quick second, the entire day flashed before her eyes. She moved her feet; she knew where she needed to go.

Anders would have been able to see this shadow coming. Gerica turned, and with everything in her body, she ran to the southern end. She was too scared to look behind her; she was not sure if she was being followed. She needed to make sure that she was not alone in the castle. As she entered the last corridor before reaching the southern end, her heart stopped.

"You poor delusional child; you cannot run from me. I have always been here. Where will you go? I am everywhere you are," Gerica could hear a voice coming from all around her. It sounded like a woman's voice but not one that Gerica had ever heard before. She looked around the corridor to see that she was alone. "You cannot see me, child. Not until I allow you to."

She continued running and made it to Ander's door as she heard the voice hissing and laughing. She pounded her fist against the hard, wooden door; over and over again until she could not feel her hand. Screaming, pounding and kicking at the door. "Anders, I need you! Please! Anders!" Gerica repeated this but Anders never came to the door; he never spoke to her and she began to grow concerned that the shadow had gotten him as well. She gave up with tears racing down her cheeks and turned her back against his door. Her head was pushed up against the door when she slammed her body to the ground. She sat with her knees to her chest, her head bent down; she was crying uncontrollably. It had only been a moment of rest before the shadow had returned to taunt her.

She heard the blood curling laugh from down the hall. "I have made myself known to you, child. You need not ignore my existence any longer; you will be mine." Gerica looked up and stared in this face that would surely be the last one she would ever see. The shadow was eye level with Gerica, with its sinister grin close to her own mouth; she felt the cold breath on her lips. She screamed the last hair raising, high pitched scream that she could drag out of her body before everything went dark.

Chapter Thirteen

"Gerica, for Pete's sake girl, wake up!" Lucille sat on the edge on Gerica's bed, shaking her by the shoulders. She had been screaming so loudly that she woke Lucille and Oliver up. They rushed into her room to see what was going on, but they soon realized that she was just having a nightmare.

Gerica laid in her bed, drenched in her own sweat, and tears; with random locks of hair stuck to her forehead and cheeks. She was always a heavy sleeper, and often had nightmares; this dream, however, was by far the worst that Lucille had ever seen. It had taken several minutes to wake her up, which caused Lucille to start to worry about her. She just laid there, screaming, crying and repeating all of their names over and over again.

Finally, Gerica opened her eyes to see Lucille sitting on her bed, and Oliver in her doorway. They both had looks of great concern on their faces and seemed very confused. They were still dressed in their night clothes; Lucille in her pink night gown with her hair wrapped up in a black scarf and Oliver was wearing green robes. They both looked like they had been woken up from a deep sleep. Gerica was unsure what time it was but her room was tinted orange so she knew the sun must be poking through her red curtains.

"What in the world was going on with you Gerica?" Lucille gasped; the amount of emotion that Gerica displayed shocked her; all she could think of was how different the King would handle things. *He is needed here; his daughter needs him; she is getting worse.* Lucille used her head scarf as a towel to dry Gerica's face; the tears had been so heavy they made lines down her face.

"You died," she whispered to Lucille before turning to Oliver. "As did you, and Horus. Oh dear, where is Horus?" Gerica cried as she tried to jump up from her bed. Tears actively rolling down her cheeks even though she now knew it had been a dream; her heart was still pounding.

"My dear girl, no need to worry; Horus is sleeping. He and Stetson switched duties mid night and it was Stetson who has been outside of your door. He ran to get Oliver and me when you started to have your dream; you scared him half to death, he had thought that whatever was seen yesterday had found its way into your room. He opened the door, but when he saw you were alone, and frightened, he came for us. The guards are taking a break watching your door, so Oliver and I wanted to check on you. I know that in your years

123

here you have had nightmares often, but I have never seen you become so involved with one before now. Care to tell the details?" Lucille, still wiping her tears, questioned Gerica.

Gerica pulled her legs in closer to her chest to give her chin a place to rest. "I walked in to your bedroom and the two of you were there, dead. You laid on the floor of your bedroom while Oliver sat in your rocking chair. Horus was dead as well, but Anders was nowhere to be found; neither were Samuel or Stetson. I yelled and cried as I ran down to Anders' wing, but I found no one. Horus was missing an eye, and his mouth was sewn shut. " Her eyes widened as she recalled the details, the dripping blood from Oliver, the pillows flying toward her head, Horus' lifeless head falling into her lap. Everything was far realer than anything she has felt, "Could this mean something?"

"Dreams hardly ever mean anything, dear. It is simply the fears that you have that come alive when you are in your most vulnerable state. Hence, while you are sleeping. You are defenseless and unable to protect yourself. Perhaps you have a hidden fear of being left alone. That would make sense; you were once abandoned. But no, I would not hold much stock in your dreams," Lucille smiled. "Well, I remember this one time, when I was younger than you. I had this dream where I was flying, but I am deathly afraid of being high in the air. That dream meant nothing, and looking back on it, it still does not make sense." It was clear to Gerica that Lucille was trying to make her feel better, but she was failing miserably. Gerica was anxious for the pair to leave, so she smiled and agreed. "Now, my dear it is not time for breakfast, I ask that you try to return to sleep. It will be a short while until the sunlight makes it difficult to sleep; you need your rest; since your father has been gone, we have gotten none of your schooling done. Which you know is unacceptable, and we need to keep on the right path. If he asks about your progress, I do not want to upset him. You do understand?" Lucille smiled. She knew that Gerica was in a tough spot, but that could not take away from what Gerica needed to get done. These dreams and notes would only get in the way of her learning, and she needed to be ready.

"Yes, I suppose you are right," answered Gerica. She laid back down, and Lucille covered her with her blanket up to her chin; she placed a single kiss upon her forehead. This was Lucille's way of always sending Gerica to bed; it was such a lovely gesture. They left the room, and Gerica was alone again. She could not be sure if she was actually alone; she felt that she was being watched.

She stared at the ceiling, and out the windows. She knew that there was something hidden in her dream; it meant something. Recalling all the images felt like a puzzle. The shadow was just that; a shadow; a face that her own mind came up with. The part that disturbed Gerica the most was that her own mind killed the only people that she had ever had in her life. There was no falling back asleep for her. There would be no way she could risk seeing all of those frightening events again. Even if she wanted to sleep, her mind would not let her, and her heart would not calm down enough for her to rest. Gerica wanted to keep some sort of journal for nights that dreams kept her awake. Gerica decided that she needed to sneak away to her father's library. There would be something there that she could use for writing. It was next to the dining hall; she needed to stay silent and bring no attention to herself.

She slipped out of bed, through the corridor and down the stairs. The castle was lit by the orange morning sun, and once she reached the library, she was careful when opening the door. She did not want to risk making any loud noises. If Lucille thought for a moment that Gerica was continuing with the meaning behind her dreams, she would be annoyed.

126

Gerica slipped through the door of the library and began to look around. There were shelves everywhere and they were all filled with books. There was a dark wooden desk filled of the quills, scrolls, candles, more books and letters from other kingdoms addressed to her father. There were no journals as Gerica had hoped for, so she reached for a scroll and a quill. Once she had both items, she left the library and made her way back to her bedroom.

What am I doing here? The cold floor felt easy on her bare feet as she curled her toes with every step her took. *The shadow could only want me because I will be queen, would it still follow me if I ran away?* Gerica had spent so much of her life wondering if she could escape what her life has become, in her heart she knew she could not.

Safety back to her room, she flopped herself on her bed; she replayed the dream in her head and took notes. Things begun to flood her mind; the rain, storm; it was dark, and she was alone. *This could mean that I will be alone when it is my time to die; or that I am the only person that can face this shadow. The dark time would symbolize that someone is keeping me in the dark by keeping something away from me. How will I know what is real?*

The next thought that came to mind, was Horus. He was supposed to be protecting her, yet he was dead. *Was he a sacrifice to get to me? His eyes were gone, that could mean he saw something he was not supposed to; or perchance the shadow took it to see what he had been seeing. And his mouth; it had stitches! Was he hiding something, like a secret? He most certainly could know things that he was not telling anyone else. Maybe it was the opposite; he said something he should not have.* It felt like a rainstorm of ideas flowing in her mind, each drop was a new possibility.

Oliver and Lucille; a clear bond between the two for them to have died in the same room. Lucille's body just laying on the floor; that was disrespectful to her; a way to symbolize hatred. Does Lucille have special meaning to this shadow?

Anders was the missing element; because he is not committed to this castle or its people. He is just here out of obligation to the King. It could be that the shadow had no grudge against him.

All of the ideas were just overloading her head; she thought that perhaps if she had answers before the King arrived home, he would believe her. All of these years that she spent being ignored would be forgotten. Most importantly, they could find out what the shadow wanted. She had no plan of attack; there was not much to plan for when you do not know who you would be fighting. She had no outstanding qualities that made her a worthy opponent. Gerica had heard stories and fairytales all of her life; and in every tale that she could remember, the good character always won. She feared that would not be the end of her story.

A light tapping noise on her balcony window interrupted her thinking. She glanced out but saw nothing. The sound was still continuing as she had gotten off of her bed and slowly walked toward the window. She pulled back the curtain and saw an empty balcony. She swallowed what felt like a rock in the back of throat and opened the window. While she was standing outside in the early morning sun, she wished she was someone else. She never chose this life, it was chosen for her. She began to cry a few tears as she looked below the balcony; she was only a child, not ready for a kingdom. The few tears turned large and plentiful as they fell from her face; she was beyond scared and could not get herself in the proper mind to face another day. The rain had stopped and she could smell fresh new air in the spring morning. Some may think that was a refreshing smell, but for Gerica the smell made her stomach turn; it was just another chance for the shadow to end her.

She knew that she had to speak to Anders; there was no way around it. No one would be able to help her but him, if there was even anything he could do. He was her best and only option. She wondered if he was awake. She was supposed to have gone back to sleep, so bothering him at this hour may get her into some trouble, but she had to take the chance. She walked off the balcony and shut the window; pulled the curtains shut and left her room with the paper and quill still on her bed. She thought it would be best if Anders did not see it. If her ideas were unknown, and he came up with something similar, she would know that she was right. She walked down the corridor and saw the Western end; the chills that went up her back sent a cold sensation to the rest of her body. Her mind went from wanting to go speak to Anders, to wanting to run and hide under her blankets. She ran passed as fast as she could. If Lucille spoke to Anders before Gerica was able to, she would tell him everything, risking any possible answers that Gerica could get out of him.

Gerica put her head down as she run down the stairs; avoiding any eye contact with the door of the Western end. She felt that whatever it was watching her not only saw her, but they saw right through her soul; her thoughts and fears did not feel like they belonged to her anymore. She pictured a hideous beast hidden away in their mountain cabin, watching her through a crystal ball. She pictured them laughing at her tears and enjoying every drop of sweat that dripped from her head during her hellish nightmares.

Gerica ran along until she finally reached Anders' end of the castle. She had been in this part of the castle roughly six times in her life. It was not as creepy as the Western end, but it never felt right. He had never made any type of attempt to be in her life; he was cold and short with her the very few times she had tried to speak to him. She found him very frightening, really. And yet, he was the only one that could help in her time of need.

When Gerica was in front of Anders' door, it took a lot to make herself knock on it; but she did. "Hello, Anders? Are you in there? I am really sorry to wake you, it is just I need help you see; and you are the only one that can help me in this matter. I do hope you are not upset with me," declared Gerica in a soft, innocent sounding voice, with a bit of desperation.

Without saying a word, he opened the door. He stood there in his night robes, holding a mug of tea. His white eyes were not to be stared at, but it was impossible not to. Gerica was always confused and interested in his eyes; she could hardly look away.

"You may come in. What is it that I can assist you with, Ms.Gerica?" Growled Anders. It was obvious that she was not welcomed; she never knew what she did to him. Or why her father cared for him.

"I was hoping you could tell me what a recent dream I had meant. It was odd and there does not seem to be much sense in it," Gerica started to go into detail until she saw the look on Anders'. "Anders, I know that you do not care for me much and I have never known why. But you do work for my father and in a sense, for me. Now, I will ask you nicely to help me but really, it is an order." Anders' mouth curled into a smile, and it only confused Gerica. He looked happy but just a moment ago, he seemed annoyed. "Anders? Is something amusing?" Gerica hissed.

"You never have asked me to help you, and more importantly, you have never spoken your mind to me in the past. It is a nice change. I will be happy to help you; have a seat, and tell me what happened," coaxed Anders.

Gerica was not expecting this outcome and she was a little taken aback by it. She had noticed that the end of the castle where Anders' room was located, was the least lit of all. There were not as many candles here as the rest of the castle and the ones it did have were not always burning. It was a dark and gloomy place that was frightening in its own right. Gerica had a seat in an oversized orange cushioned chair and sat with her legs crossed with her hands on her knees. She wanted to appear more grown up so Anders would take her seriously. She started off by recapping the very beginning of the dream. "It was night time, and there was a bad storm. I was awakened by noises that sounded like banging, or perhaps thunder. I am not really sure. I knew that Horus had been outside of my bedroom door that night to protect me, so I ran from my bed to my door. I was not able to open the door at first however, so I began yelling for Horus. Eventually, the door opened and I was able to walk out. Horus was lying on the floor, dead. Not only was he dead but he was missing en eye and his mouth was sewn together. As if he had seen something and was not able to talk about it. Then I run to Lucille's room, covered in Horus' blood; I saw her lying on the ground, dead. She was not alone in her room; Oliver was there, sitting in chair and also dead. Then there was this thing, I have always referred to it as a shadow; I do not know what it actually is. Well, it was by the window until it heard me cry. Then it left the

133

window and went around the outside of Lucille's bedroom against her walls. It was not able to come close to me, I ran away before that happened. I ran to you actually, apparently, in my most vulnerable times, I would think that you would save me. It did not happen however, you were not to be found. I kicked and screamed at your door, repeatedly, and you were not there. It's possible that this thing had killed you. I was feeling defeated at that point and I sat to rest, and cry. Then all I can remember is looking up and seeing a face screaming at me; but the face was missing something, and I cannot really remember what. Often when I awake the next morning, I have forgotten details of my dreams, and sadly this was no expectation. It is very possible I am missing things that may be of great importance," as the words came from Gerica's mouth she became unsure of herself. She looked at Anders who was silent and looking back at her; it felt to Gerica that he was looking through her. It was his eyes; they never gave her a good feeling.

Anders cleared his throat and begun to speak quietly. "I see, well this may be a hard dream to interpret since it seems that you may not have all of the details. Now, I am sure I have heard talk of you having nightmares before, is that correct?" Anders looked at her in a way that made Gerica start to feel safer, like she could actually trust in him.

Yes sir," agreed Gerica.

"Now, were any of these details consistent with any other dream you have ever had?" Anders asked

"Yes, this shadow. Although, I never had a good look of it until this dream.It never had a face," she informed Anders. "I was always being followed before this one, in this dream I was being chased. There was a voice that followed me while I ran from Lucille's room to yours. It sounded like it was talking to me from the walls. I cannot remember the exact words, but I know it was saying that it had been following me my whole life." Gerica confessed this fact that she had just now came to terms with. She looked at Anders face; he appeared interested.

"Now, there have always been things that have bothered you, but I have to ask do you think this particular dream was the result of the events that took place yesterday in the dining hall. Lucille came to tell me that there was something watching you and that it was left a note. Do you think it could have been your fear?" asked Anders with a sense of caution before continuing. "There have been times in my life that I had dreams that came to me during a time when they were needed. There have been other times where my dreams literally meant nothing, but I had something going on in my life that made this dream significant to me at the time. I know there must be something going on in this castle, but also in your mind. You need to understand that whatever is going on will be nothing you can change. Everyone in this castle is here to protect you and nothing will happen to you. I believe that you need to stay close to people who care about you; like Lucille. Do not leave her side for any length of time. It is just a gamble that should not be taken." Anders spoke with a tone that sounded more fatherly than friendly. His eyes lightened up while talking to Gerica, as if calm came over him.

"That is the advice that you have for me? Stay near to Lucille? You are not even going to try to see a meaning behind this dream?" Gerica asked in defeat. "Who shall I go to for help if the one person that is meant to do this work cannot, or will not help me?"

"Gerica, please understand. It has nothing to do with me not helping you. I cannot see inside your heart dear. I cannot see into your fears or thoughts. Dreams that I have are the only ones that make sense to me; and even those sometimes take time to break down and figure out the meaning to. If there is a meaning behind this dream, you would be the only one that could figure it out. I trust that you understand this?" Anders fragilely broke the news to Gerica. The truth was he could not help her; he did not know how to; his abilities had more than faded over the years. He could not tell her that he was useless as a physic.

"Very well, I believe it must be close to breakfast. I hope you find this day to your liking." Gerica stood up from the orange chair and made her way to his door. When she reached the door she turned to look at him, "Thank you for at least taking me seriously. I trust that this conversation stays between the two of us?" Gerica confirmed.

Anders nodded, "As you wish, my lady."

And with that Gerica made her way to the dining hall. She was surprised when she saw Lucille and Oliver already there at the table. They had the breakfast table set and filled with food. There was fruit cake, custard and fresh apples on the table with a pot of black tea. When Lucille is in charge, the food is always better than it is when the King is present. Both Lucille and Oliver smiled at Gerica as she made her way toward them. Apparently, they had no knowledge of what she had been up to

137

this morning; which took some pressure off of having breakfast with them.

"Well hello my darling lady! How was the last hour of sleep?" Lucille asked as she smiled the warmest smile that Gerica had seen in a sometime.

Gerica felt guilty lying to Lucille so she smiled and quickly thought of something else to mention. "Have you heard from father? When shall we expect his return?" Gerica hoped that Lucille did not catch on to her ignoring her question. Anders' face, his eye, and the orange chair flashed in her mind over and over again as the words "I cannot see into your fears or thoughts" replayed as a whispered to her ears.

"Actually yes; I had received word yesterday that he will be home tomorrow morning sometime. Let's hope that the weather permits," Lucille's face lite up with the mention of the King. She missed him when he was gone, and on top of that she was the one to handle all of the castle's affairs. The King did not leave often enough for it to brother her and she was always happy to help him.

Gerica sat down and looked at her plate; slowly she started to nibble on a piece of fruit cake as she fought her current state of constant paranoia. Her mind wondered to the last time she had eaten a meal here; she began to watch the doors with every bite she took. Gerica did not speak much during breakfast, in fact no one really did. Oliver was a man of few words on his best day; Lucille was the one who liked to talk. However, it seemed that Lucille had her mind elsewhere as well. The uncomfortable silence during breakfast was broken up only when Oliver made a mess of his tea. He had missed his mouth and the tea was dripping on his shirt. This lightened the mood as all three of them begun to laugh. Gerica noticed his eye sparkling when he smiled, she liked that about him. His hair had started to grow longer, and some pieces brushed into his eyes. She had never found him more handsome than just then.

Lucille took her attention away from Olivier at the least opportune time, "Gerica, we need to get focused on your schooling today. I am afraid that we have fallen behind more than I would care to admit. As I am sure you are aware, the last thing your father needs to hear is that. So, right after breakfast, please follow me to the library," instructed Lucille.

Gerica was silent and just nodded her head yes. Although she was not crazy about her school work, she thought it might be a good distraction from all the insanity she was facing; and from pining over Oliver's shaggy hair and sparkling baby blues. If she could forget what had happened with the note, then perhaps she could breathe easier. That was the most wishful thinking that Gerica had done for as long as she could remember. The truth was no matter what she did, it was in the back of her head. As she sat at the table, she realized that her mind had wandered off and Lucille was still looking at her; waiting for her response.

"I understand that things are difficult for you right now, Gerica" She began to whisper. "But I do pray that you trust me. This mess will all be over and when it is you will be glad that you did not let it stand in your way of living a normal life.

Lucille's comment annoyed Gerica; it was frustrating for her to listen as Lucille downplayed her feelings. "*Normal life, what on earth is normal about my life? Girls my age have friends, and fun. I am stuck in a castle while I am haunted by something no one believes in but me.*" Gerica had actual proof that she was dealing with something frightening. If this shadow was anything like she was predicting, they needed to get out of the castle; arm all the guards, and perhaps hire more. Yet, here Lucille was, smiling in Gerica's face and acting as if the biggest problem was teaching her to read a sonnet.

Gerica bit her bottom lip in order to hide her feelings, "I do not think you understand my dilemma Lucille. I do not think you know what it is like to have this cloud hovering over you everywhere you go! Excuse my tone, but now that you see it is not in my mind, I would assume you would have some sort of sympathy or understanding for my lack of concern over reading. We should be locking ourselves in a fully secured room, waiting the return of father. For my own sanity, and quite possibility yours, we need to keep me from having to face this thing head on, again." Gerica hissed words like she had never spoken to Lucille before. It hurt Gerica to speak to Lucille in that matter almost as much as it hurt Lucille to hear it; but Lucille was getting better, she understood.

"Again, I can assure you this is only for your benefit! Do not think for a moment that I would not do anything in my power to protect you, child. I have raised you since you were a baby; I love you as if you were my own! I can provide you this information as comfort; nothing will be able to get to you while you are in my custody and surely not your father's. I am aware that this thing has been and is still possibly within these walls, but it will be a cold day in hell before I do anything that will risk your life. If I can assure you that we will be locked in the library, with Samuel as our guard inside. Horus and Stetson outside of the door, will you then take your schooling into consideration? This is not necessarily a choice, but I will make these accommodations for you, my lovely Gerica," Lucille's words were a mix of anger, desperation and sympathy. She was not one to be questioned or augured with, but she did know when things were not as simple as just obeying. The love that she felt for Gerica was strong; there was not a thing in this world that could get in the way of how this woman loved her.

"I shall deal with that then; let us lock ourselves in the library. With the protection of three guards; I would also like any other available guards on standby. Last night I had that awful dream and that was when I was being protected. I do not want to think about what would scare me if I was not being protected. I know that despite all of this, my schooling is important. I am just worried that I will not be able to take it as serious as I should," Gerica admitted this knowing that it was almost pointless to try to focus on work. She understood however, that she had little choice in the matter.

The three of them finished breakfast and Lucille and Gerica made their way to the library.

Lucille had all of Gerica's lessons in her arms; poems that Gerica would have to read aloud, and math problems that Gerica would have to solve. It was always the same type of work but at least the company was good and, Lucille was a patient teacher. When Gerica was first learning how to read, Lucille took her time with Gerica. If it had been the king that was providing the lessons, it would not go as smoothly. He never had patience with anything.

As Gerica sat going over the poems her mind wandered, again. She wondered if the shadow was outside the room, or still in the castle. If it watched her every second of everyday; or if it had other people it was stalking. Did it want her crown, or the kingdom? This constant wandering was breaking her spirit, more now than ever before. She had never wanted a friend so badly in her life until this very day; she needed someone to talk to. She was beginning to feel insane, she needed to break free, and perhaps never return.

Lucille was staring at Gerica and she felt sadness take over her heart. Lucille had a brilliant thought that perhaps would be beneficial for Gerica to write her own poem. *Poems can be the focus point of raw emotion; it might be a good way to allow Gerica some release of stress.* Gerica did not protest to this idea, she actually thought it might help to verbalize how she was feeling in a different way. She was slightly nervous as she touched the quill to the paper; she hoped to find words that gave a better view of the pain and misery that she was feeling.

There is not a way to explain the constant pain; to be alone, an empty space.

You see the look upon my face but know nothing of pain's taste.

The smiles that lay upon your lips, sends draggers through my soul.

Knowing that this fear stays by my side, until I am weak and old.

I speak my words to closed ears and live with crippling fears.

One day, I pray you see the world through my eyes, and know that my heart is where this pain lays.

You hear nothing of my words and know nothing of my world.

Should you take the time to see, this life is not fair to me.

When Gerica was finished writing this, she was in tears. The emotions come to her and she could not control them. Lucille had stopped watching her; she had actually left Gerica with Samuel and went to get them their lunch; they were having soup, again. Gerica assumed that Lucille did not have much time to make anything other than simple food. She had her hands full with Gerica's problem; Gerica felt like it was her fault that she was made to eat soup again. Nonetheless, that problem was almost laughable at this moment. She laid her head down on the table, and when she did, tears started to fall from her eyes; faster. Before she knew it, there was a small puddle under her hand.

Sometime must have past while Gerica was sleeping, because when she woke up it was dark outside. She woke up to Lucille rubbing her hair and singing. Samuel was still in the room and nothing had changed. Gerica started to rub her eyes and wander aloud "How long have I been lying here, sleeping?"

"For a few hours, but you looked too peaceful there was no way I could disturb you. I assume that you have not had a good quality sleep in sometime. Hopefully, knowing that you were safe allowed you to sleep well?" Lucille stated with the utmost sincerity in her voice. She continued to rub Greica's hair. "I did look at the poem when I returned; I must say that I am impressed with your words. The emotion that must have gone into this poem was clear for the reader to feel. I believe that if you have things to write about, you could write great things."

Gerica appreciated Lucille's compliment, and she was right, it may be a good way for Gerica to release some of her emotions. Gerica stayed silent and just smiled. She had been well rested; she had not slept in sometime. It had been a mix of her not being able to sleep and having poor sleep when she did actually get to sleep. "Can I go to my room, now?" Gerica asked.

"Of course my love," Lucille answered; the pair got up from the table and made their way to the hall. Gerica was still very much sleepy and had a hard time focusing of objects that she looked at. When they made it to her room, Lucille turned to Gerica and smiled.

"Would you like me to sleep in here with you tonight?" Lucille whispered.

All Gerica could do was nod her head yes; she was weak and still so sleepy. She moved to her bed; Lucille followed and laid down beside Gerica.

Lucille gently continued rubbing Gerica's head as she drifted off into sleep.

All Lucille could do was wonder about the poor dear; *there had to be a good explanation for everything that was going on with her. It could be that Gerica was just a disturbed child; who knows what type of things young Gerica had seen before she was accepted into the King's life. She could have seen death and starvation. Lucille had only met her real parents once and did not know what they were actually like. The poem may have been written by Gerica, the dreams may all be in her head and her worsening mental health may be a result of something else.* Lucille thought about her meeting with Anders; she would be sure to speak to him as soon as the sun rose.

Chapter Fourteen

"Lucille, lady Gerica, the King has returned and is in the throne room. He wishes to speak to you, Gerica." Oliver informed them as he stood in the door way. Once he saw Lucille had lifted herself out of the bed, he was on his way.

Lucille poked her head up from the pillow she had been sleeping on; she saw that it was early morning. The light entered Gerica's room as the sky turned from black to orange to light blue. Lucille noticed that Gerica was still asleep; her deep breathing reassured Lucille that she still needed her rest. She excused herself from the bed and made her way down the hall. Once she reached the throne room and it was only her and the King, she jumped into the King's arms. She had never been so happy to see him. It was rare that he would travel on business, but from time to time duty did call him away. Lucille hated when he was gone, now so more than ever.

The King started to laugh, "Well, I am glad that someone is happy that I have made my way back. Where Gerica is hiding?" The King was confused why his daughter was not there to greet him.

"Sir, there have been hard days since you left us, and they have taken a toll on Gerica. She is resting now," answered Lucille.

"And what exactly does this mean?" The King was almost scared to ask; knowing Gerica there could be all sorts of things that would get in the way of her living a happy childhood. The girl being a misfit and socially awkward; she was never destined to be normal. He thought of how long he would try to hide her from the world; being a misfit would keep her under his thumb longer.

"The other day, Gerica, Oliver, and I, had been having lunch in the dining hall. Out of nowhere, Gerica glazes off into space and starts to spill her drink down the front of her dress. Next thing I know, she is running out of the dining hall and up the stairs toward her bedroom. I followed her, and when I asked her what happened she told me she was being watched. There was a 'shadow' or some type of figure watching her from the corridor. This is a normal Gerica story, however, when she run out of the dining hall, she found a piece of paper. It had said something like 'Dear young Gerica, you are not crazy. I am here, and I have been watching you. Your life is not your own, and your future is not for you to choose.' I do not think she is faking this. I saw the fear in her eyes, there is something that we have been missing all of these years." When Lucille stopped talking, she looked at the face of the man she loved. She was not sure how he would react; Lucille had always taken his side in this journey. "When she first ran away, I was incredibly anger with her, she made a mess in the dining hall; and her dress was ruined. But once I spoke to her, I could tell there is a presence over her that is unlike any other I have seen before. She needs us, Beckford."

In a second's time, the King thought of the first time Gerica had mentioned that something was wrong. She was a young girl, maybe five or six. Playing in the gardens while Lucille tended to the flowers; Gerica was silent, sitting on the gravel when Lucille found her. Her little hands were tightly grasped with handfuls of gravel and tears flowing freely from her eyes. She could not tell anyone what was happening but just acted as if she needed to be next to Lucille no matter what. "Wait; there has been someone uninvited in my home?" The King's face filled with anger as he spoke these words. "Come with me," the King commanded Lucille to follow him as he walked out of the throne room and toward Anders' end. He was silent as they walked down the corridor; Lucille was not sure of what was going on in his mind. He had the most intimidating face, filled with anger and fear that Lucille had ever seen.

They reached Anders' room and the door was already open. "Your Majesty, welcome back," Anders called from inside his room; he was sitting in his orange chair; his legs crossed as he read a book. He was smiling until he saw that the King looked mad. He stood, but his knees were weak. "Your Majesty, I think I have come to find what was going on. I searched around and came up with nothing. Until I was reading an old scroll that was in the library. It had spoken of tricks that one's mind can play on them; hearing voices, seeing things and just day to day tricks. These tricks of the mind channel something bigger going on in the person's life that they are not able to deal with; or they do not know how to deal with; disturbed people who make up problems so they can ignore their real problems."

As Anders spoke, Lucille's face turned into a frown. She did not believe everything she had seen Gerica go through was made up in her head. "Then if that is the case, Mr. Anders, how can to explain the note that I showed you. Surely if there is evidence it needs to be taking seriously." Lucille spoke these words with such distaste in her mouth.

She was hurt and confused because for once she did not doubt Gerica; this was real.

"Ah, yes. I thought of that as well. Is it possible that Gerica had written it? I know that she would have had time before you came to lunch. Also, how long was it before you followed her up to her room? I must say Lucille that this can all be explained, I just need to know more specifics." Anders noted in a cold, matter of fact tone.

The King was silent while Anders and Lucille traded words. He could not figure out exactly what was going on. It was not like Lucille to ignore her feelings, and if she had thought something was going on with Gerica she would be quick to act on it. Then there is Anders, who has never done the King wrong in the many years that he has been the King's advisor.

"I do not doubt that either one of you have your thoughts and concerns, but we need to get to common ground. It is clear that something has happened while I was gone, and I need to make sure my daughter, this castle, and this kingdom are all in good standing. Anders are you sure that you have checked every possible purpose for these events?" asked King Beckford.

"Of course, Your Majesty, I have; to the best of my ability. I know that Gerica is a bright girl, and very special. However, I do not doubt that what is going on with her is not real and is in her mind. It is possible that I have missed something, but I will continue to work to ensure her safety." Anders's eyes had softened at the thought of Gerica. It was clear that although Gerica did not feel that he cared for her much, she actually meant a great deal to him; he was able to watch her grow into the beautiful young lady. He knew that he and Lucille had never seen eye to eye on much, but he wished that in this matter she would take his word; Gerica was in no danger.

"Lucille? What are you thinking?" King Beckford asked. Lucille was standing there looking at Anders with almost a puzzled expression; she was not convinced that the answer was that easy.

"I saw that note myself, and I know Gerica's writing. Since I am the one that taught her everything she knows; I have seen her writing time and time again. That was not her writing." She bickered back. She had found that over the years that he had lived in the castle; Anders had grown into an arrogant human being. Lucille doubted that he had even looked into anything that may help them. Nonetheless, she would have to find out

153

what was going on by herself. "It is obvious that you are not here to help, I shall excuse myself as I have breakfast to prepare." With that last word, Lucille gave Anders a stare; turned on her heel and left them there.

She entered the dining hall and was pleasantly surprised that Oliver had set out the breakfast for the day. He may not have spoken much in crowds, but to Lucille, he was the most caring person she had ever known; she knew that she raised him well. She thanked Oliver for his hard work with a kiss on the cheek. Just then, Lucille's head started to spin, and there was a ringing in her ears. All the sounds in room were muffled; as if she was hearing things under water. She went to reach for a nearby chair but was unable to grasp it; and she fell to the ground. When Lucille opened her eyes, she saw Oliver and King Beckford standing over her to see if she was alright.

"I … I… What happened?" Lucille asked in a whisper; she did not know how she ended up on the floor and why they were hovered over her.

"You fainted, my dear. Can you see and hear me?" The King's voice shook as he asked Lucille this; he had never seen her sick and the sight made him nervous.

"Yes, I can." She spoke as her hands and legs started to shake.

"You need to rest," Demanded King Beckford. "Stetson, Samuel! In here at once!" The two guards came in and stood over Lucille and King Beckford. "Help Lucille reach her bedroom, she is to stay in there and rest," King Beckford ordered the guards and then he turned to Lucille. "You take as long as you need to rest up, I will send Oliver right up to your room with your breakfast."

With that, the guards picked up Lucille and carried her to the Eastern wing. When they reached her bedroom, they carefully laid her down on her bed. She drifted off to sleep almost as soon as her head had hit the pillow. She slept the most peaceful sleep but did not wake to Oliver when he came with biscuits, a fresh apple, peach slices, and a hot pot of her favorite tea. He did not want to disturb Lucille as she was sleeping so peacefully, so he decided to leave all of the food to the left of her bed, on her night stand; then he made his way out of her room and quietly shut her door.

As Oliver made his way down the hall, he thought about his life in the castle. He had never known a life of normal people. Not like Gerica once had, he had been born in the castle. He was always told by Lucille that he was meant to be a servant, but a royal servant. That he was able to have the privilege of taking care of the rich and powerful and that he was lucky to be there; but he never felt lucky, he felt burdened. He never knew who his father was; Lucille had told him that before she worked in the castle, she had been married to a soldier. The couple always lived in Leward, and his father was sent to one of the many wars to protect it. Lucille was mid-way through her pregnancy with him when she found out that her husband had been a casualty of the war. The devastating news was delivered to her by King Beckford himself. No one could ever tell him why or how the King knew that she was pregnant, but once he spoke to her, he offered her the job in the castle. He sort of took them both in for the exchange of their work. That is why Lucille told him that he was born to be a servant. *My life was decided before I was aware, I even had a life.* Taking care of the King was not horrible, and the guards take care of themselves for the most part. Things changed once Gerica was bought into the picture; she was more of a project for Lucille to take on. He felt she took his mother away from him when she got here. He had to start taking on the bigger chores when Gerica had entered their lives. Before that, he was able to be a child; to run and play. Oliver was five or so when he remembered the child being brought into the castle, and he slightly remembered her parents. When they arrived that day, he was told to run and play.

Oliver did not remember much, expect some yelling and screaming. He stayed away from them while they were in the room. The next time he saw them, the parents and the baby Gerica were leaving the castle. About two or three days later, just Gerica had returned to stay. Oliver was never given any answers as to why they were in the castle and he did not ask many questions.

Chapter Fifteen

It was sometime before Lucille woke up; but when she did, she was in terrible pain. She was not sure exactly what had happened. Confused; she sat up in her bed to recall the things that had been going on. She was feeling light headed and short of breath.

Lucille slid her legs off the side of her bed and realized that someone had gotten her food while she had been sleeping. She thought it was best to eat something to gain her strength back before she went on this quest to find answers. As she sat and ate the food that was left for her, her mind started to think of the food itself, and how it came to be in her room. It was a caring gesture and it was obvious who it came from. Oliver had always looked out for her almost like she would look for out for him. Lucille smiled to herself as she thought of what a great man he was, and how he would have made a perfect King. He was meek and quiet but incredibly loving. He took other's feelings and wellbeing into consideration whenever he needed to do so. He did not have many male figures in his life; only the King and the guards. Which he was nothing like any of them, and for that, Lucille was very thankful. She laughed to herself as she pictured King Beckford being the main male figure in Oliver's life. Oliver would probably never have the chance to marry, because he will always be in the servant position, but Lucille was convinced that he would make a woman very lucky. She was confident in the way she raised him to be a gentleman, with a tender, loving soul. It was a shame that he would never know true love, or any love besides the one between mother and son. *There are hand maids around the castle around his age, but Oliver had never mentioned them, nor has he ever looked at them. Not that I have ever noticed, and they were rather inseparable most of the waking hours.* Lucille thought of chores that Oliver could do that would allow him to speak or better yet meet these young ladies. She realized most of them were involved with guards, but there had to be a few that were not. Lucille smiled at herself yet again; she needed to find a way to make her son love the life he was given. What better way to love your life, than to share it with the love of your life? It was settled; Lucille would do some meddling and get her son a wife.

When she was finished eating her breakfast, although it was now sundown, she decided to look around the castle. She knew in her heart that there was something going on with Gerica. If Anders would not help, it was up to Lucille. She exited her room; headed down the hall with the lightest feet that she could. She knew that if King Beckford or Oliver found her, they would rush her back to bed. Her head was still spinning, like it had before she fell. Her vision was poor and blurry, but she could not let it stop her.

Lucille was bare foot and all she could think of was how cold the floor was. Lucille had no idea where she was going or where she should look; she did not even know what she was looking for. She wondered what had gotten into Anders; he had changed all these years. When he first became part of the family, he was eager to help out with anything he could. Cleaning and cooking where things he often had a hand in. Until one random day, he begun to lock himself in his room and he stopped socializing with people in the castle, besides the King of course. She did not know what turned him so cold. She remembered when Gerica was a younger child, maybe six or seven years old, he tried to leave. He had asked King Beckford permission to work for him from his own house, or back at his sister's where he was living before, he came to live here. That request was denied however, because the King was not comfortable with his life line not being at his beck and call. Lucille thought that he was unhappy giving his life to the King; by moving into the castle, he sacrificed himself.

Lucille did the same thing; however, she did not feel resentful. She was not upset with how her life was going. But she had always been deeply in love with the King, and, also, with Gerica; she was the apple of her eye. When Lucille thought of everything she may be missing while she worked as the King and Gerica's personal servant, she was not saddened. To her, she was living a married life. Taking care of her son, daughter, and the man she loved. Cleaning and cooking; perfectly content with the life she lived. She would like a solid commitment from the King, but she knew why he could not marry her; the throne was only going to be given to Gerica.

Finally, Lucille made it to Anders' end of the castle. She walked on her tippy toes so he would not hear her. She saw that his light was on in his room and two silhouettes moving around. There were voices but she was too far to make out the words. She lightly inched her way closer to his door, to make out the words. She recognized the voices as Samuel and Anders.

"I do not understand what you are saying, Anders. You did not see anything in your dreams, in your thoughts or even in your books. So it is my belief that there is nothing to fear if the ever so insightful Anders was unable to come up with answers. If you came up with no answers, no real problems, why on earth do we need to tighten security around lady Gerica. You do not seem very confident in your abilities Anders. Are you wasting the King's time by being here since you cannot even decide whether his daughter is safe or not?" Samuel hissed in his typical Samuel tone, many times he was rude or short with people; he was not found of many.

"It is not that I disagree that Gerica needs to be protected at all times, all I am saying is that you cannot seem to make up your mind. When you spoke to the King and Lucille you acted as if lady Gerica made this whole situation up in her head. If you really believed that then you will see why I am saying that this is pointless. You will also see why I am starting to think that you are not so sure of your abilities," declared Samuel; he was not going to back down from Anders that easy. These two men had been at odds before and their relationship had always been a rocky one.

"You doubt me? Well, Samuel I will say I am not surprised; nor am I hurt or discouraged. You see, the King knows that I am a man of many talents, and he knows that your talents are rather limited. We can stand here all night and throw hurtful words at each other, but the end result shall be the same. You and your men will do around the clock protection of lady Gerica and you shall do that with no less than a pleasant smile upon your face. If I need to bring this up to the King, I will do so with a large grin. And as I know you are well aware of his priorities, it is not hard to believe he will pick my side. I must admit; however, I did not see this hesitation coming from you. Stetson, maybe, the old man is a lazy one. Never you though Samuel; you have always been a man of loyalty. Apparently, that was only to the King's face, and not his right hand man. I assure you, my dear Samuel that should this information make it to the King's ears, you will not like the outcome. I trust that when you leave this room, you will make the necessary changes to ensure her safety above all else." Anders was ruthless in his delivery of these words.

Lucille stood with her back flat against the wall while she listened to this exchange of words; she had never heard Anders speak in such a tone, and it sent chills up her spine. With his last word, Lucille closed her eyes and placed her hands over her heart. She smiled and was able to breathe again; this was exactly what she needed to hear from Anders.

There were indents that lined the corridor walls, and once Lucille thought that their meeting was coming to an end, she ducked inside one of them. No sooner had she done that, their meeting was over; two men said their farewells and then the door slammed. She heard Samuel muttering as he made his way angrily down the corridor, but she was not able to make out any words that he was saying. She had never really seen Samuel mad, and she had never seen him so unwilling to help Gerica. *He had been having his men stationed outside of every room that she had been in the past few days,* Lucille did not understand his resistant attitude.

And Anders; oh Anders; how you had been doubted, Lucille thought to herself. She could not believe that for a moment she had forgotten about the man that had been there to help since day one. He had been short with her when she tried to speak to him about the shadows in the corridor, but it was now obvious that her words did not fall upon deaf ears; he had been listening. He was rude but the important thing was that he heard her, and he wanted to help Gerica. It was nice to know that Anders still felt so passionate about helping the kingdom and helping to save Gerica. *Perhaps I read him wrong; I took his tone the wrong way; or he was just rude to me, not the idea of helping Gerica.* Now that she sees that he was always trying to help, and she made things worse by not trusting him, she felt incredibly guilty. A part of her wanted to walk right in his room and hug him for all the encouraging things he had said about protecting Gerica; a smaller part of her wanted to hit him for the stress he caused her. She had her faith restored in him, but she was still unable to shake her feelings of him being odd, and she was not sure why.

She started to head back the way she came; through the pitch black castle. She had one candle in her hand, and a pocket with a few matches; she wanted to remain unseen. She was able to see more when she passed a window and moon light shined into the castle. She had an overwhelming feeling that she should make her way to the dungeon; where she had not been in over ten years. It was full of painful memories of the horror that once took place down there.

She was aware of the King killing and torturing many men over the course of her stay in the castle, but all of that stopped. It was bizarre to her how everyone knew this horribly kept secret of King Beckford's, but no one ever stood up to him; they feared more than respected.

After the balls had stopped, the events in the dungeon started to calm down, and then once

Gerica came to the house, everything stopped altogether. Lucille was at peace with the ending of those events. For a long time while they were going on, she felt like there was a dark cloud that hung over the castle; it affected everyone's daily life. Lucille never partook in the events, but she did have to clean up after them. Her stomach turned inside out as she recalled the pools of blood on the floor, and the stains that never left; no amount of scrubbing could remove them from the stone. The smell of burnt flesh hanging from the chains that were screwed into the ceiling never went away. The utensils that were used to inflict harm on these men haunting Lucille's dreams. It all came rushing back to her like it had never left and it was all too vivid; the painful memories forever engraved into her mind.

After every one of those killings, she would wonder how she could love such a man; she was resentful toward him for so many things. She always told herself that it is for the good of the kingdom, but she never truly believed it. She had heard stories of prisons that kept people captive when they committed a crime; *why torture when the men could have been jailed?* It was concerning that King Beckford took some sort of pleasure in allowing these cruel acts to go on. Whatever his reason for it, Lucille did not like that part of him.

She could have left back then, but she did not have the strength or the knowhow; she was alone with a child and she did not have many options to care for her son. Once the killings stopped, so did her resentment for King Beckford. She had been reminded of the man she had fallen in love with; to her he was kind and gentle. There were just parts of him that she could not control.

When Lucille made it to the dungeon, she was hesitant to go in. Her hand shook as she touched the black stone door; she was glad the lighting was poor; she did not want any more visual reminders of her trauma.

As she turned opened the door, she was met with a foul smell that turned her stomach into knots and filled her mouth with warm, salty saliva; she needed to vomit. Pinching her nose closed with her free hand, she continued farther into the room. She saw all of the old jars that contained parts of men; the chains, knives and blades that all laid around the room.

She did not see any clues to what had been possibly lurking around the castle; there were secret passage ways in and out of the castle that came through the dungeon. It was the main way that the King was able to get his victims in without brining too much attention to his activities. She wanted to search them and see if there was any sign of life; but she needed light. The candle that she took to accompany her on the journey was running low, and she was nowhere near the end of her search. She thought that perhaps she could light candles inside the room and not be caught. She back tracked her steps until she reached the door and gently shut it behind her. She then searched for candles within the room that she could light. There were only two candles within her reach, but that was plenty. Once she had all three candles lit, more of the room was visible and the sight was unbearable. The blood stains were all still there, the smells never left, and the feeling of hatred was so heavy, Lucille could feel it entering her body. Anywhere that Lucille shined her candle; she would wake up rats; there were hundreds of them in this tiny room. They were always kept here just to help clean the messes up. The little creatures loved the taste of blood, and for that reason alone the King never tried to get rid of them. They had never bother Lucille when they were in another other part of the house, but when they were down here, she found them to be frightening. It was almost like they could sense when death was in the air and they sat there waiting with their beady little eyes. Nevertheless, she made it to the back of the room to the portrait of the King's father that was hiding a secret door. She needed both hands to move the heavy painting from the doorway, so she laid the candles by her feet.

Once she had the hidden door open, she grabbed the candles from her feet and kept one candle there to stop the door from closing, she was worried if would trap her inside and no one would find her. There were two doors in the hidden hallway; the room on the left was the final resting place of the leftover body parts; and the room to the right had always remained empty. The hallway was small, with incredibly high ceilings; made of gray stone covered in cracks.

A putrid smell of decaying flesh filled the air, she recognized that smell all too well. *There is no way there could be a body decaying here, the room has not been used in over a decade.* Lucille pushed through the smell and continued to enter the room that was on the right-hand side of the hall. When she reached the room, the smell started to fade, and she was relieved to be able to breathe with a little more ease. There was absolutely nothing in the room; it was empty and clean like it had been throughout its existents. There were not any windows; no place to sit, and most importantly, there were no rats. Once Lucille walked around the whole room and saw nothing, she turned to leave.

She was careful to shut the door behind her without making a sound; she was not sure just how the King would react to her being out of bed and being down in the dungeon. She walked over to the left side of the hallway and then the horrible smell came rushing back as if it had never left; it burned her eyes, nose and throat. It was stronger than anything she had ever smelt before. She lifted her shirt over her mouth and nose and pushed on through the door. Once she got the door fully opened, her jaw dropped; what she saw was heartbreaking; and the smell was nauseating. It was now clear where all the decaying flesh smell was coming from, but she believed her eyes were lying to her, she knew that this sight was impossible.

Chapter Sixteen

Ten chains hung down from the ceiling; all about seven inches apart from each other. On three of the chains were human heads hanging without their bodies attached; the rest of the chains had what appeared to be whole bodies hanging from them, but they were wrapped in a black cloak and all Lucille could see that could identify these objects as bodies were the feet that were hanging from under the cloaks. Bodies that she assumed belonged to the hanging heads were lying on the floor; badly decayed. She judged by the flesh that remained stuck to the bones, they had not been there for too long. She was so confused; she thought that he had given up all the torture.

Just then, Lucille remembered Gerica always talking about the shadow being in a cloak; and now, she knew there were cloaked individuals within these walls; *had Gerica seen them? Was she being haunted by the spirits of those that her father had killed?* Lucille was not sure if she got the answers that she came for, but she was done looking for now; she could handle no more answers at that moment. Flashbacks of Lucille scrubbing up blood from the floor came rushing into her head in waves. She saw a rat running off with a piece of an ear, and a bone falling from a body hanging from the chain; she was losing her mind.

Lucille walked backwards out of that room, and all she could do was turn and run. She ran through the dimly lit, rat invested room that smelt like death had been born in it. Once she made it to the bottom of the stairs, she could not control her dizziness anymore. She fell to the ground, crying uncontrollably. Her tears fell onto the stone floor, and all she could do was replace them. She was not able to stop herself from her wails and tears. They just continued to come, until she felt a burning sensation in the back of her throat. Before she knew it, there was a fire from the pit of her stomach leading up to her mouth. Balls of sweat poured down her face like she had been in the rain. Pieces of her red hair stuck to her forehead, and then it happened. She vomited all she had eaten for her breakfast. The entire time she was expelling her food, she continued to cry. Before she knew it, she was sitting in a pool of her own bodily fluids, and she did not care enough to move out of them. She crawled her way to sit her back against the stairs and sat with her head in her hands. She had never felt so betrayed in her life; she felt defeated.

It was sometime before Lucille was able to pick herself back up and when she made it to the ground level of the castle, she began to look for King Beckford. She wanted to confront him with his lies and his actions. She was aware that he may have little to do with her once she mentioned anything to him, but at this point in his life, he needed Lucille as much as she wanted to be there with him. He would be lost without Lucille; as well as Gerica, who was not ready to be a queen; she still had so much to learn.

Lucille was not able to continue her walk down the corridor and before she knew it, her vision started to blur. Her head had been spinning the entire time she was in the dungeon and more so once she had made the discovery of all the King's extra activities. She was not able to hold her head up any longer. As her vision blurred, her ears began to ring. She reached out for a nearby table to stop her from falling, but it was too late. She fell to the ground and laid there with no knowledge of what was going on.

Chapter Seventeen

King Beckford woke up in his room, alone. It was not often that he was in bed alone. Mostly, Lucille would accompany him; and from time to time, he would enjoy the company of another hand maid, but they would almost always leave before the sun came up. It was odd for him not to wake up to Lucille brining him breakfast and chatting his ear off. He remembered what had happened with her the day before. When she had fainted, it was an awful sight; never had he seen Lucille sick or fragile. All he wanted to do was comfort and protect her in her moment of need.

He climbed out of bed and went to dress himself in his silk robes. He chose to dress in a grayish robe with a crimson stitch around every seam. This robe had not been worn in many years, and it was actually a birthday gift that Lucille had given him shortly after she came to live in the castle. He thought perhaps she would enjoy seeing him in it; she poured her heart into making that robe for him. As he started to exit his room, and he heard loud voices coming from the common areas on the lower level of the castle. It had sounded like Horus and Oliver, but the King could not make out any words. He made his way quickly to where the two men were standing.

"How long has she been here?" Horus barked at Oliver.

"For goodness sake Horus, I told you I do not know! She is still breathing, so will you please help me bring my mum to her room? This is not a time for your rubbish ego trip!" blurted Oliver; by his voice and his words the King could tell he was he was worried; there had never been a time in his life when people took him seriously until then; there was a sense of desperation in his voice that could have turned into anger very quickly.

The King got closer and realized that Lucille was lying on the floor. Her eyes were closed and there was blood on the bottom of her dress. Her red head was a knotted mess and her skin was pale as the King's good china. She was bare foot with blood and dirt covering the bottoms of her feet. She was cold; her lips had turned purple and an overwhelming smell of vomit and urine hung around her.

"What in the world..." King Beckford mumbled without meaning to.

"Your Majesty, I just found her. I do not know what has happened to her," Horus volunteered the information with a look a terror on his face.

175

King Beckford looked at Oliver who had a tear coming down from his right eye and his lips were quivering. The King spoke in the softest voice possible "Oliver, please go and get a bowl of warm water, rags, soap and a fresh outfit and return back here as quickly as possible.

Without saying a word, Oliver ran off toward Lucille's room. King Beckford had never seen Oliver run, but he had some power in his legs because it was not long before the King was unable to see him. King Beckford turned back to Lucille and bent down to touch her; she was as cold as ice. He pushed her hair out of her face and gently called her name, but she did not respond to his call. He was on his knees by Lucille's head the whole time he waited for Oliver to return. It had only been a few moments but time past so slowly while the King waited. He had played every possible outcome over in his head a million times within those few moments. He pictured the castle life if Lucille was no longer around; he pictured someone trying to hurt her. It was an earth-shattering feeling that he would not be able to shake until she was awake and spoke to him.

Oliver returned and the King thought it would be best to carry Lucille to a warmer room. The dining hall had a fireplace and King Beckford instructed Oliver to go start it. Horus, and Samuel, who had made his way to Lucille, were instructed to carry Lucille into the dining hall and place her near the fire. King Beckford had to check on Gerica quickly and return to Lucille as fast as he could. He flew up the stairs only to meet her at the top.

"Father, I was in my bedroom when I heard loud voices. Is everything ok?" Gerica questioned; she had just woken up and her hair was a mess.

"I believe everything will be fine. However, for now, I need you to stay in your room and out of the way," cautioned King Beckford. The truth was that he did not want Gerica to see Lucille this way; for more than one reason. Gerica had not shown signs of much sympathy thus far in her life; simply because she had never had to and that was how the King wanted it to stay. The less people she felt bad for, the less attached to them she was; she would still be able to rule the kingdom the way he intended her to. Another reason was that Gerica may think that something or someone did this to Lucille, and since that was not known for sure, he did not want Gerica to have any other reasons to be scared of whatever it was she was already scared of. Lastly, he did not want her in the way.

Gerica just nodded her head and walked away. The King could tell she look disappointed, but he did not have time to worry about her childish emotions. Once he watched her walk back down the corridor and she was out of sight, he turned and headed for the lower level; back to where Lucille was. She was still lying on the floor with Anders, Oliver, Samuel, Horus, and Stetson were all around her. They all looked up once they saw the King come down the stairs.

Oliver was the first one to speak up. "The fire is ready and has warmed up the room a good amount. How shall we move her in there?"

"There are six men here, I believe we can lift a woman," King Beckford rolled his eyes as he hissed his reply. The stupidity of people was never something he was able to take with a grain of salt; it always was able to get under his skin. One thing that he always felt was a curse was having to share his world with people who were not as smart or talented as he was. "Alright then, Horus and Samuel you grab her shoulders and stomach areas, be gentle. Stetson you can grab her legs, and Oliver support her head. Everyone needs to be as gentle as possible, do not harm a single hair of her head; Anders get the door, please."

All the men bent down to pick her up while Anders walked to the door and the King stood there to supervise. Once they all were inside the dining hall, Anders shut the door behind them. The four men carried Lucille until they were close enough to the fire for her to feel it. The King went to get a blanket to lay her down on; once he laid it out, the men gently laid Lucille down by the fire. All of the men just sat there and watched her as they waited for their next move.

"All of you are free to leave, expect you Oliver; you need to stay here to assist me," demanded King Beckford. As the four men turned to walk away, the King had a thought. "Anders, I will need to speak to you in a short amount of time so stay near. Stetson go outside of Gerica's room and keep an eye out for her. As for you two," King Beckford turned and looked at Samuel and Horus. "I need you two to secure the grounds; in and outside of the castle leaving no room untouched. Also, I need every other guard, hand maid, and gardener in this castle to meet me in the throne room in one hour. Go!" There had always been a lot of staff working within the castle walls, but the King did not know every single one personally. Most of them were the children of servants and guards that the King's father had employed. It was considered safer to employee the past generations' children as workers. The King was not fond of the idea that new people would have access to his life; and this way, most of these people that worked here now were born and raised on these grounds. The King did however allow debts to be settled by taking someone from a family that owed taxes, though it was rare. They all had housing on the castle grounds; most were outside in the shacks that were near the woods, but for a select few, their housing was inside the castle walls. There were Lucille, Oliver, and Anders that all lived inside the castle walls. Also, the three guards those were closest to the King. These six people aside from Gerica were the only ones permitted to speak to the King unless the King spoke to them first.

He waited until the door was shut between the guards, before he turned to Oliver. "We need to undress her and wash her up; and then we shall change her clothes. You did gather everything I asked for, I assume?" Oliver stayed silent but shook his head yes. There was a look in his eyes that made King Beckford's heart ache. He knew there was a bond between the two that he would never understand but it was powerful, and meaningful. He bent down and started to unbutton Lucille's white blouse. Oliver began taking a damp cloth to the spots of blood on her right arm. The pair of men stayed quiet as they cleaned her up; until Oliver broke the silence.

"Do you think she was attacked?" He was nervous to ask the question; almost as much as King Beckford was to answer it.

King Beckford did not answer right away; the truth was it was possible that she was attacked, and he did not want to admit it. He did not want to think that she was hurt inside the walls of his castle. He cleared his throat and answered "I cannot be sure. My hope is for her to be able to tell us what happened to her as soon as she wakes up." Once she was clean, the King called Horus and Samuel into the dining hall.

"You two need to carry her to her room. Lay her down in her bed and stay right there with her. I will be there in a moment," Ordered King Beckford; he needed to meet with Anders. "Horus, do you know if Anders is close or if he is in his room?"

"His room, Your Majesty," informed Horus. He and Samuel walked up to Lucille and gently started to carry her to her room. Horus checked to make sure she was still breathing; he was relieved to find that she was.

When the door shut behind them, King Beckford turned to look at Oliver. "Please clean this mess; then make your way into the kitchen and fix your mother something to eat. Something that will be ok if it sits out for a few hours. There is no way of knowing when she will be awake." With the last demand, King Beckford turned on his heel and headed for the door.

He quietly made his way to Anders; he realized that without Lucille, his kingdom would fall apart; she was the glue that held so many things together; he was more concerned with Lucille's well- being than Gerica's. King Beckford had truly believed that nothing of real danger was going on; Gerica had been telling the truth since day one. Only if he had listened to her from the beginning, he could have avoided this entire ordeal. King Beckford reached Anders' bedroom door and he raised his hand to knock, but before he could make contact the door opened.

"No need to knock Your Majesty. You know you are welcome in here any time your heart desires," enlightened Anders. He returned to the desk he was sitting at and looked at the King. His room was darker than the rest of the castle but at that time it had more candles lit than the King had seen in one space; candles of every size and color one could think of. They were placed on the desk, on the shelves, on tables nears the shelves, on the table near his bed, and there were even some candles on the floor. It looked like some sort of ritual had been going on.

Anders cleared his throat and rose from his seat. "I assumed you would need me to look into things for you, when you spoke in the dining hall your voice rang with desperation. I returned to my room only to find that these candles were already lit for me; so, I left them alone. Someone had been in my room during the short time I was in the corridor and the dining hall. It occurred to me that this "shadow" as Gerica calls it, is trying to make its presents known. Either that or it plans to frighten us. I cannot answer if it attacked Lucille, but I can tell you whatever it is, is watching us. When the guards and I went into the corridor after you dismissed us, I asked them to bring me back anything that look suspicious. And although they were not able to bring me back psychical evidence, they did tell me that someone had been down in the dungeon. Apparently, there were bloody foot prints leading from the corridor at the bottom of the stairs to the dungeon doors. Once inside the dungeon, there were more foot prints. One last thing was that picture of your father that hung to hide the doorway was moved. They said that it was put upside down. The oddest thing, because it would make sense that if someone was not trying to be caught, they would make sure they did not leave a trail of clues behind them. This person or thing has little worry of us finding out that they are in this castle. As you know, the power I hold is limited; I am not sure that I will be of much help." Anders' spoke with conviction in his voice.

King Beckford was starting to doubt Anders and everything he thought he was. He was so angry that he let his tongue speak before he thought about what he was saying. "What use are you? Why do I keep you here? You are seemingly more and more useless by the day. When you first got here, I saw so much promise in you, you would be a valuable friend and partner. But that is not the case, it appears to me more now than ever that you had a few lucky dreams and I have given you a great life due to your good luck."

King Beckford knew this was not the case, he knew that Anders had always done what he could for the good for this kingdom. His lips spoke from his emotions and not his head. He looked at Anders, who had a frozen face. He had his mouth opened like he was about to respond but was not able to think of anything that could add to the King's comments. King Beckford felt a knot in his stomach, and he was not able to take back his words; but he was never one for apologies, so he turned and walked out of Anders' room. He left his room with a large feeling of regret but also with a large feeling of uncertainty. King Beckford had to speak with the guards and the handmaids; he would talk things out with Anders later; when he was able to calm his anger toward everything that was going on.

Chapter Eighteen

Meanwhile, Gerica was in her room; cut off from everything that was going on with Lucille and her father. The walls in her room for as far back as she could remember felt like a prison; she is suffocated when she is stuck there. She had not had anything of significance happen to her since her father had returned home; but she wandered what had gone on that made her unable to leave her room. She started to panic when she heard a knock on her door.

"Gerica, are you in here?" The sweet, soft voice of Oliver came through Gerica's bedroom door.

"Yes, come in." instructed Gerica. There was always something calming and exciting about Oliver being near. She had always had a crush on him, and how he never figured it out was beyond her. She blushed while he was around, and she was not able to stop her palms from sweating. She could not be certain that he would even care if he did find out; but someday she would tell him. She did not know how Lucille would react to this news; she was the only mother figure that Gerica had ever known. In some ways this felt wrong to Gerica, but in so many other ways it was right. Before Gerica was informed from her father that she was not able to marry, she had just always assumed that Oliver would be her husband. There was no one else that the King would trust with his kingdom like he could trust Oliver. Knowing that he would not allow Gerica to marry, she never bothered to ask him his thoughts on the matter; she did not want to let her secret feelings for him be known with no positive outcome. In the back of her mind she thought there may still be hope for the two of them. After all, her father would not live forever.

Her heart skipped a beat when she saw him walk into her room. He was carrying a tray and it looked like it had breakfast items on it. He was still dressed in his robes from the night before and had a smudge of dirt on his beautiful left cheek. His eyes looked troubled, and that would explain why he was in here, speaking to her; he never came into Gerica's room alone. "Oliver, what is wrong?"

As he made his way over to Gerica, he placed the tray of food on the bed beside her. He took the seat right next to the tray. He had his hands in his lap and he head is bent down; he did not look at her or speak a word. Gerica started to become nervous as she waited for him to answer her. Finally, Oliver looked into Gerica's eyes and allowed his voice to escape his body and tears slowly rolling down his face, he whispered, "my mother." That was all he could get out of his lips; and Gerica was only more confused and worried by this lack of information.

"Oliver… what are you saying? What is wrong with your mother? Gerica asked with a shaky voice.

"We do not know, but she is sick, Gerica. Hours ago, when you came to the lower lever and your father sent you back upstairs, it was because she was laying on the floor; covered in blood and dirt; no one knows what happened to her. She is not awake and has not been all morning. She could have been there all night, or ten minutes. There is no knowledge of anything that has happened to her." Confided Oliver as his tears began to fall faster and heavier.

"Where is she now?" Gerica asked. It felt like her world had stopped moving and nothing was making sense. Lucille had never been hurt or sick Gerica's whole life; she never needed anyone to care for her or protect her. Lucille was the strongest person that Gerica knew and to think of her being helpless and hurt was too much for Gerica to believe. The only emotion that was present in her was love. "Can I see her?" She asked; all Gerica wanted to do was look at the face of her angel.

Oliver did not say anything; he just shook his head no.

"But why not?" She demanded.

"Your father wanted her left alone." He replied.

"And where is he?" inquired Gerica.

"That was why I came in here actually. Your father sent me to tell you that he, Samuel and Horus were heading into Bales' village. They are planning to bring back a doctor; he did not want you to think that he was ignoring you." He informed her while he was trying to fight back anymore tears.

Gerica's tone was ruder than she had meant it to be. "So, you mean to tell me that father is not here, and you expect me to follow that insane rule? No, I will be going to see her; Oliver, where is she. Is she in her room?" She was staring Oliver in his eyes and all she could think of is how she wished they were meeting and conversing about happier things. Nevertheless, she could not focus on her feelings for him; Lucille needed her more than ever. Gerica stood up and walked toward the door;

Oliver did not try to stop her, but he stood up to join her.

"She is in her room, but Gerica you must know, she does not look pleasant," warned Oliver. His face was red and white at the same time; his cheeks looked as if the sun had laid upon them for far too long. Yet, around his eyes and his forehead were as if he had seen a ghost. It was an odd combination, but it showed he was dealing with great emotions.

Without saying a word, he threw both of his muscular arms around Gerica's shoulders and bent his head into her neck. She is taken aback by this hug; nothing of this sort has ever happened between the two of them. Gerica was not able to catch her breath or stop her heart from jumping out of her chest. She had to remain focused on Lucille's wellbeing, though it would be hard with the love of her life holding her as if she was the only person that he needed. Gerica lifted her arm and patted Oliver on the back, then slightly started to rub. She wanted to tell him everything would be alright, but that was not something she could be sure of; then she thought to say something that she could be sure of.

"No matter the outcome of all this unfortunate insanity that has taken place here, I will always be here to help you. You mean a great deal to me, and I would never want to see you unhappy." Gerica whispered into Oliver's chest. The two were still interlocked into the longest hug that Gerica had ever experienced. There were so many more words that she wished she could get out of her lips but that did not seem possible.

"Gerica, you will never know what those words mean to me. Come, we must see my mother," He insisted as he released her from his arms.

The pair walked down the hall and the whole time Gerica could not fight her feelings. She wanted to tell him that she loved him and that she always had. She did not know what had taken over her. As they walked in silence, she remembered her shy and lonely days; her meek persona kept her from ever telling Oliver how she felt. It had always kept her from telling anyone how she felt. She thought that perhaps now she could tell him, but when she opened her mouth her tongue would not make the proper movements to allow her to speak. Her palms started to sweat, and she could fell her face becoming redder by the moment.

"Gerica, what is the matter with you?" he asked while his face looked confused and slightly scared.

Gerica could not speak, so she gave a small grin and just shook her head.

Before Gerica knew it, they were at Lucille's bedroom door. Oliver held out his left hand to open the door, and what Gerica saw inside was the worst sight she could have pictured. Lucille was lying in her bed and she had cuts all over her face and arms. Her hair was piled into a bun on the top of more hair, but it did not look brushed. She had dark circles under both of her eyes and her cheeks had a pale white color to them. She looked as if she was sleeping but not peacefully. She had an expression on her face that showed she was in pain. Gerica had never seen Lucille helpless; she was not sure how to react. It was clear that Oliver did not either. Gerica turned back to him and looked him in his eyes; they swelled with tears.

"We do not know what has happened to her," Oliver choked as he tried to whisper these words.

Gerica did not say anything; she just walked up to the bed. She could hear Lucille breathing; she was taking long, deep breathes. It was almost as if she needed to concentrate on breathing because it was not coming easy to her. Gerica fell to her knees and grabbed Lucille's hand. It was so cold;

Gerica touched Lucille's face with her free hand and that too was cold.

"There are not enough words I could speak that would show you the pain I feel watching you like this. Lucille, please find strength to be alright; there is not a world I can live in without you. Oh, Lucille please wake up. Please speak to me. I know you can hear me." Gerica wanted to cry but she realized that crying will do no good. For all she knew Lucille could wake up any moment and think Gerica was mad for crying at her bed side. Gerica had so many feelings running through her head and those feelings were the exact opposite that they were just moments before when she was walking with Oliver. Oliver! Gerica looked back at the door and watched him cry. There was an overwhelming sense of love in the room that mixed with the same sized sense of fear. Gerica could feel the love between Oliver and Lucille, herself and Lucille and the love she felt for Oliver.

Gerica stood up and leaned in closer to Lucille's face. She whispered "Lucille, you will be ok. I promise you. I will not let anything take you from me." When Gerica finished those words, she placed a kiss on Lucille's forehead just the way Lucille had done for her thousands of times.

Gerica got to her feet and walked right toward Oliver. Without thinking she grabbed his face by putting a hand on each of his cheeks and kissed his lips. When she pulled back away from him, she looked into his eyes; there was a tiny glimmer of light in them. "We need to be strong for your mother. Just the way that she has always been strong for us. Now is not the time to be weak." Gerica was not expecting a rebuttal or a comment so she turned to walk away. She was feeling proud of herself and yet still a little shy. She did not know what he was thinking and she did not dare ask.

As she reached for the knob, she noticed out of the corner of her eye that Oliver was still standing there; he looked dumbfounded. She walked out of the room and started to make her way down the corridor. She had not gotten far when she heard footsteps behind her; she grew nervous because in the midst of everything that had been going on, she had forgotten that there was still something that wanted her attention. She did not dare to turn around and she picked up the speed as she started to walk.

Next thing she knew, she felt hands grab her shoulders. Strong hands, hands that she had never felt before. They turned her around and pinned her against the wall. Before she had a chance to move, she felt a pair of lips attack hers. They were soft and kissed her lips gently. One of the hands made its way to her chin and held her there in such a sweet way. It was the most passion she had ever experienced in her life and when it ended, all she could do was smile. She looked at Oliver and he was staring deeply into her eyes.

"You should know, Gerica. I have always loved you. And that will never change," confessed Oliver. He released Gerica and walked back toward his mother's room. He did not even turn to look back at her while he walked away.

Gerica could not breathe; and her heart was pounding through her chest as her knees became weak. To think all these years wasted because she was never able to tell Oliver how she felt, while he possibly shared a similar feeling.

Chapter Nineteen

Gerica had no idea what time of day it was. No one was around to help her with her questions on Lucille, and because of that she felt helpless. Gerica went to one of the tall windows that were in the middle of the corridor. She sat on the sill and just stared and through the glass; she watched how the sky started to turn into a purple and red mess. The day light was leaving and the sun was falling away. She was full of confliction, she was worried, but she had promise; she was scared but she had love. The best and worst things in her young life had just happened to her within moments of each other. She was not sure how she would deal with this chaos. She needed to talk to her father; it was hard to believe that he left knowing that Lucille was sick. *Lucille would have never left the King's side if he was in this situation.* Gerica curled her feet up on the sill and laid her body down. She was staring up at the sky and she could not stop her mind from racing. The mere thought of life without Lucille made her eyes start to tear.

"There she is. I found her," a raspy voice whispered.

"Oh, how trusting of her to sleep where no one is watching her. It would be a shame if something happened to her while no one was here to see. "Another voice replied to

196

the first. *This voice was not raspy at all, but rather frightening.*

"*Oh now, you know nothing will happen to her. She is to be protected until the grand reveal.*" *The raspy voice said with a giggle.* "*Besides, she is not ready for all that will come to her. She is still so naive of her faith. We shall have our day.*"

"*Oh my dear Gerica, we will meet again. You are ours and there is a life that is promised to us.*" *The frightening voice had chanted. This time, both voices started to giggle.*

"Gerica, Gerica! For heaven's sake girl, wake up!" yelled the King as he shook Gerica's shoulders quickly.

Gerica opened her eyes to see the King standing over her with an angry face. Behind him were Oliver, Anders and Stetson. The air was cold and the corridor was silent; night had fallen upon the castle's windows.

"Father; you are home, oh goodness; I did not realize I had fallen asleep out here!" Gerica jumped up and realized her hair was a mess, and she had heard voices speaking to her, but she could not recall every detail; she could not shake the feeling that something else was going on. "Oh, father. How is Lucille? Has she been seen by a doctor?"

"You know Lucille is sick and yet you disobeyed my orders to remain in your bedroom? I shall not deal with a child that does not take my orders seriously; and especially not when I am dealing with matters of more importance." King Beckford yelled.

"But father, I love Lucille; she is like a mother to me. Surely, you can understand my curiosity, and I did not intend to sleep here." She insisted.

"Your curiosity is of little interest to me child. You need to return to your room and you are to stay there until I send for you. Do I make myself clear? Should you disobey me again, you will be locked in your room in complete solitude for as long as I see fit!" He hissed. And with that Gerica made her way down the hall. She was astonished that her own father was more concerned with the rules that she broke than he was about how she felt about Lucille.

She was still incredibly sleepy and was anxious to make it to her bed. When she lay down, she remembered those voices; *they were talking about a grand reveal.* Gerica laid on her back and grabbed her pillow with both arms; pulled it up to her chin and started to release tears. As they begin to moisten the pillow, she remembered her emptiness. Her heart would never be full, not with her father still in the castle. He does not understand anything.

Just as she started to allow more tears roll to down her cheeks, she heard a noise. The bedroom door started to creek and it was starting to open. The windows allowed the glare of the moon shine into her bedroom. She could only see a figure making its way to her bed, and her heart started to pound.

After what seemed like forever, the figure spoke. "Gerica, are you in here?" It asked.

Gerica was shook yet relieved that this figure was none other the Oliver.

"Oliver, what are you doing in here?" She asked.

Oliver did not say anything until he made it to her bed and he sat down. Gerica was able to see his face clearly now. He looked so handsome in the moonlight.

"Have you been crying?" He whispered.

"A little," Gerica admitted.

"No, dear Gerica; do not cry. Everything is ok; I came to speak to you about my mother. They think that she is exhausted and just needs rest. She has always worked her whole life to make sure everyone else was perfect. And now it has caught up to her. The doctor from Bales said that they need to watch her, but in a day or so, she should wake up feeling refreshed and normal again. I believe that she will be very hungry when she awakes," Oliver smiles once he is finished his sentence; with a look of hope and relief in his eyes; and Gerica found a peace just by seeing his mood change. Oliver made his way closer to Gerica and started to wipe her tears from her face. He smiled as he did it and whispered, "Do you remember not too long ago when mother sent me into the garden to get you for her?"

"I do," she answered.

"Well, before you heard me. I was following behind you for a moment. And I was just taking in the beauty that is you. Your hair shimmered that day and your skin had a flawless glow. I realize that I have not seen many women outside of these castle walls, but I can promise you; not one woman on this earth holds the amount of beauty that you do. When you kissed me earlier, Gerica I felt like my world had come and finally let me in. There was a piece of life that I was missing and everything made sense after your lips met mine. I went back into my mother's room and just sat with her. I stroked her hair and just sang to her. From that very moment, it felt that you were the only thing in my life that I was missing. I do hope that when you kissed me, it was out of love and not sympathy. Now that I have told you everything that I hid to myself, I would not be able to stay around you if you did not feel something for me." He confessed.

Gerica just sat there; breathless. She wanted to say how badly she had been in love with him, for as long as she could remember but the words could not form.

"Gerica, please say something; anything." Oliver whispered.

"I love you, Oliver," was all Gerica was able to get out of her lips. And with that, Oliver climbed into her bed. He laid beside her and stroked her hair from her face gently. It was like a scene that Gerica had read in a book; it was perfect. The two fell asleep and only awoke when the sun started to beam into Gerica's room. When they both opened their eyes, they realized that they were interlocked with each other. They had slept the entire night in each other's arms; it was most blissful sleep Gerica had ever had. No dreams haunted her, there was nothing watching over her or at least nothing that she could feel. Gerica sat up and turned to Oliver; he opened his eyes and gave a big smile.

"You are even beautiful upon waking up," he declared as he reached for her hand and kissed it. His lips were like silk touching her skin; and Gerica wondered how she was able to keep away from him for all these years.

"Good morning Oliver. How did you sleep?" asked Gerica. She was smiling ear to ear with her fingers laced into his. It was a perfect fit.

"Very well, better than I have ever dreamed possible," Oliver's voice was soft, almost like a whisper.

Gerica was silent for a moment. She looked at this man and realized that they could have such a beautiful life together. She thought of her father and what he would do should if he found out that Oliver had spent the night in her room; she could not bear the idea of the King banishing Oliver from the castle; she knew that this had to be kept a secret.

Gerica turned to Oliver and looked him in the eyes. "My entire life father had told me that I was not to love or marry. Now having you here with me shows that I never want a life without you. I would pick being with you over being queen. I think we should leave the castle; run away, to another kingdom; far from Leward. We could go where he could not find us." Gerica had seriousness in her voice that proved she was not to be taken lightly. She was all too willing to leave the life she was living behind her. She never wanted to be queen, she never asked to be adopted and she never stated she did not want love. The life that her father was forcing upon her was not by any means something she wanted.

"What about the kingdom, Gerica?" Oliver was uncertain what would happen to everyone they loved if the two of them vanished.

"To hell with the kingdom; I never wanted this. The pressure and stress that I find myself under is enough to drive a sane woman mad. Besides...." Gerica looked away from Oliver; she was not sure how to continue in her rant. "I cannot be sure that I am safe here, or that should I take the throne, I will not be killed for it. I know that I am not alone in the corridor, or the dining hall. I do not believe my room is solely mine. I think that whatever has been around while I have been in this castle is going to haunt me for however long I am here. Anders' can have the throne; the all mighty man himself should be able to run a kingdom." Gerica had ended her sentence and she felt the anger leave her body. She had never verbalized her exact thoughts about the shadow because she had always known that no one wanted to hear about it. "Forgive me, Oliver. Sometimes I do not pay attention to the ears that are subjected to my rants. Years of having no friends, no one to confide in, has led me to a lot of lonely nights speaking to myself. I need to remember when people are nearby."

"Gerica, this castle is not where I wanted my life to end, nor where I would have picked it to begin; the only thought that has kept me going to the idea of serving you as queen. I would give anything to leave with you, but my mother will have no part of leaving the King or the castle. And her health, I am not sure when she will be on the mend." Oliver disclosed this information with an almost apologetic look in his eyes; he was visibly torn.

Gerica was overtaken with a sense of guilt that brought tears to her eyes. "Oh, Oliver, you are right. I cannot believe the thought of leaving

Lucille in her time of need even entered my head. I assure you, I would never ask you to leave your mother. I would stay in the castle a thousand lifetimes to be at her side."

"You will be a great queen Gerica, the love in your eyes is no match for the love in your heart. Your father will never be able to mold you into his puppet. You will do great things, you have been giving a remarkable opportunity to make good of your father's short comings. I pray that you reconsider your plan to leave. Surely, I have my selfish reasons; but the most important thing is that you understand how this kingdom would need you after a king like Beckford." Oliver enlightened Gerica with ideas that she had never thought of before. She was not bound to anything that he father wanted her to do. One day, he will no longer be living, and she would be allowed to have friends, and visit outside of the castle walls. Gerica's eyes lit up like the rising sun when she realized one last thing; she could marry.

Gerica looked at Oliver and smiled. "My dear Oliver. How right you are; may I ask you something?" Her voice was reaching a higher, more excited pitch than just a few moments before.

"Anything," he agreed.

"Would you like to be King one day?"Gerica was unable to hold back her smile. She was looking Oliver in the eye and saw his emotions change from relaxed during the casual conversation to almost shooting up from the bed.

"Is this…. are you asking me to marry you?" He muttered.

"There is not another man in this kingdom better suited for the job; nor will I bother to look. If you decline my offer, I am more than prepared to rule alone. Since I have been conditioned to always think that is my destiny, it will not bother me to continue with it." Gerica informed Oliver, she was hoping that he would say yes, but surprisingly she was preparing for a no.

"I would, of course; but even if I was your servant for all of my days, I would be the happiest man in the kingdom," assured Oliver, he was smiling his famous smile.

"I think I have found how this shall work. We cannot let a soul know that we are anything. We shall speak as much as we always have, but only around people. When I take the throne, you will be by my side. Can you promise me that I will have you then, when the time is right?" Gerica pleaded.

"You have more than my word, you have my heart," Oliver confessed with a smile and a kiss to Gerica's cheek.

Gerica basked in the love she felt from Oliver, but one thought interrupted this moment for her. "Now, how shall we sneak you out of this room"…

Chapter Twenty

Moments later, Gerica had found herself walking to the throne room; she needed to address her father. She thought about her life with Oliver and what that would mean for a girl that never even had a friend. There was no denying the chemistry that was between them; it felt like lightening had shot through the core of Gerica's body.

There was a heavy presence that hung in the castle. Gerica was not sure what it was but she had a feeling that nothing besides Oliver was going to result in a happy ending. As she stepped down from the last step, she could hear voices coming from the throne room.

"But you are not being clear with me. Is Lucille going to be alright?" Demanded the King. Gerica had heard her father angry on many, many occasions but not like this. Not only could she hear anger in his voice, she could sense worry and confusion. She knew that Oliver would be able to leave her room without being noticed, but now she saw that was not a happy accomplishment.

As she slowly made her way closer, she could hear a second voice; but she was not able to recognize it. It was deep, yet pleasant and it made attempts to confront King Beckford. "My lord, this is nothing I have ever seen before. This type of affliction is not one that has been documented. I would be happy to take her into the town, keep a close eye on her. Surely, I could do it here, but I feel that having more of my tools around could help me better serve her."

"Then I shall come too. I will not allow her to be left alone without someone from her life to comfort her. I will have my guards help bring her into town. I need just a few moments with my daughter and servants to make my leaving announcement." The King sounded like he was passing a law for all of Leward; he was not to be taken lightly when he spoke in this manner.

He made his way around the corner and saw Gerica standing there, listening. Gerica's eyes begun to water as she saw the look of devastation on her cold-hearted father's face; her father loved Lucille more than he loved his daughter.

The King was not wasting any time. "Gerica, I need to follow Dr. Patten into Bales. He is to nurse Lucille back to health; and when she is rested and refreshed, I want to be there. She needs to know that we love her. You will not be able to join us on this trip, and I do hope you understand that this may be a matter of life or death." As his voice started to trail off, his eyes looked behind Gerica. "Ah, Oliver, perfect timing; please make your way over here. Your mother needs to be taken into the town of Bales to receive the proper medical attention. I will be making the journey with her, as traveling alone would not be easy for the doctor to do. I need you to look after Gerica, of course, cook and clean as you normally would. Oliver, I understand that this may be difficult for you, but this need not interfere with your work. I promise all that can be done for your mother will be done; but this kingdom and castle still need attention. Gerica, you are to act as if you were queen in my absence. Nothing of importance should arise but if it does, I assume you can handle it." The King looked at Gerica; she had wide eyes and a thin, quivering lip. She shook her head yes and did not make a sound. Then, he looked at Oliver, and he looked like he had seen a ghost.

They stood there and both were in a daze. It had seemed a lot of time had passed before Oliver took the lead and spoke up "Of Course, Your Majesty. I am here to do anything to help." He gave a small smile then turned on his heals to exit the hall. He looked like he was walking toward the kitchen area, Gerica assumed that he meant it; he would continue to handle everything.

"Father, would you also like me to help with Lucille's work in her absence? I am more than willing to lend my hands." She was hoping to help ease some of his worry but judging the look on his face, it did not seem likely.

"Very well, Gerica. Hurry along now, I must go." His voice was tired and he did not to want to chat.

She also turned to walk away; her eyes fought back tears as she walked to the dining hall. She heard Samuel and Horus make their way into the throne room, and the four men helped carry Lucille out of the castle. This had been the saddest day thus far in Gerica's young life; she walked down the hall with her head down and her steps heavy. Her world had seemed to change somewhat overnight. Gerica was distracted from all of her fears and filled with emotions that contradicted each other; she felt lost. When she finally made it to the dining hall, all she could do was sit and allow the tears to flow.

Gerica was not sure how long she was sitting in the dining hall, but she knew that the day needed to be started. She had not eaten nor studied, she had to keep her mind off the things at hand. She stood up and wiped her teary eyes; she had no appetite and did not remember the last time she had eaten.

Stetson walked into the dining hall and he had looked more serious than Gerica had ever seen him. "Gerica, what are you doing in here alone?"

"Nothing, Stetson; I was taking a moment to myself." Gerica muttered as she looked up from the floor. She saw Stetson standing in front of her in a black robe, and he looked scared, or tired. Gerica had not really looked at Stetson; she had never taken the time to see his wrinkles or the color of his eyes. She always had stayed away from the guards as much as she was able to.

"I am not sure you realize the danger that you are facing being out of sight of those who are here to protect you." Stetson warned with a warm voice. "I am sure you realize that things are very different around the castle, and now is not the time you need to be alone."

"You have a job to protect Stetson, and not give orders. I assume you realize that your words are meant to help, not annoy." Gerica was not sure why she was being so rude to Stetson. He had never done anything wrong to her, he had always been polite and kept his distance, but she was out of sorts. The words that he spoke were not meant to hurt her, and although she knew that, she could not stop herself.

Stetson's face dropped and his eyes looked worried. "Very well, Ms. Gerica. I will leave you alone, I will not be far however, just in case you need me." Stetson walked out of the dining hall and Gerica was heartbroken; now she was hurting people that did nothing but want to protect her.

She had remembered that she had not had a thing to eat all day, and she could smell food cooking. She made her way to the kitchen and once she got there, she saw soup on the stove and a bowl of stewed tomatoes on the table next to it. She was not overwhelmingly hungry, and she figured that small amounts of both things would be more than enough. She gathered two bowls and a soup spoon from the nearby cabinets and she poured herself some breakfast. She then found a tray and placed everything on it. She did not want to go eat alone in her room, so she made her way back to the dining hall. She sat down by the fire place and stared at her food. All she could do was drag her spoon through the soup; she took small bites between each swipe of her spoon.

She sat at the table long enough for her soup to become cold, and unappetizing. She thought about how little her problems seemed now that Lucille was hurting. Gerica finished all the food she could bear and stood away from the table. She started to make her way out of the dining hall, still feeling dazed. It had been some time since she had walked through the garden, and all she wanted was fresh air; she opened the front doors of the castle and felt actual sunlight for the first time in days.

Chapter Twenty One

King Beckford sat in the carriage next to Lucille; he watched her face sit still despite the bumps that were on the roads. She had no movement and her skin was still cold. Her red hair, though a mess, laid against the floor of the carriage perfectly in the King's eyes. He was not saying anything to anyone, and only looked at her. No one spoke, mostly out of fear of saying the wrong thing to the King; no one was used to seeing the King this upset.

Dr. Patten was the first to break to the silence. "With all the new medicines and treatments, I am hopeful that something will make sense." Dr. Patten was the most highly respected doctor in Leward and all of the surrounding kingdoms. At the young age of only 33 years old, he was heavily sought after and was very hard to get in contact with. He had a long list of accomplishments for being just a young man. He had very pale skin, mostly in part because he was never able to see day light. He had short, brown hair and big brown eyes. He was not unfortunate looking, but he was not popular for his looks alone. There was no reply from any of the men after the doctor spoke.

After several hours, but they had arrived at Dr. Patten's home. The outside looked very well kept, the trimming on the shutters were a bright yellow that one could see from a mile away, and the sills all housed pots of sunflowers to brighten one's mood. Inside was just as bright as the outside; the large walls were painted a light blue with golden trim. It smelt like apples upon entering; and King Beckford was calmed by the atmosphere. They were greeted by Dr. Patten's wife, Tess and small son. Tess opened the doors to Dr. Patten's office for the men, where she had already had a fire going. The room was lit by the sun light that came in through the large windows that wrapped around the room.

"Tess, can you please draw the curtains back and light some candles? This is a private matter and I do not need peering eyes." Dr. Patten asked his wife who nodded her head and without saying a word lit the candles.

There was a bed with white sheets and a green pillow that sat in the middle of the doctor's office. "Please place her there, gentleman." Dr. Patten instructed; his tone was soft, but very professional. The guards did as the doctor had asked, and carefully lifted Lucille onto the bed. Tess came up behind the men and placed a white cotton blanket over her. She covered Lucille up to her neck, only exposing her head.

"There. Between the fire and the blanket this poor dear shall in warmed in no time." Tess noted as she turned to her husband. "Is there anything else I could get for you, Jed?"

"Perhaps a bite to eat for the King and his guards; they have been on a long journey and will need to regain their energy," informed Dr. Patten.

"Oh, of course; would you gentlemen wish to follow me?" Tess asked with a pleasant smile on her face as she walked out of the office. The guards followed her and they made their way past the King, who still stood in the doorway almost as if he was scared to enter. In his mind, this was all a dream; he was not watching his love lay at the hands of a doctor.

"Your Majesty, if you wish to stay that is fine but I would like to close the door. The warmer we can get her the better chance of her waking up." Dr. Patten assured the King.

"Right," King Beckford muttered as he stepped in and closed the door behind him. "What will we do now?"

"Well, I will check to see her pulse, and heart rate. All the normal signs of a live person and then we will give her awhile. When I reached your castle her body temperature was just below normal, and that can cause her blood vessels to become narrow making it hard to get blood to different parts of her body. To make sure that she is still with us, is the first step." Dr. Patten started to put his fingers on Lucille's wrists and neck. Then he placed a single hand on her stomach to make sure to rose every time she took a breath. "She is still here, but her breathing is shallow; I need to check her temperature." He turned to get his thermometer. "Ah, 96 degrees; we are getting somewhere. For a few moments, let's just sit and wait."

"So, this is promising?" asked King Beckford.

"Very, it is possible that she was not awake because she was so cold. Your body can start to shut down when it becomes too cold in some cases. It is possible that she will wake up once her body becomes warmer." The doctor reassured King Beckford.

"That is good news; thank you Dr. Patten. I do not know what would have become of Lucille had it not been for your help. I have faith now that she is in your hands." King Beckford smiled the tiniest smile he was able to make and took a deep breath. His mind, although still worried, was no longer racing as fast as it had been hours before.

"Tell me again what happened to her," engaged Dr. Patten. He did not need to hear the story again, he was only hoping to get King Beckford into a conversation and distract him while they waited for Lucille to wake up.

"She was just lying on the floor; cold, dirty and bloody. Whatever happened to her before that moment is unknown. I do not know how long she was there by herself and if she was injured before she got there." King Beckford had to choke back his tears; he needed to keep his tough persona.

"Ah, I see. But you mentioned that hours before this she had not been feeling well?" Dr. Patten was hoping that he had all the facts right, but he was unable to recall everything. When he arrived at the King's castle, King Beckford was speaking so fast it was hard to note everything that was told.

"Yes, she had been," confirmed King Beckford. "But I am not sure why she was not feeling well."

Just as he finished his sentence there was a knock at the door. "You may come in," called Dr. Patten.

Tess made her way into the room very graciously; King Beckford had not noticed her before. She was average height for a woman, with a smaller build; her skin reminded King Beckford of cream, it was very pale; much like her husband but hers was covered in dark freckles. She had long, thick, black wavy hair almost loose curls; dark green eyes and very white teeth. She was very warm and welcoming; she was used to strangers in her house. She spoke very softly while looking at the king. "I am very sorry to bother you, but I was curious if there was anything I could get you gentlemen?" She smiled, and King Beckford gave a small smile back.

"A pot of tea; if there is any, and perhaps some crumb cake? We may be in here a while, she has to warm up before we try to wake her." Dr. Patten answered as he smiled at his wife and she turned to leave the room.

"She seems like such a lovely woman." King Beckford acknowledged.

"She is indeed. She spends all of her days being here for my son and me. I truly cannot think of my life without her. I assume Lucille takes care of you in a similar way? You look at her as more than just an employee." Dr. Patten jokingly accused.

"It is true; very true. She is a friend, a lover and an employee. She is the only one that has ever gotten near my heart in such a way that seeing her in this state pains me. I am not familiar with emotional pain. Only one other time in my life have I known that fear of losing something that meant a great deal to me. I do not do well with pressure like this." He admitted openly why Lucille's life was so important to him.

There was a slight knock on the door and then it opened without having permission. It was Tess again, and she carried a tray with two mugs, and large pot of tea, two small plates, what looked like to be two small salad forks as well and a delicious looking crumb cake. She gracefully sat the tray on the stand that was closest to her husband and left the room without saying a word. The two men stopped talking for a moment to eat the cake, and they could hear the noises from the other rooms in the house. The doctor's son started to cry.

"I am sorry for my son's behavior. Heath is a special boy, but he needs a lot of love and attention. I fear he is not in the normal mental state that other three-year-olds are. He had trouble with learning and such; but Tess is very loving and understanding. She takes her time with him." Dr. Patten stated.

"You have been very blessed, Doctor." King Beckford added. The room fell silent again and it left time for the King to think to himself. He had wondered if he had ever had his own children if he would have been able to love them. He knew that Gerica knew he did not love her the way a father was supposed to love a child. He never worried about that because Lucille had always been there to pick up his messes when it came to Gerica. His only concern was if she was turning into the correct ruler. Having Lucille hurt had brought up so many feelings for the King and it was abundantly clear that he had not been a good person.

"Ugh, my head!" groaned Lucille. Both men jumped up to their feet and looked at her. The King almost smiled the moment his eyes saw her face. "What is going on?" Lucille sat up and screamed in agony. "My head; I feel like I am dying."She laid right back down and curled into a ball.

The two men jumped to be by her side, Dr. Patten dragged over a stool to sit by her bed side. "Lucille, I know that you are confused right now, but I am only here to help you. I need to know what is going on with you and how you are feeling." The Doctor announced. "Can you explain to me how you feel at this moment?"

"Nauseous and thirsty; my head feels like it has weight on it. How long have I been here?" Lucille tried to explain while in a coughing fit.

"Would you like some water?" King Beckford asked her.

"Very much so, yes please." She answered.

King Beckford turned and walked away. When the door was open Lucille could hear him ask a woman for a glass of water.

"Lucille, what is the last thing you remember?" Dr. Patten questioned in hopes of finding out something that would help him.

"I was walking in the corridor," she began to answer until she realized that she could not tell the doctor about the dungeon and what she had seen. She needed to speak to the King but for now that part needs to be omitted. "I had been in bed for an extended length of time, I believe I had fainted and I was placed there. Although, I am not sure; I remember my son had left me food by my bed, I sat and ate it. Then got out of bed to walk around; I had been lying in my bed for some time and my body started to ache. I believe I was on the first floor of the castle and that is the last thing I remember, and now I am here looking at you." She did not lie, but she was curious where they had found her. She knew she made her way from the dungeon, and she hoped that she was not caught. She looked at the face of the doctor and he did not seem to suspect anything from her.

Just then the King walked through the door and without saying a word, handed Lucille a tall glass of cold water. She lifted her head enough to reach the glass; she did not try to hold it, she allowed the King to pour it into her mouth. She had never tasted anything as delicious as the cold and pure water. Everything on her face was dry, her throat hurt and her lips felt chapped.

When she was done drinking, she moved her mouth away from the glass. She lowered her head back onto the pillow and began to take long deep breathes. It was hard to breathe and she could not figure out why. She looked at the two men standing next to her bed; the King, looked at her with teary eyes and his right hand covering his mouth as if he was stopping himself from saying the wrong thing. He seemed upset and Lucille had never seen him this way before. And the doctor, who Lucille still was not sure if she knew or not, was studying her. He just looked at her like any movement she made could tell him the answer to what was wrong with her.

Before anyone could say anything, Lucille turned to her side, away from the men and begun to vomit. There was only the water in her stomach, and yellow bile that came up with it. She was drained even though she had just woken up. The two men stood and waited for her to finish vomiting before they spoke. Once she was done and she had rolled back onto her back, the doctor ran to the door. "Tess, please bring some cleaning supplies in here at once, we have a mess to be cleaned." And he walked back from the door leaving it opened.

A woman that Lucille had never seen before with black hair came in with a bucket and several rags. "Where is it?" she asked. The doctor pointed her in the direction of the vomit and without a word she cleaned up Lucille's mess.

"Oh no, no dear; I shall clean that up!" Lucille insisted; she could never bear the thought of someone cleaning up after her.

"Nonsense! You lay there and rest, love. I am here to help take care of you." Tess replied. The two women exchanged endearing smiles and the King took comfort in this. He could tell that Lucille and Tess had things in common and would make great friends. The King was going to mention who Tess was; but Heath begun to cry. Tess finished up her work and rushed out of the room.

"My memories are slowly coming back, but I may have gotten sick in the castle." Lucille mentioned.

"I do believe you did, dear." King Beckford agreed.

"It concerns me that she is not able to hold down water. Perhaps you drank it too fast Lucille, would you be willing to try again. Only sip smaller sips and over the course of say twenty minutes?" The doctor was hopeful that she would be able to make progress. "It may have been that your body was not ready to handle all that water at once upon just waking up. I will go and get you a smaller amount." And with that, he turned and walked out the door, closing it behind him.

King Beckford tried to touch Lucille's forehead; until she spoke up "get your hands off me you murderer." She demanded.

He pulled his hand away and looked at her with a puzzled face. "I beg your pardon?" He muttered.

"I saw your secret room in the dungeon; I know what you have been up to. I thought you were a changed man. Do not touch me." She repeated with a certain amount of strength in her voice.

"Lucille, you do not understand what you are talking about" King Beckford informed in a stunned voice. He had no idea that she had seen his secret room. He was ashamed that she had found it; for once he could explain what was happening in there. Many times before it was his ego that lead him into that dark room to complete the evilest tasks known to mankind; but this time was not that simple, and he was nothing close to evil. "I was trying to protect Gerica." He confessed, and as soon as he did the door opened and the doctor came back into the room. The King stared at her with eyes that filled her with compassion without knowing the full truth. It was a hold that he had over her and no matter how sick she was; it would not go away that easily.

Lucille figured that she would allow the conversation to end for now. Since it was no one's business but her and the King's, she closed her mouth. She had to worry and wonder about the last sentence that King Beckford disclosed. He was protecting Gerica, surely if that was the case Lucille would look past this as she always had; she felt that anger that she had kept in since she woke up start to slip away.

"Here, take a sip or two. Slowly, please." Dr. Patten instructed as he held the glass to her lips. Lucille did as she was told and placed her head back down after.

"My body aches like I have never felt before. It is sore to the touch and I feel that I need to get up and move around," insisted Lucille.

"Not at this very moment, you need to rest and I need to monitor you. Now, I need to take your temperature. Please open your mouth." Dr. Patten was back to the poking and touching of Lucille; and he placed his hand on her forehead to receive her temperature, he looked relieved. "Ah, as close to perfect as we shall get; now that you are on the mend, I need you to stay here for at least two days. I need to make sure that you are able to continuously drink fluids without vomiting. When you have attained that, we shall start making sure you are able to eat normal food. I need to know if your pain gets worse. For that matter, I also need to know if it gets better." He turned to look at King Beckford, "Sir, I would assume you will want to stay here, we do have a guest room, can I offer you that?"

"That is kind, Dr. Patten, but no. I wish to sleep in here with Lucille. Please give Samuel and Horse the guest bedroom." King Beckford replied.

"Ah, yes the guards! I knew I was forgetting something; or someone rather. Right, well as you wish Your Majesty. As it is nearing bed time, I will get you a pillow and blanket. You can sleep in my chair if that is alright? Not exactly fitting for a King..."

"It sounds lovely," agreed King Beckford. Lucille was stunned by the humbleness that took over his monstrous form; she was looking at a different person.

Dr. Patten nodded and left the room. Lucille turned to King Beckford and with a soft voice whispered "I am sorry, I did not know that Gerica's safety was your reasoning. May I ask what had happened?"

"Another day you can, you need to rest. I will be right here if you need me, but we shall not talk about anything until you are well." He bent over her bed and kissed her forehead. "You have no idea what you mean to me, I did not know what you meant to me until today. I am not willing to lose you for anything and I will do anything and everything to see that you pull through whatever is causing you discomfort and pain. Lucille," the King took a deep breath and closed his eyes. "I love you."

Lucille was speechless and stunned. She had heard King Beckford say millions of words over the years she had known him, but never any that had this much meaning. Never any that took her breath away. "I have always loved you" she replied.

He just sat back, "I know," he assured her.

The door opened and in came Dr. Patten with a blue and green blanket and a white pillow. "I am sorry this is all I have to offer; my wife made this blanket herself. Normally, we have more to choose from but we rarely entertain this many guests at one time."

King Beckford shook his hand, "no need to explain, this is plenty." They smiled at each other and just before the doctor went to turn away, King

Beckford said in a deep, powerful voice, "Thank you, Dr. Patten, you do not know what you have done for me." Doctor Patten smiled back and walked out of the door; closing it slowly behind him. King Beckford walked over to the chair and begun to make his bed. He looked at Lucille, who was half asleep, but she was able to give a slight smile before she drifted off completely.

King Beckford laid in the chair and just thought to himself; his whole life he had thought of himself as a hardened man; someone that would never allow anyone to make their way into his heart. He actually did not know that Lucille meant this much to him until she was laying on that floor and he was not sure if she would make it to see another day. He thought of Gerica, and how he hoped she and Oliver were okay in the castle alone. They had Anders and Stetson, but they are unstaffed and that was concerning. He was used to having such a tight grip on everything that when he did not, he felt out of out of touch. He was not sure what would happen, but he knew that Lucille was the here and now and what she needed from him needed to come before his kingdom.

Chapter Twenty Two

The next morning started when Dr. Patten walked into the office; which woke both Lucille and King Beckford. "How did everyone sleep?" He asked as he searched for his instruments to check Lucille's vital signs.

"Fine," answered King Beckford. He was not a morning person and waking up in a strange place did not help him any.

"And you, Lucille?" Dr. Patten turned to face Lucille. She still looked mess, but it was clear she was feeling better. "I see more water from your cup is gone and no vomit on the floor. That means that the smaller sips are working for you then?" He asked Lucille, he wanted to engage her in conversation so he could hear if she had trouble breathing.

"I slept fine, actually, rather well despite all the sleeping I had done before night time. And yes, the smaller sips are easier on me. It seems to help my throat as well; it was hard to shallow in the beginning." Lucille's voice was noticeably tried but did not alarm the doctor. He was poking her and looking her over as she spoke to him and her breathing was fine. He stepped back and found his stool; he pulled it closer to her bed. "Can you tell me how you are feeling today? What has changed from last night or what has stayed the same?"

"My head pounds like a hammer to a wall; that has not gotten better at all. My stomach still feels like it is doing flips; although, I do feel like I could eat. I have not been able to rid the chill yet, even though I am wrapped into this blanket. Honestly, Doctor not much has changed." Lucille sounded defeated.

"Lucille have you ever heard the phase 'no news is good news'? Well, in this case no change is better than a change for the worse. You are in a stable condition and since I do not know what type of condition that is exactly, stable is right where I want you." He gave a slight smile in Lucille's direction and then addressed the King as well. "Tess will be making breakfast, is there anything special you would like her to make? Lucille, please keep in mind that your stomach might not be able to handle much. I would recommend something simple like a biscuit or bran muffin."

"Either is fine thank you." Lucille assured him as she tried to sit up slowly. She could feel all the blood rushing from her head to the rest of her body causing her to feel slightly light headed.

"King Beckford?" addressed Dr. Patten.

"Oatmeal is fine, and perhaps a biscuit. Thank you." He answered as nicely as he could for being in a grumpy mood.

"Coming right up" the doctor replied and walked out of the room.

There was an awkward silence between Lucille and King Beckford. Although Lucille did not know the whole story of what was going on in the dungeon, she knew she could not let it cloud her mind. She thought that there could be something very wrong with her, and she worried about her health. She laid in the bed and looked at the ceiling; she could not let it go however and she needed to ask. "How was Gerica in danger?" She bit her bottom lip as she asked and closed her eyes. She was expecting him to snap at her.

King Beckford looked scared, as if he did not want Lucille to know what had happened. "I will tell you, but you need to promise me that you trust I have it under control."

Lucille became scared, his tone made her nervous and she was not sure what to expect. "Yes, I will trust you."

King Beckford took a deep breath and looked at Lucille. "You know the trip I took recently?" Lucille nodded but she did not say a word. "As you know that was very impromptu. Anders had visited me in the throne room the previous night because he had information. In the kingdom of Topsland, there was a militia forming; this militia was planning an attack on Leward. These idiots were stalling, until I pass away. They know that I am up there in age, and they also knew that Gerica would be taking over for me when I was gone. From Anders's story, they were going to make their way into the castle once Gerica took over reign; and they were planning to kill her. In the most tortuous ways, much like I had done to many men in my past. This was not going to happen, and I had to stop it. It was possible that it would not have happened for years to come but to know that there are people that continuously try to over throw me and now my daughter, was just too much. Perhaps because the rumors about my ballroom days have ceased; perhaps people have forgotten the lengths I will go to protect what is mine. Either way, I will not entertain any of these thoughts. Anders was unable to give me specific names, and therefore it is possible innocents were murdered; but that is a small price for a bigger gain. When the guards and I left, we traveled for a while until we reached the kingdom. It was a tiny place, with not much to offer; I could see why they would want a kingdom like Leward. When we reached the castle, I waited by the horses. I am not one to go where I am not invited. Soon, the guards returned with several men, all with sacks over their heads. We chained them together and dragged them alongside the horses as we rode them; they were made to walk the entire journey. We knew that would exhaust them; and that would make for an easier time to torture them. I did not want you or Gerica to know where I was, and although I did not actually take place in the torture itself, I was there to witness it. I know that long ago we had talked about this type of behavior when Gerica was first bought into the castle, but I want you to know that I had intentions of remaining well behaved. I could not picture anyone hurting Gerica. Should they try to over throw me while I am in power that is one thing; but to think of hurting a child, that is not something I could bare. Those men were taught very quickly that no one is to cross my kingdom. I do not regret what was done."

Lucille sat with every thought that came into her mind, racing through it at once. This story scared her, but also restored her faith in the King. She had never seen him worry about the fate of anything but himself and his kingdom. Lucille asked him the only question she could, "why did they have to die such horrible deaths; some did not have heads. At least that is what I think I saw; my memory is strange right now. Could you have just thrown them in prison?"

"It was possible, yes; but if they escaped then they would have another reason to come for my kingdom. Odds are, at some point we would be vulnerable to them." King Beckford informed as he sat there with his head down; this was not an act of an evil villain, but an act of a desperate father.

Lucille had nothing more to say, and she was starting to feel pain in the stomach. She groaned quietly and rolled to her side. She lived most of her days inside the castle or on the grounds. She was rarely out where the general public could infect her with their colds, flues or diseases. She was growing older and more fragile; she did not like to admit that. The door opened and in came Dr. Patten with breakfast. Lucille, although in pain, was very hungry. She was hoping that she would be able enjoy breakfast without getting sick.

A whole day had passed, and Lucille had not been out of bed; she was still so weak. Dr. Patten was reassuring that being able to eat was a good sign, and that before long she would be able to get out of bed. She had some sharp and some dull stomach pains, but as the day went on those pains started to end. Lucille had stayed at the doctor's house for three days before she was able to return to the castle.

"Now, Lucille when you return home, I do not want you to focus on cleaning. You need to focus on regaining your strength and health. I am still unaware of what caused you to be sick, I need you to come back if you feel sick again. Any of the same symptoms or any new ones." Dr. Patten instructed. With the permission from the doctor, the King, Lucille and both guards got back in to the carriage and made their way home.

Chapter Twenty Three

"It is almost time," the raspy voice whispered.

"I can hardly wait for her to be ours." The second voice was softer, and clear.

"All in due time, everything that we have ever wanted will be ours. She has no choice." The Raspy voice noted.

"What about the King; what if he does not go along with the plan?" The softer voice asked.

"Do not be silly, he will not have a chance to choose a different path."The raspy voice answered.

Both voices started to laugh; Gerica's blood ran cold. She was lying in bed, listening to these faceless voices talk about her future; paralyzed from the fear. Her bedroom was pitch black and she could not even use the moon light to see what was in her room with her. She did not have Lucille here to comfort her and Oliver was in his own room. She did not think before she sat up and stepped out of bed.

She stood next to her bed with her palms shaking and sweating. "Hello?" she called out; but there was no answer. "Just face me. You have made your presence known; do not be a coward now." She was hoping that she was hiding the fear in her voice. She took a step forward, and as soon as she did, she heard giggling and her bedroom door opened and slammed shut. She started to allow the tears to roll down her face, but she was not making a noise.

Gerica walked toward her door, and with a shaky hand she turned the knob. When she made her way into the corridor, she was able to see but it was still very dark. She looked both ways but did not see anything. She started to walk and just when she made her way from her door, she heard a door slam shut. She turned around, and it was what she feared; the western end's door had slammed.

"Dear Lord, please watch over me." Gerica whispered a small prayer when she had realized that it was time to make her way into this room. Her whole body was shaking but she continued to walk. The door sprung back open and she could feel the cold air hit her face like a small breeze.

"Gerica?" The raspy voice called.

"Yes, that is her. She has come to find us! But she cannot see us," giggled the softer voice in a playful tone.

"Even if she finds us, she will not be able to see us." The raspy voice informed.

"Silly young girl" laughed the softer voice.

"Stop it! Come out of the shadows and face me!" Gerica began to scream. "You have robbed me of my childhood, and I will not stand for it anymore!" She was choking back tears and she was allowing her anger to take over her emotions.

There were no words coming from the voices, there was only laughter. It was the evilest thing Gerica had heard in the entire life. "Stop it! Stop it!" she yelled at the top of her lungs.

No sooner had she said that, lightening stuck the castle and lit up the corridor; and in the doorway, she was two cloaked figures She had always thought there was only one, but she saw differently now. She turned on her heel to run but froze.

In the doorway of her bedroom stood two more cloaked figures. She whipped her head back toward the western end to see if the first two figures had moved. But they did not; they were still in the doorway. Gerica was seeing four shadows; she fell to her knees and screamed. She had nowhere to run, and she knew this was the end.

"Gerica, Gerica?" called a familiar voice. "For Pete's sake, Gerica, answer me!"

She had no idea what was going on, or where she was. She felt something on her shoulder, shaking her. When she came to, she opened her eyes and saw Oliver. They were in her bedroom; she was lying on her bed while he was sitting up. She sat up and had never been more confused.

"It is about time you faced the day light sleepyhead! You did not make it down for breakfast, so I bought it to you." Oliver declared happily with a large smile on his face.

Gerica could not make sense of what had happened. Her head felt as if there were tiny people inside it using hammers against her skull; the pain was making it hard to keep her eyes open and it must have been showing on her face.

"What is wrong, love?" Oliver asked with concern in his voice; as he rubbed the hair out of Gerica's face.

"My head is painful at the moment. How long have I been in bed?" Gerica asked.

"It was late last night; I spent the night in here with you. Do you not remember?" Oliver was now just as confused as Gerica.

"I am sorry Oliver; I must have been very tired. I also had an awful dream; there was or someone in my room. Watching over me and talking." As Gerica started to tell Oliver the events of her dream, she looked at his face; it was one of concern and caring. Unlike everything that Gerica ever grew up with. "Saying something to the effect that I was theirs; I am not sure what lead up to the next thing that took place but the next thing I know, I was in the corridor. It was pitch black expect the light coming from the thunder that was outside. There were four cloaked figures surrounding me. The last thing I remember was dropping to my knees and screaming." Gerica was forgetting the details as she tried to tell Oliver what had happened.

"Dreams can be insane at times, Gerica. I know that they always seem so real and that is what makes them so frightening." Oliver looked like he wanted to talk about things that he had seen but did not want to make the conversation about himself.

Gerica felt better that she was not the only person to ever have a nightmare. "What have you had for dreams?"

"There was one time I dreamt that I was running through the woods, bare foot and without a shirt. I was being chased by a man; but this man had a face of a demon or something. It was red and covered with scares. It had followed me around everywhere in that dream. I actually had that dream more than once, all right around the same time. I thought I was being haunted for a while after that."

"Wait, haunted you say?" commented Gerica.

"Yes, of course. Something you see in your dreams that frightens you will make you wonder when you are awake. It is my belief that we have dreams because there is something we are missing in life. It can be something bad, and evil as well as good. Take the sun for example, you dream that you are running around and the sun is beaming down on you from the heavens. When you wake up and you notice that the sun is coming in from your windows. Perhaps, your eyes have already seen the sunlight of the day, and it is trying to make your brain remember it. I mean, your body and your mind are one, but do not always work together. Have you ever had your heart and mind go into different directions?" Oliver realized that he had made his point and that he was getting off the subject. The truth was he did not totally believe what he was saying himself; the dreams he spoke of happened when he was five and he was no longer scared. He just wanted to relate to her to calm her.

"Yes, I have." She answered.

He had to think of something quick to say, he was not expecting the conversation to go in this direction. "Well, dear Gerica. It is similar to that. Your body, heart, eyes and the like do not always work together in perfect harmony. Now, will you have your breakfast?" He asked. He changed the subject as quick as he could, but it seemed she was not ready to let it go just yet.

"The dreams are not always the same thing, same idea but different places. Something following me, hovering over my head like a cloud. Making me feel as if I have an audience no matter where I go. I heard the remark, I cannot quite remember how it was delivered, but something along the lines of my life is not my own? Or that I belonged to someone else; maybe both, heaven knows I was scared out of my mind. It seems that I could be dreaming about my life not being my own because I will be queen, even though it is not my choosing. That could make sense, do you agree Oliver?" Gerica suggested in a half cheerful voice. Oliver could see the thoughts running though her mind even when she was not saying them aloud;

she wanted to believe she led a life of normalcy; even if she did not. She looked at Oliver; he was staring back at her with an empty look in his eyes.

Gerica could not help but laugh at Oliver's blank face; but mostly, she laughed because she had a sense of freedom. Her world that had never made sense to her before was starting to have a brighter outlook. "Oh, Oliver; has anyone ever told you that you are positively gorgeous when you are confused?" She giggled.

"I do not believe that has ever come up in day to day conversation; but I am glad to see there is humor left in you somewhere!" He smiled back. She could tell that his smile was probably the sincerest thing about him. She had only seen him lie when they were young children. There was one time; she remembered that he lied to Lucille. She had been walking through the kitchen and there were fresh cinnamon muffins lying near the window to cool. She saw Oliver, kneeing by the window as he reached his hand up to grab a muffin; and before she had a chance to get any closer, he had eaten the muffin. She asked him to grab her a muffin, and just as he reached his hand up to grab one, Lucille came into the kitchen and Gerica ran away.

"Oliver, what on earth to do you think you are doing? For heaven sake boy, these are for the morning!" She yelled loud enough for Gerica to hear from the corridor.

Oliver was quick on his feet. "I am sorry mother, but there was a raccoon outside my window last night. At least, it looked like a raccoon. I know he was looking for food, and the poor bugger was not able to find any. I just wanted to put muffins out for him." Oliver lied, and he lied because he knew his mother had a soft spot for helpless animals.

"Oh, Oliver, I am so sorry for the harsh tone. My sweet boy, you are always so kind to those in need. Bless your heart; here, you go on and take two. That is one for the raccoon and one for yourself." Lucille gave him the muffins and kissed him on the forehead; and just like that, he ran down the hall to where Gerica was waiting.

He gave Gerica a smile that changed her life, and from that moment on, she knew what he sounded like when he lied. She was able to see pain in his eyes and hear fear in his voice; he was very easy to read.

"So, what should we do today?" she asked Oliver. She was hopeful that they could embark on an adventure together.

Oliver chuckled a bit, "Gerica, you know I have cleaning to do while mother is away. My day will be like every other."

"I see; that is not a life at all, is it? All work and no play, that will drive a sane person mad. No, that is not how I see you spending the rest of your life." She declared.

"It was what I was born into; there is not much choice to change it." His voice sounded defeated. Much like Gerica, he never had a choice in life. He was told that he would be a servant to the King and at some point Gerica; in return of everything they allowed him to have. He needed to be thankful; it was something that both he and Gerica shared. The King, in a sense rescued them both in exchange for their services for life; at times, both were bitter about their situations.

"Silly Oliver, if you do not run away with me, I will be queen. Do you see me keeping you as my servant; or do you see yourself as my King?" She was in awe with how modest Oliver was being. She thought that he would have understood that once she is queen, his servant days are over.

"Gerica, I know you believe that, but things will still need to get done around the castle, and you will still need to eat. There is no telling your demands once you have the throne. I am just trying to be realistic in thinking." He clarified; he was not trying to offend her, but power can go to one's head; and she might forget everything she is telling him at the moment as soon as she becomes queen and decides she wants a rich king for a husband.

"I will just prove you wrong." She declared in the harshest voice he had ever heard her use. He found it rather attractive for her to be aggressive; she was always so sweet. He had to kiss her; he moved closer to her and grabbed her chin with his right hand. When his lips touched hers there was an instant spark; something that traveled through his entire body.

"I should have told you how I felt years ago. Why did I spend so many lonely nights wishing you were in my arms when I could have had you this whole time?" He muttered.

"I feel the same way." She admitted and smiled at the memory of feeling isolated. Gerica ate her breakfast and they both sat in blissful silence.

Meanwhile, down the corridor Anders was preparing for the King's return. He knew that it would be soon and he was positive that something had been done with Lucille. He knew that she would not be sick when she returned, and that the King would no longer be distracted. Anders knew what most of them did not. He knew that soon there would be a shift in power throughout the castle walls, and he knew that the King would soon no longer be with them. He thought it was a pity that some of his last days were being spent to make sure Lucille was going to pull through her sickness, when he should have focused on himself. But Anders could not tell the King this, simply because it would cause panic and keep the King from handling any important business. There was nothing that Anders could do to stop the King from passing away, but he could encourage the King to get his affairs in order. Anders thought of Gerica, and how she was another reason that he could not tell the King he would not be with them very much longer. She had not finished her training to become a queen in King Beckford's favor; it was best to leave it that way.

When Anders had his original vision, Gerica's caring and compassionate heart would have won over the citizens of Leward. That would be how she would come to rule, but now that she was raised by a man that did not think twice before he stole fathers from their children and took their lives away, Anders was hoping she would still lead with such a pure heart.

He had faith in Gerica; she was a smart and insightful young lady. For years, Anders kept his distance from her, but he watched her every move. He knew of the love she carried in her heart for Oliver before even she knew. He had no doubt that she will make a fine queen when the time comes, but for now, Anders had to focus on the King. Since the King was sick, there would be nothing anyone, including doctors could do to stop it; Anders felt that that would drive the King mad. Death shall come to the King when he is not expecting it, and Anders felt that would be the best way to get the most out of the King's remaining time with them.

The truth was, the King had been sick for months now, but a man of his pride, he chose to ignore it. If he would have listened to his body, he may have been able to fight whatever was taking over his organs; but as it is said, there is no rest for the wicked. Anders had hopes for the kingdom once Gerica took it over; he felt that he would not be confined to these walls any longer, and that freedom was just in sight. He knew that she will have to face things that she may not be able to handle alone, and although he is sure that she is scared of him, he wants to change her mind about him.

He sat in his orange chair and thought of everything Gerica had gone through. Her parents, who clearly loved her, but would not have been able to support her. Her adoptive father, who clearly did not love her, but could support her. She would never have been able to have the best of both worlds, and Anders felt that that was a waste. As he started to reflect on his own childhood, he remembered the day he lost his mother, leaving just him and his sister to find their own way in this world. His father was taken from him when he was a young boy and that put the family into poverty. Had his father never left, Anders' life would have been very different. His father was always a hardworking man and provided everything he could for his family. He had looked up to his father like he was a King. And his mother, who died in a tragic winter storm, was the most loving woman he had ever known. The pain of losing his parents had always kept a place in Anders' heart. Anders had to stop himself from thinking about the loss of his parents, it always gave him a hallow feeling in his heart that he was not strong enough to fight.

Perhaps it was why he was always cold and annoyed with Lucille. She reminded him so much of his mother that he could not bear it. He did not want to be close to her, and she needed to know that. Anders did not enjoy being rude to Lucille, he knew that she was a great woman, and he knew that she would take care of him like she did for everyone else, but he was not able to allow that to happen. Anders knew that he could not bear to lose someone like her again from his life, if he was close to her; so he kept his distance.

While Anders was sitting there, he started to hear voices coming down the hall and he knew that Gerica was out of her room. "How would you like to take a break from cleaning and go for a tour of the garden today? I believe father should be home soon so this may be your last chance to accompany me on a fun adventure." Gerica hinted with a smile in her voice. Anders did not have to see her to know that what face she was making. He was willing to bet, that she was batting her eyes at Oliver.

"Well, I supposed this opportunity does not come often, so just this once I will take a break and join you in the garden." Oliver's voice was smiling back as he agreed, and Anders was very sure that Gerica jumped into Oliver's arms and gave him a kiss on the check. He knew these two were going to be together someday and he was glad the wait for it to happen was over.

He knew that having two children grow up together, almost in solitude, would force them to have feelings for each other. Anders had a feeling that he was looking at the future King of Leward every time he looked at Oliver. The one thing that King did not want to happen was for Gerica to marry, he wanted her as stone cold and as unhappy as he was, but little did the King realize that he pushed them together by not allowing either to them to have lives outside of the castle.

The King was never able to see the big picture, he never paid mind to anything that could be a problem for the kingdom in the future. Had he taken note of more things around the castle, he would have realized that a love would blossom between Gerica and Oliver. He also would have seen that Gerica is not that girl that King Beckford had hoped she would be at this point in her life. He would also notice little things; Horus stealing coins from the King, in small amounts, for years. It was never a lot, but if Horus had been saving it over the years, he would be a very wealthy man. The King also did not realize that right in front of his face, he had a woman that would lay down her life for him at any given moment. It is surely a shame that he was not able to see all that was going on, because had he paid more attention, he could have stopped so many events from taking place.

The King was fueled by so much greed and power that he could not see past himself; paying no mind to his failing health would be his biggest mistake to date. *It was a shock, that he made the trip with Lucille into the city part of Bales.* There seemed to be fear in the King's heart and he was not able to leave Lucille alone in her time of need. This was impressive, but far too little and much too late. Anders did not know how much time the King had exactly, but he could see in King Beckford's eyes that the time was nearing.

Anders had struggled with the idea of warning Gerica, without actually saying what was going on. He wanted to pull her aside and simply tell her that she needed to have more of a presence in the throne room. She needed to know how a kingdom should be handled. She could learn a lot from her father; after all, no one was ever able to take his kingdom away from him. Instead of having her see everything first hand, King Beckford was having Gerica waste her time with reading lessons and such. Gerica needed to know how to read, but she had other things that she needed more.

Anders feared that if and when she was put into a position of making a life or death choice for another person that she would use her heart to choose for her; not judgment or logic. She would allow someone who was not deserving of life continue to enjoy living. He knew that she would not listen to his reasons; she may not listen to him at all. She may not want the guidance from Anders that King Beckford had demanded all these years.

For Anders to be without a place to go or a job to do was not a thought that he could bear. He had never really left the castle after he had taken Gerica to the King. Not only would Anders have no place to go if he had to leave the castle, but his people skills are less than normal. He thought about leaving the castle so many times before, but he knew that he was not the person that he was when he arrived there. He was distant and cold now, and he planned to stay that away. He did not plan on leaving the castle, so he had to show Gerica that he could be a friend to her.

Anders stood up and made his way to the corridor; he knew that Gerica had already made her way to the dining hall so he would join them for breakfast.

Just as he entered that dining hall, he saw something he was not expecting. In the middle of the room, Oliver and Gerica had their arms around one another and their lips were locked. Normally, romantic affection turned Anders' stomach, but this is something he could use. He was aware that a relationship had blossomed between the two of them, but they did not know that he knew. Anders saw his opportunity to earn Gerica's trust.

Anders leaned against the door and cough incredibly loud. He could not help himself and he giggled when the pair jumped up and away from each other. Gerica's arm had hit a glass mug containing tea that shattered when it hit the floor.

"Um, Hi, Anders…" she choked; her face was frozen with her eyes wide.

"Good morning my lady, would you like some help cleaning up the shattered glass?" Anders asked with a smile.

"Uh…" Gerica looked down at her feet. "Oh, dear heavens; no Anders, I am fine to clean it alone. Thank you for the offer."

Anders eyes wandered to Oliver, who was just standing there, with a look of terror on his face. They acted as if they were caught by the King instead of Anders; he found that unsettling.

"Oliver, good sir, what is there for breakfast? I wish to join the two of you. I assume that you have not started to eat since you seemed rather busy." Anders' lip could not stop curling into smiles. He was not smiling at the young love; however, he was smiling because he just found his ticket in. He should have known that he was being paranoid for no good reason; he was not going to be made to leave that castle, at least for a while.

"Crepes, sir; and oatmeal with fresh berries," Oliver stated as his face has come back to normal, but he still looked uneasy.

"May I have a bowl of oatmeal, and black tea, please Oliver." requested Anders. Oliver nodded and started to fix Anders' food, as Anders made his way to the table. Just as he sat down, Gerica was done cleaning the glass and she sat down as well. Anders could see her hands were shaking but he thought it was best not to speak of anything; he would wait for them to mention it.

The three of them sat silently until about half way through the meal. Then Gerica broke the silence. "Are you going to ask any questions?" she asked Anders.

Anders looked up and gave her a confused look. "Do you believe I need to?"

"You are not curious?" she muttered.

"I never found myself being curious," Anders boasted.

"So, did you know?" Oliver spoke up.

"I have always known," Anders informed them.

"You have always known? Why did you not tell us?" Gerica blurted in a harsh tone. "I mean, if you knew that we loved each other, we could have saved so much time. Neither of us ever spoke up because we thought the other did not feel the same"

"I am aware Gerica." Anders noted.

"Well, I suppose father already knows as well?" she whispered.

"No, I do not bother him with things that do not affect the kingdom. At least... nothing that affects the kingdom in a positive way." Anders smiled and locks eyes with Gerica.

"So, our relationship will have an effect on the kingdom?" Oliver asked; scared.

"Such a silly question dear boy; do you think you can be romantically involved with the soon to be queen and it not have an effect on a kingdom?"Anders asked.

"I have nothing to do with the kingdom, only the cleaning." Oliver claimed.

"Gerica's eyes tell a very different story young sir. The woman that you have by your side is not full of power or greed. Her heart is fueled by far better things than money can buy, and I assure you, you will have a place in this kingdom." Anders announced.

"I shall never marry if I am to become queen, you know father's rules." Gerica confided.

"You are such a smart girl; how can you believe that you are still under his rule once he is gone? Did you think Lucille or I would stop you? Lucille pines for a daughter and a lover for her precious son. In her heart she regrets bringing him to a place that he may never find that. And you Gerica, you are the apple of her eye after Mr. Oliver. Lucille has honored your father's requests thus far but she will not honor the two of you denying yourself of true love. Your father's law will die when he does, there will be no one to enforce them unless you see them fit. I trust that you will not see denying yourself love so you can remain being a tyrant fit?" Anders knew he had their attention, and he was glad; the truth was that he wanted to see Gerica happy, he had always wanted that.

Gerica shook her head to Anders' question and looked at Oliver. She smiled and giggled, "Perhaps running away to be together was a rushed thought." She turned to Anders. "What will father do if he finds out you have known all this time? Are you going to keep this a secret still?"

"Your father will not find out, mainly because he cannot stop it, and because I have known this whole time, I will surely be punished. To be honest, I would prefer to keep my head. I do ask that the two of you do not continue to sneak into Gerica's room late at night and refrain from touching in the common parts of the castle. Bear in mind, if he catches you, I may not be able to save you," concluded Anders.

Oliver and Gerica both smiled and nodded. "Now, if you will please excuse me, I have some things in my room that need my attention." Anders declared as he stood up from the table to move toward the exit with his food. When his back was fully turned, he smiled; he had gotten himself a permanent place in the castle.

"My heart was racing for most of that breakfast." Oliver whispered while he grabbed Gerica's hand.

She pulled her hand away. "Mine as well but remember no touching in the common areas" She smiled. "I believe father could be home any time now, and this is not a risk I can afford to take. I fear that if he found out now, he may banish you from Leward, or worse; we need to behave."

"Well, I went most of my life loving you but not touching you, I can manage to wait until we are alone; but to be clear, I do not want to." He smiled.

"Neither do I," Gerica insisted. "Now go! You have work to do." She laughed and walked out of the dining hall. Since Lucille had been gone, she had been left with next to nothing to do. She was not able to keep busy and her mind had started to wonder; she still felt like there was something going on that she cannot shake. Those voices she heard in her dream meant something; the Western end door being opened meant there was something there.

She swallowed and felt a lump in her throat as she made her way to the Western end. Her hands started to sweat the closer she got, but she could not turn around. As she got to the top of the stairs, she saw the door, and her heart beat faster. She placed her hand on cold knob and pulled it open; her heart was racing out of her chest when she slid in the doorway. The mirrored floor reflected everything on the walls, and even the clouds from outside the windows; she looked up at the strangest ceiling she had ever seen. It was round all the way up and came to a point; that is where Gerica saw a crystal chandelier and beautiful paintings of birds. It was odd to have such a painting on a ceiling; they all looked like they were flying around the room in a circle. She did not know that her father even liked birds.

Chapter Twenty Four

There was nothing special to this room, and by the time that she was standing in the middle of it, she realized just how silly she had been for being so frightened by it. She moved to the closest window and sat on the sill. She had looked out many windows of the castle, but she had never seen the view from this window. She was disappointed when she saw nothing but trees; this area of the house was not only neglected on the inside but the outside as well. There was some type of garden in the yard of every other end of the house, the north end had the vegetable garden, and the south and east had flowers and herbs. It was depressing to Gerica that there was nothing going for the Western end. It was such a lovely room; she loved the mirrored floors and high ceilings.

Gerica got up from the sill and walked along the wall; her hand grazing all the sills as she walked. She saw something shiny out of the corner of her eye on the other side of the room. As she got closer, she could feel her jaw start to drop, and her heart start to pound; there were two crystals. Just like the crystal that she had found years ago in the garden; both had the crimson line through them. The first crystal that Gerica had found gave her a calming feeling, as if all her troubles would soon be over, but these two gave Gerica the most uneasy feeling she had ever felt. She had always thought that her crystal was a sign and that is was special because she found it among a pile of ugly rocks. She did not dare touch the others, she felt like it was a trap. She had seen nothing in the room which had cleared her of her fears; finding the crystals made things worse. She had no answers, only more questions. The agony of never knowing was eating away her soul.

She walked back to her room and picked up her crystal. She turned it over in her hand several times; she still received a calming feeling from it.

She needed to take it to Anders; he would be the only one that could put ease into her heart. She wondered if whatever was watching her placed this crystal where she could find it. The odds of her picking up a random rock and keeping it for years would have been nonexistent; the shadow must have known that. She would not have even taken the one if she did not think it was unique; she felt betrayed by the crystal. She had sat in her room holding that crystal many times over the years and she felt like on some level, it had been a friend to her. Now she was left with the feeling that it was all just part of some sinister plot. Once again, she was reminded that something had power over her life. Gerica felt empty when she reached Anders' door. It was cracked open and Gerica barely had to knock.

"Yes?" He called

"Do you have a moment?" She asked him.

"I do, come in." Anders sounded relaxed and welcoming; there was a new level of trust between the two of them now and Gerica was hoping that it would come in handy.

Gerica took a seat in the orange chair; keeping the crystal in the palms of her hand. "Years ago, I was walking through the garden and something caught my eye," she begun from the beginning, so she did not miss a single detail. "There was a crystal lying in a pile of rocks near one of the flower beds. It was not just a normal crystal; it had a single crimson line that reached all the way through it. From the moment I picked it up I felt calm, a rushing sense of peace take over my body. My life has been made chaotic by my fears; but this crystal, took those fears away whenever I held it. It was like magic, and it became very special to me. Recently, I choose to take a walk into the Western end. There had always been some uneasy feelings that would take over me whenever I even looked in that direction; and I was feeling curious."

"You went into the western end, Gerica?" Anders interrupted.

Gerica nodded and continued her story. "You see I had no idea that it was empty. There was nothing when I first got into the room; but as I moved further into the room, I noticed a shimmering object off near the other side of the room. When I walked close to it, I saw that it was two crystals just like the one I found in the garden. I had always thought that the one I found in the garden had special meaning, and I am sure you can imagine my confusion and disappointment when I found that it was not at all unique. In fact, the two that I found had the very opposite effect on me; I felt overwhelmed with uneasiness. Like someone had wanted me to find that one crystal long ago. I do not understand how several crystals were all in the same place but only one managed to find its way outside. I need to know where they came from or why they would be here."

Gerica held out her hand with the crystal and gave it to Anders. Anders took in gently and moved his fingers around it; he was silent for just a moment. "This is not actually a crystal, dear Gerica. It was a piece of a chandelier. Are you familiar with what the Western end was once used for?"

"I am not; father just always said it was off limits. I was always too scared to ask questions." She held her head down as if she was ashamed.

"The Western end on the second level of the castle was once a ball room. It was before my time, but shortly after I got here is when the chandelier broke. From my understanding, there had been balls here every week, grand gestures to show the King's softer side. And one night a prince of a different kingdom, had tried stealing from your father. He was caught and banished from the castle. Being the man that your father is, he chose to never allow people in his castle again. He closed down the Western end, and made it forbidden to enter for anyone in the castle. It is my belief that he has some regret closing it down because that was the high time for the kingdom; he has always lacked a source of happiness. Ah, but that it neither here nor there. Once the Western end was closed, it was abandoned. There was not regular care that was taking place, and then one night we all were awoken by a loud sound of glass shattering, we all were running around in different directions until Lucille found where the noise had come from; the chandelier had fallen. She had cleaned up the glass; she must have missed a few pieces that night." Anders' information made perfect sense, but Gerica was not satisfied with this answer; she knew in her heart that something was missing to this story.

"That does not explain the crystal that I found in the garden," Gerica noted.

"No, it does not, does it. I would assume that magical monkeys entered the Western end and stole that single crystal just to confuse you my dear." Anders' face had a slight smirk; this annoyed Gerica a great deal.

"Anders, I do need to ask you why you have an arrogance about yourself. You speak to others as if they are beneath you. For most of my life I have tried to avoid you until recently. For a few brief moments you seem to enjoy the company of others, but those moments seem few and far in between." Gerica realized that she is taken out anger on Anders that was not meant for him alone. She was angry that Lucille was sick, she was angry that something was happening in this castle that no one would enlighten her about, she was angry that she still felt so alone but lastly, she was mad at Anders.

"Gerica, I think you are looking too much into something so pointless. There are millions of ways the crystal could have made it to the garden. Perhaps while it was being cleaned, Lucille dropped a piece on the way to the rubbish. Maybe, a servant girl thought that it was worth money; so she stole a piece, ran through the garden to make an escape, and it fell from her pocket. I do not think this one crystal, as you call it, had much meaning. The truth is, sometimes things happen and there is no reason for it." He returned the annoyance and attitude to his voice.

"It was just placed there so perfectly, it makes no sense to me how this would be there by mistake." Gerica answered and looked down; she felt foolish now that he made such valid points, but she still did not believe it.

"Maybe you took it as a sign because you needed one at the time. Can you recall the day you found it perfectly; were you upset, or frightened?" Anders had concern in his voice.

"I do not recall, often times when I walk in the gardens, I have things on my mind." She admitted.

"You may have needed something to brighten your day when you found it; it is beautiful!" Anders smiled at her and handed her the crystal.

Gerica nodded. "Thank you" she whispered and rose to her feet. Anders just sat there and watched her walk out. He never had much experience with children, or teens but he knew that Gerica was difficult; special nonetheless, but incredibly difficult.

With an empty heart, Gerica made her way out of Anders end. She started to day dream of running away and just starting over somewhere else. *I do not understand why anyone would want a life of royalty; it is isolating and cold.* Her fingers trailed the wall as she walked, until she came to a window sill where she took a seat. She looked up at the ceiling, with the crystal in her hand, and her eyes filled with tears. She was trying to make sense of nothing; this crystal, her dreams, none of that meant anything. Gerica did not know that as she sat on the sill on the window, her father, Lucille and the guards had found their way back onto the castle grounds; until she heard Oliver yell.

"Mother!" Oliver cheered as he ran to the front doors like a child who was about to receive a gift. His child like ways amused Gerica and she found herself smiling. She stood and wiped the tears from her eyes as she watched the men carry

Lucille into the castle; she looked better from the last time Gerica had seen her. Lucille's face regained color, her hair was neat, and she was not covered in blood. Gerica slowly walked to meet them, and when she got close; King Beckford looked in her eyes.

"Hello, dear Gerica. I trust that everything went smoothly while I was away." King Beckford inquired.

"Yes, sir; not a single problem, the castle remained quiet and uneventful." Gerica nodded as she spoke.

"Good, I trust that it can remain this way for several more days while Lucille continues to heal?" The King stated in the form of a question, but it was really a demand.

"How are you feeling, Lucille?" Gerica asked in the softest tone she could.

"Better. Thank you for caring Gerica; you are such a wonderful young lady." Lucille took Gerica by the hand and pulled her in closer; she planted a kiss on her forehead. Lucille never had to tell Gerica that she loved her, any time she did this simple act Gerica knew it was out of love.

Gerica felt a sense of relief when Lucille returned to the castle in good spirits. Gerica was standing in the corridor near the throne room when she looked up and her heart dropped; or it was butterflies in her stomach; she was not sure which one. She saw Oliver coming to see his mother for the first time in days. It was possibly the hardest thing to do for Gerica, keeping her love for Oliver a secret. The two of them tried not to look at each other, but the moment their eyes met, they both would smile. Oliver stood across from Gerica on the other side of Lucille. He leaned down to hug his mother and Gerica could see a slight smile on Lucille's face.

"Well, Oliver. I am glad to see you missed me." Lucille noted and everyone gave a little chuckle. Oliver was a reserved man; he was quiet and no one ever knew what he was thinking.

"I did mother, I was very worried. What did the doctor say?" Oliver whispered, with a worried look on his face.

Before Lucille could speak up, King Beckford spoke up "He does not know what is wrong, or what was wrong with your mother; but he is confident that she is regaining her strength and has successfully beaten whatever caused her to be ill. So she is home but she is not going back to work, she will remain in her bed until she feels ready to start working again. I do not care if it is days or weeks, Oliver and Gerica, I trust that I can count on the two of you to continue taking care of the castle?" assumed King Beckford.

"Of course," Gerica spoke up while Oliver just nodded. They gave each other side glances and Oliver grinned at Gerica; Gerica bit her bottom lip to stop from smiling. Luckily the King did not notice either of one making eye contact; he was too busy watching Lucille. Lucille was not looking at anyone, but she was looking down the corridor.

Lucille had a feeling when she entered the castle that something was not right; she could not put her finger on it but it was clouding her mind. She wondered if someone had been able to sneak into the castle since she and the King were away. Lucille realized that she was thinking like Gerica; the times that Lucille told Gerica that she was crazy and that there was nothing going on came back into Lucille's mind. She believed she was going mad.

Lucille was taken by the men to her bedroom; she was laid on her bed with Oliver sitting at her side. He did not want to leave her alone; he had missed her so much. He also had to tell her everything that was going on with him; he knew that he and Gerica should keep everything a secret but he wanted to tell the world. He thought about Gerica all day and could not wait to see her.

Before Oliver could say a word to his mother, she spoke up. "My dear Oliver, I am so glad you are here with me; I needed my boy the whole time I was gone. Is everything ok with you, love?" Lucille did not know what was going on, but she could tell by the way her son was acting that he was not his normal self.

"Yes, well sort of. Mother I need to be honest with you, but before I can you need to promise that whatever I tell you stays within these walls and can never leave your lips to anyone. Not even King Beckford." Oliver stated this demand in such a serious tone, that it scared Lucille; she had never kept a secret from the King.

"You have my word boy, now what is it." She answered and she gathered enough strength to sit up; she was nervous because Oliver had never had something that needed to be kept from the King. In fact, he never had any secrets.

"I am in love with Gerica, and she loves me back," He blurted; he waited to see his mother's reaction and he was pleasantly surprised when her eyes lit up and she smiled.

"When did this happen?" She asked. She had a million questions for him; she never would have seen this coming. Both of them meant the world to her, and there could not be a better lady for Oliver in this world than Gerica. However, Lucille was concerned with this as well; she knew that the King would never go for a marriage between the two; but Lucille could see how this changed her son, his smile was the most honest smile she had ever seen on his face.

"The night you fell sick. I knew that I had always loved her from afar, but that night she confessed the same to me. It was a surreal feeling; I could not keep it from you, I know that if I had not told you, you would have found out on your own soon enough. A smile comes to my face when she is around no matter how hard I try to hide it." Oliver confessed.

"I am so excited for you, but I do have my concerns as I am sure you know. The number one being how will you be together if her father does not approve?" Lucille made a good point, but it was not going to stop Oliver from what he wanted.

"He never has to know; he cannot be here forever and sooner or later Gerica will be able to do as she pleases. He cannot stop her from living her life forever." Oliver spoke such harsh words that were hard for Lucille to hear; she did not want to think that the King would not be there forever. She found Oliver's rebellious attitude a bit concerning; he had always been the kind of person that would never speak ill of someone and he was never really one to break rules.

"Oliver, I must admit that I was thinking that you were at an age where a love interest would be appropriate but never did I picture it being Gerica. I am not saying that I do not approve you know I love her like she was my own daughter but the way your thinking is coming across harsh; it seems a little much for me to handle. Now, the King has always thought the world of you, what makes you think that he would not change his mind? You never know what one is willing to do until you ask them." Lucille informed Oliver in hopes that he would take a different approach to dating Gerica. Lucille would keep this from the King for Oliver's sake, but she would never be happy about it. She pictured Oliver asking the King for Gerica's hand in marriage and the King saying yes. "I know that the King's position on Gerica getting married has to do with not wanting her to think differently than the King. He has long thought that if he allowed someone from another kingdom or a common villager to marry his daughter that she would not keep the kingdom in his order. I believe that if it was you that she was to marry things would be different; you are part of the King's inner circle, he can teach you any and everything he was going to teach Gerica. I see a great team forming between the two of you with the King's help. Please consider asking for her hand." Lucille knew that there was more to the story that Oliver was not telling her, she could see distance in his eyes. "What is the real reason that you do not wish to tell the King?" Lucille questioned.

Oliver sat and stared at Lucille with wide eyes. "Gerica does not wish to rule the kingdom. She has spoken of running away and living in the city side of Bales." Oliver almost regretted those words as soon as they left his mouth. He knew that was supposed to be a secret between himself and Gerica; he knew that his mother would not tell the King, but he knew that she would not be happy with Gerica.

Lucille sat for a moment and stared at Oliver with blank eyes. She did not understand why that child would not want to be queen. Lucille spent many years in the castle wishing for the day the King would marry her and make her queen. She longed to sit on the throne and watch over the kingdom; her wishes were not sinister but perhaps a bit selfish. Gerica had been taken from a family that was not able to give her as much as the King had and she could not see how lucky she was. In all of Lucille's life she had never heard of a King adopting a peasant child and allowing her to become queen and yet, that is exactly what happened for Gerica.

Finally, Lucille broke the silence. "How could she be so selfish? What does she think will happen if the kingdom falls with no leader? Surely, she does not think that Anders or Samuel are capable of taking over the throne."

"Mother, I do not think she has given it that much thought. I just know that the idea of becoming queen does not appeal to her. To be honest, I believe she is a fool for wanting to give it up, however, I do understand her hesitations; she was never given a choice of any of this." Oliver remembered the conversation that he and Gerica had had with Anders. Anders told him one day he would not have to worry about the King and that he would be King himself; but he was not sure if he would ever see the throne, because if Gerica ever left, he would follow her.

Lucille sat on the bed, and just listened to what Oliver was saying. She was able to see the love he had for Gerica, although new to her, it was a real love. She was not going to be the one to stand in the way of their happiness. Lucille held out her arms for Oliver to hug her. She needed to hold her baby boy for a moment and embrace him; she had to have faith that everything would work out in his favor one day.

"Your secret is safe with me; no matter what you choose to do with your life, Oliver make Gerica and yourself as happy as can be." She declared as she kissed his forehead.

"Thank you, mother" Oliver whispered; he was full of relief and gratefulness that his mother was able to support him.

"Now, run along and do your chores. I still need my rest you know." Without a word he nodded and left her room.

Lucille laid back slowly onto the bed and just tried to picture a life where her son would be King. Lucille would find great pride in being able to say she raised a King, but she was also full of fear for him. So many times, people had challenged King Beckford's life; many people were killed for the thought of it. Oliver does not have the heart to take on the King's tasks; running away from the throne was perhaps the best option for the pair.

Lucille drifted off into a deep sleep while she was picturing her son's happiness.

Chapter Twenty Five

King Beckford sat looking out his bedroom window. It was a sight that he rarely ever saw, but one that he loved so much. From his side of the castle, he could look at the village of Bales. He could not see much, but what he could see made him happy enough. The thoughts that ran through his head while he looked out the window were innocent enough, by his standards at least. The village had things going on, people in the streets, businesses helping customers; and all the King could think was it was great to own all of that.

The King was not alone in his room, but no one was talking. Samuel made his way around the King's room making sure all windows were locked and that everything was in perfect order. It had been days since he was able to check on the security of the castle. Samuel moved quickly around the room and even though there were a lot of windows, he made great time in checking the locks.

He turned to King Beckford, who was still looking through the windows. "Sir, everything seems to be in fine order. Is there anything else that you would like me to do?" Samuel asked in a quiet voice. He knew that there had been so much going in the castle, and he felt like he needed to be sensitive to the changes.

King Beckford turned from the window and looked at Samuel. "No, Samuel; I think that everything just needs a bit of peace now. Things have been beyond hectic and this castle is used to order." The King had a thought just as he spoke those last few words. "Actually, Samuel I do have one favor to ask. Lucille had told me that she visited the dungeon and may have made her way into the torture chamber, could you be sure to see if everything is in order." King Beckford thought about ending his request with a please but realized he was losing his tougher touch. The love he had felt when he saw Lucille hurt opened him up to care more about others than he would care to admit.

"Of course," Samuel replied, then turned to leave the room.

As he was left alone in his room, King Beckford took one last long look out of his window and closed his eyes. With a deep breath; he took in all the smells of his kingdom. He had everything he could want but it pained him to think that one day, he would have to hand this over to Gerica. He doubted that she would be ready; he knew that she was too weak; too much of a meek and a nice person. He questioned why Anders would have had a vision that she could over throw him, she was not wise or daring. The King felt discouraged in his hopes that she would have made a good ruler; *but there is still time,* he thought to himself. He picked himself up off of the sill and made his way to his bed. He had pulled back his gold bedding and lowered his body to lay down.

Just as he was about to close his eyes and drift off to sleep, he felt a crippling pain in his stomach, and the sudden urge to vomit. The pain reminded him of someone ringing out a wet cloth and twisting their hands in opposite ways to release as much water as they could. Each side of his stomach was being twisted with amazing might. He could not make it fully out of his bed; when he began vomiting on his bedding. With vicious coughing and choking, the King released the contents of his stomach on to his golden blanket. When he looked down, he was unable to understand what he was looking at; it was dark red blood that was mixed with water and bile from his stomach. There was not any food and he had not had wine in days. The pain had faded once he had vomited but there was a knot in his stomach that did not go away.

Since he had so many blankets, he decided to get rid of just the one he had gotten sick on. He was not interested in bothering Lucille with this minor issue; she had enough to tend to and he knew that this would worry her. He would hide it for now and have someone take care of it in the morning.

Chapter Twenty Six

Before too long, Lucille was back to perfect health and King Beckford returned to his throne to rule over Leward. Anders remained to himself and kept out of the eye of everyone. Gerica and Oliver had their love blossoming into one from the fairy tales. Gerica knew that she would have a tough choice to make when the time was right. Her lessons picked back up about two weeks after Lucille recovered and it was the normal daily life. Her main focus was Oliver; she saw nothing beyond him; her eyes were so full of stars that she did not pay attention to the shadows in her room. She slept blissfully through the night; day after day she was unaware that she was still being followed.

Gerica woke with a faint knock on her door. She opened her eyes and saw the sun shining through gaps in her curtains. She rolled toward her door and with a raspy voice muttered, "You may enter."

The door opened and Lucille walked in with a pleasant look on her face, one that showed through her eyes. Her green eyes were shining as bright as the sun through Gerica's windows. "Did I wake you?" She asked.

"Yes, but that is alright, why did you knock; in all my years, you have never knocked." Gerica was used to Lucille making her way into her bedroom on her own free will.

"Dear, you are a lady now; and a lady needs to have privacy. Plus, there was no telling if Oliver was in here with you or not." Lucille smiled as she spoke.

"Oliver, why would Oliver be in my room?" Gerica questioned, trying not to let on that he had been in her room before.

Lucille did not respond, but she looked at Gerica with her eyebrows tilted up in a manner that made Gerica feel like she had been caught.

"No reason to worry dear. You are growing into a woman now! Do you think for a minute that you have to hide anything from me? I was once your age and when I was your age, I was in love too. Before you know it, you will be queen. Should you choose to go through with your father's plan. Now, I know that your father does not want you to marry, and he wants to keep the kingdom in his rule; but you can choose for yourself." Lucille knew that she was going against the King by having this conversation, but she could see the trouble boiling in Gerica's eyes in every class that she took. Gerica was not going to abandon the idea of love, and although the thought made Lucille heartbroken, when that time comes that Gerica will rule the kingdom, the King will no longer have a say.

Gerica did not say anything as she sat on her bed in disbelief. She could not understand what she was hearing from Lucille; surely, Lucille was testing her. Lucille knew how the King felt about Gerica remaining alone during her ruling of the castle. Gerica had always been too nervous or frightened to think of doing anything against his wishes. She looked around her room and noticed that her closet door was opened but Lucille was not picking her clothes out.

"Have you gotten my robes for today?" She asked in hopes that this would change the conversation.

"I have not, would you like me to?" Lucille asked; as she made her way to the closet, she noticed the doors were ajar. In all of her years in the castle neither Gerica nor the King had ever picked out their own clothes. "Odd, it looks like you have already gotten into your closet. Was there something that you were hoping to wear today?" Lucille questioned.

"I suppose it would be fitting to dress in robes fit for a queen." Gerica announced with a smile that spread from ear to ear.

Lucille knew what she meant; Gerica was making the choice to rule over Leward. She was taken aback by the sudden change of heart in Gerica but she was sure that her smile was from the heart. "Oh my dear Gerica." She sobbed as she ran into Gerica's arms. Lucile was crying tears of joy; and a bit of sadness as well. "Am I able to stay while you are queen?" Lucille joked. Gerica just hugged her tighter and Lucille got her answer. They had a bond that was deeper than most people could understand.

"Now, get you royal robes on and meet me in the dining hall for breakfast; and make sure to keep this closet door shut, it looks awful when people can see your lady wear when they do not want to." Instructed Lucille.

Gerica got out of her bed and dressed in a bright pink silk robe that fell right above her knees. The sleeves had ruffles at the end of each arm and went to her elbows. The neck was white lace and covered in diamonds; she had always felt pretty in things that were covered in diamonds. As she made her way down the stairs, she could hear voices talking from the floor below.

"Why was there blood on the corridor floor, Jace?" demanded Lucille.

"I am unsure, ma'am. I found spots while I was walking to feed the horses." Jace answered. Jace was a servant that the King had taken from the poorer part of Bales. She was in her mid-twenties and most pleasant. She had black hair that reminded Gerica of a raven; it looked silky and shined whenever light touched it. It reached midway on her back and was straight with little life to it. She had tanner skin than most people that were in the castle, and different facial features, too. Her eyes were a bit smaller than everyone else's and they were dark brown. Gerica had always envied Jace's thin lips. She was a petite girl in her height and weight, but her personality was large. Whenever Gerica walked by a room that she was working in with any other servant; she would have a laugh that was loud and infectious. Gerica was not sure about her history before the castle, but she had heard bits and pieces over the years. Jace was offered to the King by her father to settle a debt on taxes that he was unable to pay.

"You need to find out where that came from. It is very disconcerting that something of that nature was left where anyone could have seen it or stepped in it." Lucille demanded; her tone seemed one of annoyance. She was a little harder on Jace for the simple fact that Jace was pretty. Lucille was a beauty of a woman, far more beautiful than most; but when there was someone else almost as beautiful, she became jealous.

"Of course, ma'am," Jace agreed and turned around to walk away.

Gerica began to look at the floor when she walked; she was not interested in stepping in blood of any sort. Her eyes darted from the side of the floor to the middle of the floor and back. This went on until she got to the stair case, and out of the corner of her eye, she saw the Western end; a cold chill went up her spine that could freeze water.

Chapter Twenty Seven

In the dead of night, the castle was a peaceful place; Gerica had woken many nights to see the light from the moon and was never bothered by any sounds. She would lay in her bed as she thought about life in every form; but this night was different. She could not see the light from the moon as she laid there listening to whispers. Fast whispers that were unrecognizable to her ears; as she tried to make sense of the noise, she noticed that her eyes were shut, but she was wide awake. She tried to open her eyes but a ripping sensation fell over both of her eyes lids and they remained shut. She started to panic as she lifted her hands to eyes. Upon touching her eyelids, she felt little strings that seemed to be tying her eyelids shut; without thinking she tried to pull the strings, and the pain increased. She opened she mouth to scream, but her mouth stayed shut. Her hands shook as she slid her right hand down the side of her face to her mouth. Just as she feared, her mouth was kept shut by strings as well.

She slowly slid her legs over the edge off her bed and placed them flat on the ground and lowered the rest of her body to the cold, stone floor. She crawled on her hands and knees; she had not realized how cold the room was while she was laying down but from crawling, she could feel the cold air much more. She was crawling so slowly that she doubted she was making her way anywhere, but she kept going; until her foot hit something. She stopped dead in her tracks; paralyzed by fear. She took her right hand and moved it slowly to her ankle. She felt something hard and smooth but most importantly, familiar. As she held it in her hand, she turned it from side to side; running her fingers over the smooth surfaces. She could feel every tiny knick that was in it; she could not see the item, but she knew what it was. Her memories came rushing back to her like they had never left; it was the crystal she had found in the garden. Anders had said it was nothing, but she knew that it had been something all along and now here it was again. A thought that she had tried to push out of her mind came back. It was the shadow; or whatever it was. It was playing with her, taunting her with something that she felt a connection to.

Gerica wanted to run, and scream; she moved her hand to her side to feel what she was wearing. It felt like a nightgown that Lucille would have dressed her in, but in an odd circumstance, she found a pocket. She slid the crystal into it and kept crawling; she believed that she was lost in the Western end because no other room in the castle was as cold. She just crawled and crawled without finding her way to a wall or to a door.

"Would you look at that, she has woken up! Bless her heart; she is a strong-willed girl, isn't she?" A voice spoke that Gerica recognized as raspy voice.

"Are we going to let her crawl around on these floors; what if she cuts herself?" The softer voice asked in a concerned tone.

Gerica stopped crawling but was still on her hands and knees, she reached out as far as she could and began hitting the floor like a mad woman. She was just trying to reach for anything that may be there.

"Do you think she has gone mad?" questioned the softer voice.

"Not yet, but almost," replied the raspy voice.

"The poor dear, she has no idea what has been going on within these walls. Do you think in time we could…"

"GERICA, GERICA! In the name of everything Holy girl, snap out of it!" Lucille screamed as she shook Gerica. Gerica had hit her in the face several times as Lucille tried to wake her. Gerica was no longer cold but wet in sweat.

Gerica did not say anything to Lucille and she kept her eyes closed as she moved her hand to feel them. She did not feel any strings; she slowly opened them. She saw Lucille sitting over her bed in a pale blue gown, with her hair tied back into a lose knot. When she realized that her eyes were not held shut, she opened her mouth.

"Lucille…. I just had the most real frightening nightmare I have ever had." Gerica whispered because she did not have energy or courage to speak loudly. "Thank you for waking me."

"This seems like a normal dream then, ya? You are forever having your sleep disturbed by some form of dream." Lucille looked at Gerica with loving eyes that hide a great secret; and she was not sure how to break the news to her.

"It's very true, Lucille. No matter how I try, it is never totally out of my mind." Gerica confessed as she reflected on seeing the shadow in her dreams, and then in person; it followed her everywhere.

Lucille stood up and made her way to Gerica's closet, she needed to pick out her dress for the day while ignoring the feeling in her stomach and holding back tears from rolling down her cheeks. Lucille reached for Gerica's black silk grown when she lost her balance and fell into the closet. She braced herself by putting her hands in front of her body as she fell. When her hands had lightly pushed on the back of the closet, the wall moved. It did not come totally off, but it was off enough to see a room behind her closet door. Lucille had the worst thought possible; Gerica was not alone when she slept and someone had been in her room. Lucille remembered when they bought Gerica home; she made her room for her. She moved, decorated, and painted everything herself; the back wall of the closet had been as solid ass every other wall within the castle.

"Lucille, are you alright?" Gerica asked softly, but rather loudly.

Lucille knew that if she were to say anything to Gerica that it would frighten her more; and Lucille could not put her through that. Lucille stood up and reached for the gown again. Now not only was Lucille fighting back tears, she also had to hide her fear from Gerica. She ushered over to Gerica, placed the gown on her bed; forced a smile and kissed her forehead. "I am fine, just a tad clumsy in my old age. Now, get dressed and come to breakfast."Lucille turned to walk out; her hands were shaking as she heard Gerica's sweet voice tell her she loved her. Once she got into the corridor; she clutched her stomach and begun to cry. The tears just came down like rain with no stopping. She could not breathe, and a part of her did not want to try. Her back was against the bedroom door and she was worried she would make noise while she was crying, but her body could not move.

Lucille walked away for Gerica's door a few moments later; making her way down the corridor and past the Western end. She looked at the door that once was a symbol of happiness and she felt pain strike her heart. She knew that her health was just barely normal, but she needed to venture out into the unknown once again. As she made her way down the stairs, she tried to think of a way to get Gerica out of the castle, and away from her room long enough for Lucille to investigate. She would not have much time, she knew she needed to be there for the King; everything that he had protected was at stake in what seemed like moments.

She ran into Samuel on her way down the stairs; he stood against the wall and looked rather idle, the perfect person to watch over Gerica. "Ah, good day Samuel, not out watching the grounds today?" Lucille addressed him as nicely as she could. She was not friends, per se, with everyone; although, she did feel a special friendship with Samuel because he was one of the King's oldest guards.

"Morning, Lucille, what is being prepared for breakfast?" He replied.

"Would you believe me if I told you I do not have the slightest idea? I had to comfort Gerica this morning; she had a night terror, again. The dear would just not snap out of it, it was heartbreaking. I am sure breakfast is something amazing as it normally is. Samuel, I need to beg a favor from you. You see, Gerica has never liked to be alone and she had mentioned to me her desire to ride Whalen today, just around the forest line. Would you be able and willing to accompany her? I would feel much better knowing that she had you to watch over her; I know she would feel as safe as one could." Lucille held her breath while she waited for Samuel to answer. Samuel was a nice gentleman, but he was disciplined and he did not like straying away for his daily duties. Samuel looked at Lucille, and his eyes looked cheerful and seemed to have found the only ray of sunshine that was beaming in through the glass windows. They had become sparkling diamonds, which was a pleasant surprise. He had a great soft spot for Gerica, as did they all; but he had not spent too much time with her. He was always off on some adventure around castle.

Lucille noticed that he was hesitating. "I ask you this favor, because you are the one that will care for her best. I fear that she is falling deeper away from everyone. She has been in a box of sorts, and soon she may be queen. The King's health is failing and I cannot see…"

"Ay, what did you say? There are issues with the King?" A shocked tone came from Samuels' lips and the diamonds left his eyes. "Explain what you are saying."

"It is unsure, but for several weeks, he has slowly started to lose his strength. I am afraid there is more going on than I know. He has taken ill ever since I regained my health. This is all more than Gerica should know. I do not wish to burden her with any more troubles." Lucille informed Samuel in a nice manner, and very hopeful that he would see her way.

"I do agree, I think its best she is kept out of the loop. Do you think he is at risk of someone hurting him?" Samuel questioned with great concern.

That was not a thought that Lucille had considered, and she thought for a moment. "No, the King has not fallen victim of anyone." Rather annoyed that she had to insist that the King's power was not being questioned, she answered with a snarky tone.

"Aye, Lucille, I meant no harm or worry, love. I am curious if my role would change from here on. Should I be on the lookout of anyone that may storm the castle is all. After breakfast, I would like to take young Gerica for the horse ride you suggested." Samuel agreed with a slight smile and walked away to the dining hall before Lucille could reply.

Lucille stood pondering that last exchange of words. At first, she was taken aback but Samuel would be one to think that way. He had been a guard at the castle for many years, perhaps it would have been more concerning if he had not asked about the King's safety. Lucille at once felt a presence of guilt come over her like a gray cloud before a storm set in. Seemed fitting, because a storm was coming for them, and she could feel it.

She braved a strong face in front of Samuel, but she knew this was going to end badly for them. For who, she did not know; but for some of them, life would never be the same.

Gerica made her way down the stairs before Lucille could make her way to the dining hall. Lucille was still worried and she knew it showed on her face. She did not dare speak to Gerica, so she made her way after Samuel. Her steps turned into a slow run as she hurried to catch up to him.

"Samuel, she is down here. Invite her please!" Lucille whispered through heavy breathing.

Samuel turned and looked at Gerica, and he turned toward her without responding to Lucille. Lucille watched as the two exchanged words and she could see a beautiful smile spread across Gerica's light pink lips; the pair made their way closer to Lucille. She still was unable to get any words together for Gerica, so she gave a loving smile and made her way back up the stairs.

Chapter Twenty Eight

Lucille knew that she needed to see what was in that closet of Gerica's. Ever since finding that the wall moved, Lucille felt a pain in her stomach of hundreds of swords dragging their sharp, ridged edges down each wall until it tore though. With shaking hands, she opened Gerica's door, and made her way inside. She moved in silence; she did not want anyone to know that she was coming or going. As she got to the closet, she carefully pushed everything to the right side. She looked at the back panel of the closet and studied it for a moment. She could tell that it had been moved before but it did not look too much out of place. She used the tips of her fingers to gently push the door loose but before it fell, she slid her hands to each side and stopped to the door from falling to the floor. She moved it to the side, and to her surprise, without making much noise. She poked her head through the opening of the closet.

There was not much room for her to move; she thought by the quick glance that it was a room but as she pushed her body through the closet, she saw that this was more of a tunnel. A manmade tunnel that she could not stand up straight in. She got on her hands and knees, and as she started to crawl, the only light that shined was from Gerica's room, and it was growing dimmer. It was next to impossible for Lucille to get out now; her curiosity was overpowering any feeling of pain that she had felt.

She crawled over wooden beams that laid across that floor. The walls were narrow and the ceiling was very low. There was dust that covered the beams and with every movement forward that her hands made, she felt dirt fall from them. She could not see anything in front of her; it was as if someone had put a black cloth over her eyes. She could hear laughing and joking, and what sounded like pots banging around. She had to be over the dining hall, which meant that whoever made this tunnel had access to a lot more than just Gerica's bedroom. The thought brought back the pain in her stomach as her thoughts raced with concerns of Gerica, Olivier, and King Beckford's failing health that happened so suddenly.

Lucille's eye adjusted to the darkness and she was able to make out more of the tunnel. She looked to her side and saw movement from what she figured to be rats running along the corners of the walls. She thought back to the rat invested, blood stained dungeon that she had to find her way around. She had forgotten the anger she felt from that day, but a bit came back to her at that very moment. She began to see sunlight through cracks in the beams and she had left the rats behind as she was nearing the end of the tunnel. She saw a square piece of wood with what looked like sunlight highlighting the edges. It had been cut out of its place, or it was placed there to hide the hole. Lucille needed to push that out of her way and without knowing what was on the other side, she was hoping for the best.

She was close enough to the wood to rest the tip of her nose on it. She did not breathe or move for a moment so she could focus on any noises that were out there. There were no sounds to be heard, and this gave Lucille the courage to start to move the wood. She found the biggest space between the wood and the wall and slid her right index finger into it. She gently moved her finger from side to side, testing the stability of its placement. It only wiggled a sight amount and she was forced to find another hole. She stopped moving again and held her breath; carefully listening for any movements outside of the tunnel, still no sound. Her eyes scanned each side for another hole big enough for her finger. Once one was located, she did her best to fit her other index finger into it. With one finger on the side of the wood, and the other finger at the top, she shook the wood with more might.

As the sunlight started to pour in she slowed the shaking down. There was more room for her to move both of her fingers out of way and place her hands there instead. She braced herself on her knees as best as she could, she was afraid that she may lose her balance being in the tight spot. She could feel little pebbles digging in the skin on her knees as she put all of her body weight in their trust.

Once both hands were in place, she pushed the piece of wood out of her way. Still holding on, she guided it to the floor without making a sound;the piece of wood stood upright and perfectly still. Lucille noticed her reflection looking back at her from the floor; she was looking into a mirror.

She lifted her head so that she could scan the whole room; she was in the western end. Her eyes darted from the windows, to the mirror floors and to the longer ballroom that once held parties to be envied by all. Lucille could not wrap her head around how the tunnel took her to the abandon part of the castle. She sat on her behind and moved her feet toward the opening to let then dangle into the empty room. She was too afraid to jump down unto the mirror, so she turned over to her stomach and slowly let herself slip into the room. She was inches away from touching the floor and her arms began to shake until she let go.

She gave a light hop, trying to spare any noise that she was going to make. When both of her feet touched the mirror, she felt a cold shiver travel from her toes up her spine. She began talking to herself like she was a mad woman. "Something is very wrong here; no one is to be in this end." She had treated Gerica like she was crazy all those years; but it was Lucille who was the fool. She walked in a straight line toward the other end of the room, looking everywhere. There was nowhere for anyone to hide; had there been someone lurking in the corner, Lucille would surely see them.

The windows that went from the ceiling to the floor light the room up as if there were no walls to block the sun at all. She slid her right foot out and her left foot followed as she did her best not to make a sound during her inspection. She walked over to the door that lead back into the castle and noticed nothing out of place. She did not want to be seen walking around the Western end, and she did her best to avoid any windows, until she heard voices outside of the castle.

"Are you for certain, Stetson." Questioned Anders. Lucille could see Anders pace back and forth along the stone wall surrounding the ground tulip garden; his left hand over his mouth with his index finger pointing straight up the left side of his nose.

"Indeed sir; I need to inform Lucille but there is not any sign of her. Strangely enough, Samuel took Gerica on a horse ride, without Lucille or Oliver." Stetson felt it was important to lead with the fact that Lucille was not attached to Gerica's side and that she was not instructing Olivier to do it either. That alone was very odd behavior for Lucille.

"A horse ride with Samuel? How odd, perhaps it best not to have Gerica around on the day the King takes his last breath." Anders admitted in a fact of matter tone that showed little emotion.

Lucille stopped breathing; her heart was attacked by a thousand jagged edged swords piercing through it with every word that left Anders' mouth. Her ears bleed as her mind played the words "last breath" over and over. She looked down at both men and they were calm, no emotion on their face! Lucille ran toward the opening in the wall; the mirror became slippery as her warm tears fell from her eyes and splashed onto the mirror.

She jumped in head first into the opening and put her arms out in front of her to stop from failing. Once her entire body was in the tunnel, she crawled as if she had been a prisoner escaping from a jail cell. She was weak but had more than enough energy to make her way through the tunnel. It was a short time before she reached Gerica's room. When she reached the closet door, she did not bother putting the wall to the closet back, she left the closet and tunnel open for anyone to see. As she climbed out of the closet, she noticed the pale blue dress she had been wearing was covered in black dirt and dust and had a rip on the right side near her hip. She planted both feet on the floor of Gerica's room and began to run. She had always carried herself with grace and discipline, but at this very moment any servants or guards that saw her would think that she was a mad woman. She was headed to the throne room.

As she made her way closer, she saw the doors were closed and Horus blocking them. He was standing perfectly straight with the most serious face that Lucille had ever seen on him; until he saw her running. Horus looked at Lucille and her red curls flying around her head, with every step closer she took the messier her hair became. She was covered in black dirt, her dress and her arms looked like she had been rolling in it. What interested Horus the most was the look on her face; she had looked like she had just seen an evil spirit rise from the dead and she was trying to get away; it was so intense that Horus was afraid to speak to her. He pushed his back off the wall and started to run towards her. For a moment, he had forgotten why he was in front of the throne room doors.

"Lucille, what happen to you?" squeaked Horus; as he ran to meet her half way in the corridor. She did not say a word as she just kept running; she looked right through Horus. "Lucille!" He yelled once more but got nothing in return. He turned his body as he watched her run past him toward the room that kept the King. Before he knew it, she was using her entire body to open the tall throne room doors. They were heavy for Horus to open by himself, but the strength that came from Lucille's body was remarkable. Once opened, Horus could see King Beckford's dying body laid out of red satin sheets. There were tall white candles lit all around the room, signifying peace and closure. The throne room had blood red curtains that were similar to the color in Gerica's room, and they were closed. The room was a dark red with sparkles of light, and there was a presence in the air that left Horus feeling uneasy. Horus looked to his left and his heart broke; the King's throne had never looked so empty and hopeless.

Chapter Twenty Nine

The king was gone; never to breath in the air of Leward again. Lucille sat dazed as she tried to make sense of everything happening around her; before she could stop herself, she fell to her knees. Deep cries came from her body that made everyone else in the room cry harder as well. She looked at King Beckford and remembered all the love between the two of them; his face looked at ease, and unknowing.

Anders stood over the King and took a deep breath, one that sounded as if he was relieved. He had little pity on his face, and his eyes were dry. He took the satin sheets that covered the King's body and pulled them over his head. "Well then, an era has ended." He declared loudly to all the servants and guards that stood around. Lucille, still kneeing on the floor beside his bed, looked up at Anders with hatred written on her face; her eyebrows raised and her lips were tightly held.

"How do you manage to keep such a cavalier tone, seeing your best friend lay died before your eyes? Do you not have a heart, Anders?" Lucille Snipped.

"Cavalier, have you ever known me to give concern or emotion too much, Lucille?" He asked.

"The most important time to be concerned would be now, are you mad?" Lucille stood up and become eye level with Anders; she looked in his white eyes and saw nothing. She had never looked at him this closely and did not know that there were light pink splashes around the pupil of his eye. She watched the set of metallic white pearls stare back at her, but they were soulless. She studied his face more in depth and realized the young man that once busted into the castle with all the energy in the world; looked like he had aged at lightning speed. Wrinkles took up the corners of his eyes and his forehead; and the skin on his cheeks began to sag. Lucille took two steps back and took a deep breath; Jace went up to Lucille and placed her hand on her back in a loving manner.

Jace had seen the exchange of stares between Lucille and Anders and she knew that Lucille needed to be comforted. Anders' attitude toward the King's death changed the atmosphere in the room from heartbreaking to intense. There was a shift in the elements and Jace could tell nothing good would come from this.

There was commotion toward the back of the throne room that took Lucille's attention away from Anders. It was a noise that she was unable to recall ever hearing before. When she and Jace looked past Anders, they could see the tile from the floor moving, something was pushing it out of place. They saw a square white tile come up from the floor and move out of the way.

"What on earth…" Jace's voice trailed off as she walked closer to the moving tile, but Lucille did not move. Once Jace got closer, she must have seen something that frightened her, she jumped back with all the power she had in her body.

Lucille was filled with confusion when she witnessed people emerging from the floor boards. They were dirty, and in torn clothing. First, a woman climbed out of the floor and when she was able to stand firmly on her feet, she bent over and helped the second person out of the hole. Once the second person had climbed out, they both stood and looked at the King. Lucille's body was filled with fear, and confusion; her hands started to tremble with every breath she took.

"Ah, they have joined us. Lucille, I would like to introduce you to the reason that I am, how did you say it? So… cavalier." Anders looked at Lucille with the evilest grin a man has ever had the ability to make, and he turned to the floor dwellers. "If you would not mind, Lucille needs to meet you."

As they both made their way closer to Lucille, Jace ran back over to be by Lucille's side. Horus was still standing in the doorway; confused. They all heard more footsteps running into the doorway of the throne room. Samuel and Stetson ran into the throne room as fast as they could. Lucille was unable to take her eyes off of the floor dwellers; there was something about them that she could not put her finger on. She had seen them before; perhaps it was at the ball that ended the Western End. Her eyes stayed focused on the woman, she had blonde hair with thick strips of gray, and dull, dead eyes. They were a deep brown, and they reminded Lucille of a well from her childhood. One that she would throw rocks into, but never heard any noise in return; the well was empty, much like this woman's eyes. Her robes looked like they had been yellow at one point, but now they were dirty and torn. Lucille's eyes darted to the second floor dweller. At first, she did not get a good look at him, but when she began to study him, she realized where she knew them from. He had changed a lot in the past years, he was skinny, and a head full a gray hair; not a black hair in sight. Her heart dropped when she made the connection; she did not understand.

Samuel made his way to Jace and Lucille. He placed his left hand on Lucille's back. "Lucille, I came as fast as I could, what is going on?" He managed to question between heavy breaths.

"Where is Gerica?" Lucille asked Samuel while turning her head back to Anders.

"With Oliver in the garden, Lucille, what is happening?" Samuel knew that Lucille was scared, he had seen a look on terror on her face.

"Allow me to explain." Anders interrupted in a pleasant tone. "You see, this is my sister, Lena and he husband Earl; you may remember them as Gerica's parents." Anders smiled.

"You killed Gerica's parents when you stole her; you came back with her the day of their murder." Samuel was angry, he was not making sense of the news that Anders was explaining. "Anders, start making sense, before I kill you myself." Samuel threatened in a bone shaking tone. He was the King's guard for a reason; Samuel was ruthless when he needed to be.

"You may want to take a seat, in fact," Anders started to yell. "You all may want to take a seat." He took several steps backwards and spun around in a circle like a mad man. "Father, would you care to join me over here please?" The room filled with whispers; Jace looked at the servants who were standing against the walls, Lucille looked at Horus, then back at Samuel and Samuel looked at Stetson; but no one moved forward. "Father do not be scared now, he cannot hurt you anymore. We have worked on this for years! You are free!" With the room still whispering, Lucille heard the rustling of feet behind her.

Stetson began to walk toward Anders and Lena. The room fell silent; no one could move but Stetson. He embraced Lena with a hug so tight that she was lifted off of the floor. "Hello father," she whispered.

There was a roar that left Samuel's body that was nothing short of terrifying, "Stetson!"

"Oh, Samuel, you should sit down now." There was an arrogant tone to Anders' voice. "Let's begin, shall we? You see, my father was a wonderful provider, a loving husband and a remarkable father; until the King allowed his greed to interfere with our lives. To settle a debt, King Beckford took the one man that would protect and provide for us. I was a child, and the only son; I had to take on the man of the house role at age nine. Not having means to support my family, my mother fell ill and died. It was my sister and I left alone to face the cold world. We were homeless, and starving; until Lena met Earl, he took us in but even he could not provide for us. I dreamed of gold and pearls; breakfasts of grapes and bread. Do you know want we had? Crumbs and raisins; the leftovers of another starving townsman trapped in the destitute of Bales. Rats running along the street corners had more to eat than we. Have you ever noticed my eye color? I lost the pigment in my eye from lack of nutrition. It's actually an incredibly rare effect, but it was able to work in my favor. You see, one day, my father was walking the streets of Bales, when he noticed a teen eating from the rubbish left on the street by a local pub. When he noticed it was me, and noticed my eyes, he knew he had to help us. He met Earl, and we figured out a plan to take the very thing the King loved most and murder him. Gerica would have been dead if she was not raised in the castle, and she was the missing puzzle piece to taking what we wanted. Over the past decade, with the help of me and my father, Lena and Earl have been able to watch Gerica grow and learn. Always lurking in the walls; they wore black robes that covered them from head to toe. Gerica was right about being followed; you all were too stupid to believe her."

Anders looked around the room at the confused faces and started to smile. "Samuel, if only you had paid any amount of attention to things, you may have sense that something was off.

You were there from the very start; your journey to the farm house was actually our meeting to discuss the next phase in the plan. That was not their farm house, and the horses were in no danger of being stolen. You listened when I told you to stay behind too easily," Anders finished in a condescending tone that made Samuel run after him in an attack.

Samuel wrapped both hands around Anders neck as quick as a snake would strike an unsuspecting mouse. Both men fell backwards and Samuel landed on top of Anders, with his neck still in Samuel's hands. Samuel had begun to shake Anders as he choked him until Stetson punched Samuel in the head; Earl and Lena went into release Anders from Samuel's grip. Samuel was by far the strongest of the guard, but he was not ready for the punch when it connected to the back of his head.

"Get him locked up, father. Horus, make yourself useful and help my father bring this maniac to a holding cell. We shall deal with him later." Anders instructed as he tried to catch his breath and regain color to his face. Lucille watched Horus hesitate to help Stetson. "Horus, are you sure you want to disobey?"

Horus did not respond with his words, but in his eyes was a look of hatred. Samuel was his friend, and he would not take that lightly. They two men dragged Samuel's body out of the room; and just as they entered, Gerica was heard walking through the corridor.

"Dear, heavens." Lucille choked as she looked at Jace. Jace was about to turn and head to stop Gerica but it was too late.

Gerica walked into the throne room to see a bed covered in red satin sheets, and a room full of people all looking at her. Her eyes scanned the room and she saw all the regular servants, Lucille and Anders, but her father is missing. There are dirty people that she did not recognize, standing in the middle of the room. Lucille ran over to her and hugged her in a protective manner; to shield her from everything that has taken place. As Gerica tried to free herself, she looked up at Lucille and saw that she was crying. "Lucille, tell me what is going on." She demanded. Lucille tried to speak but the words would not leave her lips. She felt like there was a rock clogging her windpipe and a tie around her vocal cords; all she could do was release tears. "Lucille" Gerica cried. Jace ran over to the two of them, and as she went to speak, Anders interrupted her.

"Gerica, we need to tell you a few things. Life is going to be different now; but please, do not worry, you are safe. The King has passed on; and there are some people over here that would love to meet you." Anders said as he walked over to Gerica and gently tried to grab her arm.

Gerica started crying when she had learned that her father had died. She was frightened, and she began to act like a small child being taken away from their mother. She held on to Lucille with all of her might. "No." she whispered. She put her head onto Lucille's shoulder, much like a toddler who fell asleep on their mother would.

"Gerica," Anders whispered. "Please, this is important to your future." He looked at Lena when he saw that Gerica would not go with him and motioned for her to make her way toward them.

Lena made her way over to Gerica and Lucille. Lucille looked at her and yelled, "Do not come any closer to her. You have no reason to ever come near her."

"I gave birth to her; that is my child! You are not to tell me when I can have contact with her." Lena yelled in a high-pitched tone.

"You abandoned her for your own selfish reasons." Lucille whispered; she was trying to keep Gerica from learning anymore heartbreaking truth.

Gerica lifted her head and looked at Lena. "How are you my mother?" she asked. Her face was covered in tears, and her eyes were puffy.

"Gerica, have a seat; there is much to discuss." Anders insisted.

Gerica grabbed Lucille's hand and stood upright. "Tell me." She declared.

"Let's go back to my room; with your mother and your father." He begged.

"My father, my father is dead." She yelled.

"No, your real father; he stands right over there." Anders points in Earl's direction.

"Lucille is to stay with me. I need her; she is my mother." Gerica announced.

There was a look of pain in Lena's eyes when Gerica spoke; it was one of betrayal. She spoke up, very softly, "Gerica, my love. Please listen to what we have to say; this will all make sense to you, love. I promise." Lena pleaded.

"Tell her, go on; tell her how you murdered her father!" Horus demanded as he burst into the room while no one was looking. "Tell her Anders; how did you kill the King?"

Gerica looked from Lena to Anders and stared him in the eyes. "Is he telling the truth, Anders?" Gerica Whispered; she was hit with a shock that went through her whole body. She started to tremble, and her vision started to blur from the tears that continued to fall from her eyes.

"Gerica, please; It is not the simple." Anders began to beg; he loved Gerica and had only been cold to her all these years to keep himself from letting her know of any information prematurely.

"Is it now; was he murdered by his most trusted friend. Tell me now!" Gerica screamed as loud as she could; her throat burned after and she could not stop from crying.

"Yes, for you." Anders admitted.

"Do not say it was for her, it was for your own sick, twisted gain that his body lays there lifeless." Lucille hissed.

Gerica could not breathe when she learned the reason her father met his early demise. She looked around the room, at the people claiming to be her parents, and at Anders, and began to feel faint. Before another thought entered her head, she turned and run out of the throne room. Lucille, Horus and Jace followed her; the rest of the servants were all too scared to move. Lena went to run but was not able to get far, Anders grabbed her wrist. "No, let her go; she will come back, she has nowhere to go. She will be cold and hungry; let her return of her own accord."

Chapter Thirty

Gerica made her way down the corridor and out the front doors of the castle. She was met with cold air that touched every spot on her body, and rain drops falling from the sky, that covered every inch of her flesh. The thoughts in her head were starting to gain imagines that she was able to piece together. She could see Anders, in all his glory, falsifying his friendship with the King. The cold and calculating ways these pictures entered her mind forced her into more tears that she could not control. She was only dressed in her robes and she had nothing on her feet, as she made her way down the rock path outside of the castle. She looked to the garden on her left and remembered when she found her special rock. That rock, for unknown reasons, meant the world to her. It gave her hope when she needed it the most. Hot tears were running down her face faster than they were when she was in the castle, and before they were able to fall to the ground, they were mixed with the ice cold rain. She became soaked and with every step she took, a strand of her cold wet hair would slap against her face; bringing a different thought to mind each time. She never wanted to be queen, until just recently. She still needed to look to him for guidance; but he was dead; the man that raised her would never be able to teach her anything again. She began to feel overwhelmed by the pain of his murder, and a sense of betrayal. She met her parents; her blood relatives, and although they were strangers, she still felt betrayed by them. They owed her everything, but nothing at the same time. She had not gotten the answers she needed, but she knew that they did not love her enough to save her. They abandoned her, and then allowed Anders to kill the one man that had provided a life for her.

Gerica ran the entire length of the rock path but her legs did not stop when she reached the end. They were making her run even though she was long past out of breath. She had chills going from the end of her toes to the scalp of her head. She could feel every hair on her head, every rock under her toes, and at the same time, she felt nothing at all. Her body was numb and her mind was crazy. She made her way into the forest and before she knew it, she was jumping over sticks that laid on the ground. The forest was as dark as night; the trees were as tall as the castle, and the branches were long enough to touch the tree branches next to them and they grew attached to one another, creating a ceiling that covered the forest.

Although Gerica had cold chills that covered her body from one end to the other, she begun to sweat. Her eyes dried from the tears, but her face was covered with beads of sweat that mixed with rain.

The rain was coming down harder than it was when she left the castle. The sound of the storm overhead made it impossible for Gerica to hear what was breaking underneath her feet. Suddenly, something caught her eye as it moved in the distance. She was still running but trying to listen for any noise that was being made. She could only hear the rain, but she knew it was coming closer to her. She was alone, underdressed and without weapons; she tried to run away.

"Ahhhhhhhh!" She cried a blood curling scream while falling to the ground when it escaped her mouth. She felt the pain of a stabbing sensation in her right foot; but her eyes never left the creature. It looked at her and begun to run away but before it was gone, it moved just right into the light and she was able to make out a deer's body. As it ran away, she was able to hear braches breaking under its feet.

She positioned herself so she could look at the cause of the piercing pain taking over her foot. She saw a jagged stick that went right through her foot, and both ends covered in the darkest, thickest red blood she had ever seen. "Ahh!" She screamed one last time before tears fill her eyes again. She did not dare touch the stick, and her foot was starting to lose its feeling. The numbness in her body was leaving and she felt her heart banging against her rib cage like a prisoner trying to be free after he was wrongfully jailed; it soon became loud enough for her to hear.

Gerica looked up at the sky, as rain drops fell into her eyes, and she screamed "How could You allow this to be my life?" She screamed as loud as her burning lungs would allow her to. She went on between her deep cries and shortness of breath. "I have asked nothing of You. I never wanted to be a queen or be without my parents." Her words turned into sobs that no longer could be understood. Her throat burned as bad as her lungs did when she yelled. She could no longer sit upright, and she felt herself falling. Her head fell back and she body started to shake; she was not sure if she was shaking because the rain drops felt like ice falling on her bare skin, or from fear. Chills were still running up and down the length of her spine until they reached her neck; with every chill was a sting that took over her spine. She slowly rolled over on her side and pulled her knees into her chest. The stick was still piercing the flesh of her foot, and she was preparing to lay there until an animal smelt her blood and chose to make her

327

their meal. She had felt hopeless before, many times; but this was more than hopeless; she had a feeling that this was the end.

As she laid on the freezing ground, with puddles around her body getting larger by the moment; she was ready for death. The only pictures she could see clearly in her mind were of Lucille and Oliver; they danced around in quick flashes. Oliver looking at her, reaching for her hand in one picture, and Lucille would be kissing her forehead, as she tucked a younger Gerica into bed at nighttime. They were the only people that Gerica could say loved her whole heartily; without a doubt in her mind. She could only hope that they both knew that she loved them, just as much.

Gerica wanted a life with Oliver, to wed him and spend her life with him. That all seemed like the sweetest dream as she slipped away into unconsciousness. She saw him at his wedding, and he was dancing. Only he was dancing with a blonde haired girl with porcelain skin; she looked nothing like Gerica. And although Gerica was watching her love, love someone else, she was eased by this picture. She took comfort in knowing that he was an amazing man and he will love again. The last picture that she saw was of his smile, his thin, light pink lips curling into a shy grin as he whispered, "I love you…"

Chapter Thirty One

As Lucille ran after Gerica, she passed Oliver in the corridor and pulled him off to the side. In the smallest voice she could allow to come from her mouth she murmured, "They have killed him. Anders is a murderer."

Oliver looked at his mother with a puzzled face; he slightly closed his eye lids and whispered back to her. "What on earth do you mean, he is died; who?" It was not until this question was slipping out of his mouth that it came to him who was murdered. He saw the look of devastation in his mother's eyes.

She grabbed Oliver's hand and led him into the dining hall. They needed time for Lucille to explain what had taken place; as she tried to wrap her head around the idea that Anders had orchestrated the King's murder. She was painfully aware that his murder was pre-planned, and she knew that she was going to need to face the castle's demons; with Oliver's help, and with a bit of luck, Gerica's help as well. Lucille knew that things would end in a blaze of fire that would change everyone's lives forever. She had always had a feeling that the King's action would result in the decay of the castle and the kingdom; the good in his heart was only toward her.

Oliver sat down and laid his hand over his forehead. He took a deep breath and asked as calmly as he could, "Mother, what do you mean he was murdered?" He did not understand the news that he been given; the King was not someone who was weak or powerless. He had the makings of a warrior; cold, headstrong and demanding; with a temper that was unlike any man Oliver had ever seen. Making himself vulnerable to an attack was it just was not possible. Oliver's head started to feel light, and dizzy with his next thought; Gerica. "Where is Gerica, does she know?" the concern in his voice was heard clearly because he had taken his face out of his hands; an intense look of fear spread over his face.

"She knows, and she ran from the castle before anyone could stop her." She confirmed.

"We must find her." Oliver demanded

Paranoia set in with Oliver's words as Lucille pictured millions of ears listening to every word they were saying. She could not allow another word to slip from her lips that involved Gerica's departure from the castle. She did not know if Gerica was alone, or in the hands of those floor dwellers, and she needed to find her. Gerica was now the queen and there was no telling what kind of doors that may open for people to attack the gentle girl.

Without saying a word, Lucille reached out her arm and grabbed Oliver's hand. Slowly, she put a finger to her lips, motioning to him not to make a sound. She walked out of the room as quietly as possible and made her way quickly through the corridor. She led Oliver through the front doors of the castle and allowed them to close quietly behind them. There was a burst of artic air that froze their skin the second it touched it and the rain felt like thousands of pebbles were being dropped on their heads. Slipping their feet down the stone staircase, they quickly lifted their hoods over their heads and run off to the horse stables. The farther from the castle they went, the less tense they felt. Lucille jumped bareback onto Kav, the King's prized stallion. Oliver went to lead Whalen to the forest; Whalen was Oliver's horse and it was a gift from the King when he was only ten years of old.

Whalen was not the youngest, touchiest of stallions, and Oliver wondered if he would be up to the task of finding Gerica. Oliver was picturing them looking day and night for Gerica. Nonetheless, once on Whalen's back, he took off into the forest. Out of the corners of his eyes, Oliver saw millions of tiny pictures all smashed together as they run through the trees. Leaves and sticks were flying by in the wind; branches waved in the breeze, allowing just enough sunlight to shine through. He was frightened that he would see things that he did not want to see. Oliver held his head high, despite the rain covering every piece of hair on his head and managed to keep his eyes wide open as the water from his hair dripped down. His mother was far in front of him, and he could barely see Kav's white tail moving in the distance, but he knew his mother was just fine.

The forest was busy and still at the same moment. In Oliver's head, nothing was moving. He was gliding through the path, without any problems; but in reality, he was caught in the middle of a horrible rain storm. He scanned the ground, in hopes that he would see a sign of his love; but there was nothing to be seen amongst the rocks and leaves. He wanted to yell her name until his lungs bleed, but he knew that they were too close to the castle. The forest was the size of a village; he wanted to veer off into another path but did not dare lose sight of his mother.

Meanwhile, as silence took over the throne room, anxiety began to grow in Gerica's mother's body. She began to pace back and forth with her arms folded closely to her chest. Lena had a knot in her stomach that made it hard to breathe. Earl was watching out of the window, with his heart beating uncontrollably. He had not even had a chance to speak to his daughter, to hold her in his embrace. It was not the family reunion he had dreamed about for years. While both parents were feeling the effects of the day's events, Anders sat without a care in the world; his feet upon the table, as he leaned back reading a novel. No one had spoken words in what felt like a century, no one quite knew what to say.

Anders had planned the revenge on the King since he was a young boy forced into manhood. Anders was nine years of age when his father was taken by the King. Since that young age, hatred grew in Anders heart daily, until the day that he took his "vision" to the King. Every morning he had to wake before dawn to travel into a village that did not respect him as a man; he became a vile teenager. When his mother died, he lost any good that was in his heart. He did not blame himself, he blamed that disgusting pig that stole his father. Anders was unable to provide aid and care to his mother, and as much as she tried, his sister was limited with medical knowledge. Anders remembered his mother as a beautiful light in his life until she laid on the cot, with ice cold hands and closed her eyes for the last time. He was thinking of the way she held him when he was sick and he could feel the emotions taking over when Lena finally spoke up and killed the silence in the room.

"She does not understand what we did for her." Lena announced in a declaring tone. She looked at Anders and continued to make points. "She could have everything she has ever wanted." Anders saw the same look of hurt and confusion in Lena's eyes that he saw the day his mother died. Lena knew that this was a lot for Gerica to take in, but she never thought Gerica would react this way. At the very least she thought Gerica would ask questions; but surely, she would understand the sacrifices that they made for her.

Lena looked into Anders' eyes. He smiled and softly promised, "She will still be queen, Lena be still. No one can take away what we worked for." All the planning and years of living with the tyrant that Anders had to endure was not going to be in vain because a child had hurt feelings. This will work out in his sister's favor, and most importantly, his own.

Lena looked away from Anders's white eyes, she hated looking into them. They were a mix of lies and devastation. "But she has left us, Anders! She ran away and we have not gone after her! She needs to be found, she needs to understand! This is not how you led us to believe things would happen! You told us that she would be happy to see her parents alive and well; and that she would understand why we gave her to that man. She needs to know that we allowed her to be raised by him to ensure that she would have a better life, a life that was beyond our reach. She should be happy that he is gone, never to control her life again. She is now queen; there is nothing that she will ever want for again!" Lena walked toward the King's lifeless body and stared. His skin was paler than ever before, his cheeks used to have a bit of pink to them, now they looked like a colorless cloth thrown over his bones. His skin just hung there, loose and wrinkled. She hated his entire being; she could feel the hate throughout her limbs; mixed with the blood that ran through her veins. His eyes were closed, but she could feel him watching her. "You ruined my life for the last time," she whispered as she reached her hand out and slapped him hard across the face; leaving no mark on his pale flesh. She had a feeling of relief wash over her. That was something she had wanted to do for so many years. He stole her father, her life, and she felt that he stole her baby.

"Are we going to search for her?" Asked Stetson; he had been standing by the window along with Earl. He had seen Horus and Jace running from the castle; he assumed they went looking for Gerica. Anders did not move, and Stetson became annoyed. He walked over to Anders and placed a hand on his shoulder. "Son, we must do something."

Anders stood up and looked around; his father was the only one looking back at him. He watched Lena walk over to her husband and pull him into her arms. Anders lets out a sigh, "What shall we do?"

"We should find her; there is no telling where she is." Earl answered.

"Perhaps she never left the castle?" Anders hints. "I know that we have had little success in our attempts to rectify our lives and at this dismal moment, life seems bleak; but I need the three of you more than ever before to stand your ground. Understand that this is just a minor bump in the road; but on the up and up. Father you are no longer under the control of King Beckford and Lena, you and Earl do not have to hide in the Western end any longer. You are free to walk around the castle and reveal your faces. No more cloaks, no more hiding. Just understand that she will come back; that child was, and quite possibly is, still very much afraid of her own shadow. She will not get far." Anders had a tone in his voice that always sounded certain of whatever he was advocating for; he was persuasive, and confident.

"So, you want us to sit here. Is that your big idea, eh?" Lena snarled her upper lip as she questioned his suggestion.

"Indeed, I do; I have gotten us this far, haven't I? I managed to convince that King of the most ridiculous of ideas and he fell for it. I did have help from father, thank you for that by the way. I am not sure that if those doors did not close behind me that he would have been so trusting. Even adding Samuel as a pawn to watch the horses worked out nicely. Nevertheless, I think it is important that we do not freight over this. She has nowhere to go, let's take advantage of all the castle has to offer, shall we?" Anders smiled as he made his way closer to Lena and Earl. "Rejoice! There is no more sleeping on a floor! There are enough bedrooms here, pick the one you want the most. I do want the King's room however." Anders turned away from his family and started to make his way to the King's bedroom.

He was unable to hide the devious smile that spread on his lips as he pulled his head away from his family; he had done it. After years of being a noble friend, or at least acting like one, and weeks of poisoning the King, he had killed him. He thought about the backlash from the people of Leward, and he immediately began to think of ways to calm their sprits. Sure enough, taxes would be fewer and there would be more help for those in need. He did not doubt that he would make a great King;and that he would become Gerica's right hand man. Lucille might be a problem, but then again, she will need to learn her new place in the castle if she wished to continue to spend her life here. Anders was filled with hope and satisfaction for the first time in ages.

He reached the King's bedroom door and threw the doors open. Although he had his own part of the castle to himself, this was where he felt that he belonged. "Jace!" He yelled at the top of his lungs. He did not want to sleep in a bed that did not have clean sheets; "Jace, I need you at once." She was always around whenever the King needed her at first yell; but as he went to yell for her a third time, he realized that the staff may not respect him, therefore, they may make becoming King harder than he had thought. They too, will need to conform.

He was no stranger to changing a bed; he would allow Jace this one night. Tomorrow marks the beginning of a new era for the kingdom of

Leward. He peeled back the sheets on the King's oversized bed to see red spots on the golden sheets. He leaned his head in and realized that it was blood. The more he peeled back, the more he saw. This sight turned his stomach; he knew this was a side effect of the King being poisoned. Irony, the King was murdered the same way he wanted Anders to kill Gerica's parents. Hemlock water, in his soup; every night at dinner time. It had been easier than expected because the King would only use a crystal set of soup bowls while the rest of the castle used porcelain. Each night, Anders would sneak into the kitchen and act as if he was looking for a glass for wine or a plate; he was never questioned. He would gain access to the soup and put three drops into it. The hemlock water was so strong that any more than 3 drops would kill him that night; but over time, the three drops turned the King's organs into mush. It attacked the liver first; then kidneys and ate away at his stomach. It ruined his body from the inside out; there was nothing anyone would have been able to do to stop it. Perhaps, if the King did not expect a five coarse meal every night and was able to skip the soup, it may not have built up in his body. Just one more reason that he deserved to die; he was greedy.

Anders made his way to the linen closet and got fresh sheets and a quilt for himself. As he walked past the windows in the corridor, he noticed his reflection. He was thin and tall, as always, but tonight he looked different. He felt untouchable and worthy of the finest silks, but he was dressed as a normal person. His hair was matted, and there were wrinkles around his eyes that were not there before he came into the King's life. He looked and felted poorly aged, and this feeling annoyed him but he knew that hc had the chance to change it. He smiled to himself and made his way back into his new bedroom.

Chapter Thirty Two

Lucille's fingers were going numb from the freezing rain that had kept them wet throughout the night. She was unaware of the time and knew that it had been night long enough. She was sure the sun would make its appearance. She had pain all over her body and was shaking from the cold. She could tell that Kav was losing energy, but they needed to keep going. She was not sure where they were, how far they had gone and if they were even on the castle grounds any longer.

"Gerica, Gerica! Mother, she is here!" Oliver announced in a thrilled voice as he directed Whalen closer to Gerica.

Lucille had been just a few minutes away from Oliver; but she heard his cry very loud and Kav had already started to run to him. Kav ran fast through leaves and rocks, and once he made it, Lucille jumped off of him as fast as possible.

Horror took over her body and mind; she saw a sight far grimmer than she was expecting. Gerica laid on a pile of leaves, her hair was frozen to the ground, and she laid in a pool of frozen blood. She was in her robes, but they did not cover all of her, and the parts that were left uncovered were a light purple. Lucille was standing next to her body as Oliver kneed by Gerica's chest; he had his hands on her face.

"Mother, she is frozen…" Oliver cried.

Lucille dropped to her knees and placed her right hand on Gerica's chest, over where her heart should be beating. Lucille started to panic as she did not feel a heartbeat. "We have to lift her up."

They both slide their hands under Gerica's motionless body; Lucille at her shoulders and Oliver around her waist. They managed to lift her up, until her head was not able to go any higher. Oliver looked down and noticed that her hair was going to need to be pulled out from the around. "Lay her down for a moment, mother. We need to peel her hair from the ground." As they lowered her body, Lucille kneeled down and reached for her hair; locks of her curls broke off and stuck to the ground. It broke Lucille's heart to see the beautiful locks that she once brushed where no longer on her head. Lucille was not sure if Gerica was alive or not, but she imagined that if she woke, she would be upset over her hair.

Once all of her hair was unstuck from the ground, they lifted her again, and took her to Kav. They laid her on his back, her head was on one side of his stomach and her legs were on the other.

Oliver struggled with seeing her body, laying limp over an animal; his heart ached as he looked at her purple cheeks. Her hair was sticking out everywhere and is had a thick layer of ice around each lock. Her lips were gray, and looked like they were turning black. He was not as cold, so he walked with his hands resting on her cheeks.

They were not sure what direction the castle was in, and most importantly, they were not sure if being in the castle was the right thing to do. They walked aimlessly in search of a place to bring Gerica. Lucille was crying when the rain finally stopped; she could see the sky turning orange in the mountains that were ahead on them. The weather had grown warmer, but it was little relief for Gerica.

"Mother, what if she is gone? I never had a chance to say goodbye." Oliver declared in an announcing tone; his voice cracked when he spoke the word 'never', Lucille felt that it was a final word, and that Oliver was making an end to everything in his head.

"Oliver, we do not know what is going to happen. We do not know where this trail will take us." Lucille stated as she tried to keep a positive outlook; but deep inside she knew that if Gerica was dead, and the castle was housing Anders, she would not be able to be a citizen of Leward any longer. She would run, and never look back. She had been unable to mourn the death of the King; she was never able to say goodbye to him. She was getting deeper into depression when she looked up at a shack with smoke coming from the roof top. A picturesque scene from a fairy tale book that Lucille would have read Gerica; a tiny cottage tucked away in a forgotten forest.

Their pace picked up as they were traveling closer to the cottage. Once they reached the door, Lucille knocked; Oliver was not going to leaving Gerica's side. The door opened in the oddest manner. First, there was a long pause before the door moved, and then when it did, it was opened at the slowest speed Lucille had ever seen a door open. Once opened, there stood an older man, just a few inches shorter than Lucille, but a large build. He was not fat in the least; he looked like he had worked hauling lumber his whole life. He had blonde hair that hung right below his nose and a large patch of gray at the roots. He had wrinkles that surrounded his eyes, with enough extra skin that another face could be made of it and a beard that reached his shoulders. Lucille saw hair everywhere, in his nose and his ears. He had glasses that hung on his nose but did not cover his eyes. His eyes were a dark brown, and they matched his robes. He wore a brown robe that at one time could have been white, or yellow. He smelled of liquor and cinnamon.

"Sir, I am very sorry to bother you, but this was the first cottage we came upon. We have a young girl with us, who was lying in the woods. She was found frozen and bloody." Lucille thought it best not to mention who they were, and more importantly who Gerica was. There was no need for unnecessary questions, or someone's distaste for the King getting in the way of Gerica receiving the help she needed. Lucille stepped out of the way and pointed to Kav's back. The man took a look at Gerica and his face changed.

"She needs to come by the fire. Would you like help carrying her?" He asked. There were no questions of how or why. Oliver did not say anything to the man but began to take her down; both men carried her into the house, and Lucille followed.

Once they were all inside, Lucille closed the door. She watched the men lay Gerica in front of the fire on a rug that looked like animal fur in front of it. It was a small, one room cottage, and Lucille began to scan the contents. She saw pots hanging from the ceiling, and dishes piled on the table. It looked like it had never been dusted and it was very dark. The sun was peeking through the four small windows that were spread out along the four walls. There was a candle lit on the table, and of course the fire was burning. Despite the appearance of the cottage, and the hairy man that dwelled there, Lucille was not concerned; she felt at ease and somewhat safe.

"What has happened to this child?" Asked the man; and before Oliver could say anything, Lucille shot him a look that warned him not to mention a thing.

She spoke very softly but to the point, "We found her, laying there on our nighty ride through the forest." She had her hands holding each other in front of her stomach to stop them from shaking. She was cold but more importantly, she was nervous. "We must have walked all night; we were lost when we found her

Oliver said nothing, he was not sure why his mother was lying but he trusted her. He sat next to Gerica and rubbed her iced cheeks. "She is a beautiful girl." He admitted out loud.

"Indeed. Beautiful and bloody. Let's get her cleaned up, shall we." The man suggested as he rose to his feet and made his way to a pot, and then walked out the front door.

In the lowest voice that Lucille was able to make, she whispered "He is not to know who we are, and that Gerica is the queen; no one knows who she is. We do not need trouble. We do not know her, and should she wake up, she will have to play along."

Oliver knew his mother was a smart woman and that she had a reason to lie. He agreed to not speak a word and went on with every detail that Lucille gave the hairy man.

The hairy man came back into the house with the pot filled of water. "The well is full this morning, thanks to all that rain, eh." He announced when he put the pot on the fire. "That'll heat it up, and I have some blankets for the two of you. Right over in the corner, behind ya." He had a bit of a weird accent that Lucille could not place. "Come on in woman! Sit down. I have got a pot of tea brewing. I was just about to head out to the woods; I am in need of lumber. The both of ya are welcome to stay here."

"Thank you Sir, may I ask your name?" Lucille asked as she sat down next to Oliver.

"Ramselyn; but you can call me Ramsey. I never fancied Ramselyn much; I was named after an old relative that I never met. Anyway, can I get something to drink for either of you?" Ramsey asked.

"Water, please for the both of us," Lucille answered; she saw him get up and head to the kitchen to grab to cups for her and Oliver. He poured water from the pot into each cup and sat back down.

"Poor girl, tough tellin' if she will make it," Ramsey noted and Lucille could see a shift in Oliver's face.

"We have hope." Lucille said, as she bit her tongue not to say anything rude. "We just need her to wake up and give us answers so we can make sure she is safe. Oh, this is my son Oliver and my name is Lucille. Is the water ready? I will wash her if you do not mind."

"Here ya go, and a cloth, I forgot the cloth; one moment." Ramsey got up and headed back to the stock of pots. There were cloths hanging near the window. He grabbed a light green one and made his way back; without a word he handed it to Lucille.

Lucille began to wash the blood away from Gerica's foot. It was everywhere on her body and it was dried on so Lucille had to scrub to free her skin of its presents. Oliver had removed the stick when Gerica was still laying on the ground; no new blood had come from it. This action was breaking Lucille's heart as she washed away the blood and dirt. Her mind traveled to a time when she bathed young Gerica and sang to her the whole time. In the back of Lucille's mind, Gerica was the product of her and the King's love affair; she was their child. Not those monsters that had lived in the walls of the castle. "I will need more water, Oliver, could you help Mr. Ramsey with more?" Oliver shook his head yes, even though he did not want to leave Gerica's side and walked away with Ramsey. Lucille let out the cry that she had been holding in since they reached the cottage; her darling Gerica may be dead.

Chapter Thirty Three

"Oh, for all things good! Anders, you made yourself at home in the King's bed? What are you thinking?" Lena yelled; she was growing annoyed by the minute with her brother. She felt that Gerica was the most important thing and Anders was not concerned at all. She had let herself into the King's room and made her way over to the bed. She noticed a pile of golden sheets left in the corner, and Anders laying in a silk robe amongst royal blue quits and satin pillows. "Living highly now, I see. Come on then, get up. Gerica never came back; she still is nowhere to be found!"

Anders lifted his head from the pillow and tried to focus his eyes on Lena. His blonde hair was spread in different directions. "Lena, she will be back." He yawned and attempted to get out of bed; but the King's bed was much more inviting than his own and he did not want to wake or move from it. "Have you looked outside?"

"No, I have not; we have watched the windows on the Western end, but there was neither sight nor talk of her return this morning. Earl and I believe that she is out there." Lena declared.

"The Western end, good heavens; why would you turn there? Have you not seen your share of those walls all of these years?" Anders asked in an annoyed tone. He knew his sister was worried, he understood but she needed to have patience. They only knew Gerica from a distance, they did not know her the way Anders did. Anders knew how Gerica was frightened by her very own shadow. It was likely that she was curled in a ball in some crawlspace in the castle. "Give me a moment to ready myself, I will meet you in the dining hall soon enough."

Lena did not respond; she just walked out of the room. As she made her way down the corridor, she watched out every window that she passed along the way. She noticed the pond; that was where Gerica learned to ride her horse when she was just six years old. Lucille was there to help her up when she fell and to kiss any scrape that she may have gotten. Lena watched from the trees, dressed in her usual face covering black robe. She loathed Lucille, and yet, was thankful that Gerica was taken care of. Lucille was able to do everything with Gerica that was meant for Lena. Lena was supposed to give Gerica love and teach her different types of flowers and birds.

Lena had always wondered how their life could have been different if she was the one that raised Gerica. A large part of her doubted that Gerica would be alive at this stage in her life. They were living in a one room shack in the middle of Bales; Earl did his best to make ends meet by working as a well digger, but because of taxes, there was not much left of their money.

She recalled the day that Anders had hatched this insanely brilliant, but very frightening plan. It was a mid-winter day, and the temperatures were frigid. There was a wide spread famine, but that was the case throughout all the seasons. Lena was sitting next to the fire with Gerica snuggled up to her breast as she fed. Anders came into the shack with a wild expression on his face; he told her he had a surprise for her. She stood up, with Gerica still attached to her breast, "What is it, Anders?" He opened the front door and behind him was a man. Lena looked closer and saw their father. Lena gently woke Gerica up, pulled her blouse back up close to her neck, and laid Gerica in her bassinet. She then ran to her father who embraced her in a lengthy hug. They had not seen him in over a decade. Lena laid her head on his shoulder and began to cry. "I have missed you. Where did Anders find you?" Lena took a deep breath. She took in his smell, which was much

353

different than she remembered. When she was growing up, anytime she hugged her father, she would smell dirt and sometimes smoke; but right then, he smelt so clean and groomed, with a little scent of lavender; something that only a person of royal stature would have access to.

"He was walking, collecting taxes for the King. I have never stared at someone as much as I did when I laid my eyes on him." Anders answered.

Lena took note of how different he looked; he was old, with graying hair and a pot belly, but he still had eyes that made her feel like nothing in the world would hurt her. "How have you been? Your granddaughter is there! You have a granddaughter!" Lena shouted in excitement.

Stetson started to choke on his words as Lena pulled away from him to allow him to see Gerica. "I have missed you two beyond a point of words. I am sorry that I have not been here for you. May I hold her? Who is her father? And where is your mother?" asked Stetson. His lips were filled with questions and his heart filled with love; but his mind was full of fear. He knew by looking at his children that their life had not been easy. He was holding on to hope that his wife was doing well.

"Father, after you left, things got hard. Anders tried his best to keep things in order; being that he was only nine years of age that was rather difficult for him. Mother fell ill sometime after you left. I am not sure of the actual time line; but she did not make it, she passed away in the dead of winter." Lena's eyes begin to moisten with tears as she mentally lived through that day again. Gerica was handed to Stetson, and she was wrapped in the blanket that Lena's mother had made for Lena when she was born. It was the only blanket small enough to wrap Gerica's tiny body up snug.

"She is dead?" Stetson whispered as he sat down with Gerica in his arms. He did not cry at first, the tear ducts in his eyes were numb. He had known something was off when he walked into the house. Overcome with emotion, he did not dare to speak on what might be. He sat down and stared at the baby. His beautiful granddaughter and just thought, "No, this cannot be right" over and over in his mind. Anders came and sat next to his father, and put his hand on shoulder.

As his father began to allow tears to drip from the corners of his eyes, Anders whispered, "I am sorry, father."

Stetson looked up at his son, and began to cry harder. "My dear son, you have not disappointed me; no need for a sorry. I have failed my family. Many nights, I laid awake in the castle, and thought about escaping. I could get away with it, but the King's threat played over and over in my mind. I did not want my family murdered. This was no fault of anyone but my own." Stetson took his chubby fingers and rubbed Gerica's little cheeks. "She is beautiful, Lena. Just like you and your mother."

"It was not you father; it was Beckford. He stole you from your home, your wife and us. There was no regard for the lives he would ruin. I have lost count of the number of nights I have dreamed of his death. A painful, slow, and cruel death; a death to match the life he made me live and taking over his kingdom. To put our family in the royal chairs has always been a thought in the back of my mind." Anders admitted; he glanced at Gerica, and then back at his father. An idea was formulating in his mind that would scare and excite both his sister and his father. "Father," he looked into his father's eyes, "what does the castle have for guards keeping watch."

Lena was pulled out of her memories by her husband's raspy voice. "Lena, there you are, I have looked in every corner and end of this castle for you. Have you found Gerica?" asked Earl.

Lena bit her lip in a sign of annoyance. "No." She did not need Anders' permission to find Gerica but something was telling her to listen to him. She knew that she could walk out the door, past the gardens and past the guard chambers on the edge of the forest; but her body was not allowing her to run. "Anders should be here to lend a hand soon, I would imagine, as soon as he makes his way out of bed."

"Lena how is it that you are able and willing to allow your brother to continue this ruse? I do not feel that he is keeping his promise." Earl confided in his wife.

"I believe you are correct, my love; but I believe we need to keep a close eye on the castle. Oliver and Lucille have not returned to the castle. Which means they have not found her, and I believe she could be hiding. We had done it for so long, we were never found." Lena reminds Earl of how they spent their years in the castle.

The pair made their way down to the dining hall; they could smell fresh muffins, and excitement filled their mouths. For years they were only allowed to eat what they found on the tables after everyone else was served; and on their desperate days, they would look through the rubbish. Even the nights they had to search for their food, it was better than anything they had eaten while in Bales. They were almost fully past the throne room when something caught Lena's attention. She saw feet in front of the throne room; a spark lit in her heart that began to boil her blood. Was the King alive?

Gerica let out a scream that could wake the dead, as the knife began to cut into her flesh. She tried to kick her feet and with every movement, they pushed to keep her held down harder. Her wrists were tied over her head by a wire that was cutting into her skin. She could feel the warm blood run down her arms. They were trying to force their way into her body through her chest. Between her yells, she would scream the only word that her lips would allow her to make, "why."

She could hear the raspy voice talking to someone else in the room, but it soon turned to her. "You need to do as we say, Gerica. You were not meant to leave the castle; these walls are your home. You belong to them; you belong to us." A sinister laugh left the raspy voice as Gerica heard a second voice chime in.

"Gerica" it called. "Dear, Gerica."

Gerica started shaking, uncontrollably; her whole body was wrenching and trembling. Until she opened her eyes, and saw Lucille and Oliver standing over her. She felt the pain in her foot, and the ice fingers that touched her own body. Gerica jumped into a sitting position, and as she did that, her head began to hurt.

"You are awake! Oh, no, dear lay down. Oliver get her another blanket." Lucile demanded. Gerica laid back as her eyes would focus on Lucille's face...

Author's website

https://antha0408.wixsite.com/srobichaud

www.blossomspringpublishing.com

40776247R00217

Made in the USA
Middletown, DE
31 March 2019